Ravens Ruins

By

Catherine Gruben Smith

Illustrated by

Emilie Gruben

Sola Deo Gloria

"Therefore being justified by faith, we have peace with God through our Lord Jesus Christ:"
- Romans 5:1

This book is dedicated to my parents, the teachers who have given me such a loving home and pointed me to Jesus every day of my life.

Note to Readers:

Sign language is another language, not just a form of English. A signer thinks in pictures, they sign what they see, not full sentences. I translate Joe's dialogue as I would any language; making it smooth and sensible in English, just as someone would do in their mind when watching a signer.

Contents

Chapter One: Confusion 16

Chapter Two: Between Worlds 33

Chapter Three: Disintegration 40

Chapter Four: Another Way Out 54

Chapter Five: A Crack of Hope 71

Chapter Six: The Ravens 79

Chapter Seven: Joe and Beau 94

Chapter Eight: Notes and Resolutions 106

Chapter Nine: Stars in the Dark 126

Chapter Ten: The Wild Lands 137

Chapter Eleven: Vision Keepers 151

Chapter Twelve: Hunted 167

Chapter Thirteen: Taken 182

Chapter Fourteen: The Guardians 195

Chapter Fifteen: New Beginnings 213

Appendices 233

Introduction

The doors crashed open. Their bang mixed with the whine of Enoch's priming laser and filled the vaulted room. He spun to face the sound, his heart hammering, one hand grasping the stock of his Brunhiem rifle. Titus's chuckle mingled with the laser's whine and Enoch's shoulders slumped in relief. The Judge, leader of the government for one of the most important kingdoms in the world, strolled over and slapped his guard's shoulder.

"You need to learn how to relax, Enoch."

"Relax!" It was a bark, husky and tight, and Titus lost his smile. Enoch Mickelson wasn't a man to bark at his boss.

"What's wrong, why did you call me here?" Titus asked. Enoch moved aside, allowing a sight of the Pillar of the Book. Usually a huge, tattered, leather-bound book lay on that pedestal. The gold filigree had long ago rubbed off the cover, but the words "Holy Bible" could still be seen indented in scrolled letters. Usually Titus Hillson looked at that pedestal and felt his lungs expand and his tight shoulders loosen, encouraged just to see the book that made his job possible. And not just because it was the basis of the government and the kingdom; the promises and truths, the knowledge of God revealed there, filled his soul with encouragement.

Today, Titus's jaw dropped two inches, his eyes bugged, and his lungs locked. No book lay on the smooth marble.

"Enoch...tell me you removed it for security reasons," Titus whispered, his voice husky. Enoch's mouth opened, his chin trembled, and fear sparked in his eyes. It told his boss all he needed to know.

"My lordship..." Enoch started. He stopped and cleared his throat to get rid of the tremble in his voice and then went on with forced composure. "As Judge, I felt you should be the first to know what we discovered when making our routine checks this morning. Peter Lovine–"

11

The doors clanged against the walls again and both men spun. A tall, beautiful woman in her forties swept in, with a handsome young man beside her, and a spritely gray-haired man bringing up the rear. The old man paused to close the doors as the others swept toward the pedestal. The woman's hand went to Titus's arm and clutched it as she saw the bare stone.

"Your ladyship, Mr. Daniel, Master Samuel," Enoch nodded at them, his veneer of calm on strong.

"Oh skip the civilities, Mickelson!" the young man burst out and spun to Titus. "What happened, Dad?"

"A robbery, Mr. Daniel," Enoch answered stolidly. "As simple as that."

"Simple?" Daniel growled. "I remember going over the security measures with you, this robbery could not be simple."

"Perhaps so, sir," Enoch said. "But this is what we found when the guards ran their routine check this morning. Just an empty pedestal. The book is gone."

Silence prickled in the vaulted room like a live thing. Goosebumps rose on Titus's arms. The quiet hummed and buzzed in his ears, louder than the clanging door.

"I think," Samuel said quietly, one hand running through his silver hair, "we had best find a substitute to put on display immediately–"

"Substitute?" Elizabeth broke in, her voice shrill. "There is no substitute for a book, Samuel! There are so few in existence the world over–"

"He knows, my dear," Titus broke in gently, patting his wife's arm where it still clung to him, fingers digging into his flesh. "I think he means something that would allow people to think it's a book. Can you manage it, Enoch?"

"Of course, sir," the guard nodded. "I will keep Peter Lovine on guard here as he's the one who found it missing, and gather a series of blank pages and a piece of leather. It will do if we keep people at a distance."

"For how long?" Daniel Hillson murmured, and again that

heavy silence fell.

"We can't survive as a country without our book," Titus finally said, his voice thick. "We must have it to exist, no kingdom is allowed without a book at its base. And for us, the world hates us already for speaking the truth, if the tiniest hint of this gets out..."

"Disintegration," Daniel finished it grimly. "The rest of the world will step in and smash us, and stay for occupation to glean the fat from our people. I think that diplomatic journey I was leaving for this morning ought to turn into a series of discreet inquiries about who might have taken our Bible."

"Yes," Titus nodded, his eyes still fixed on the empty pedestal. He felt a breath rattle into his wife, her fingers loosening with an effort.

"Be very, very discreet, Daniel," his mother urged, her voice quiet with forced calm. "I know you can be cunning and brilliant when you want to. Be careful."

"If you think it wise..." Samuel murmured, leaving the words hanging in a way that said he thought it anything but wise. "Remember any inquiry, no matter how cleverly done, is liable to get someone talking. And speaking of talking, may I ask if your lordship means to explain the matter to your two youngest?"

"Good heavens, no!" Titus burst out, and even in that tense moment everyone in the room relaxed in amusement.

"It really is unfair to be so adamant, dear," Elizabeth commented. "Anna and Nehemiah may be young, and talk a good deal, but they have nearly as much sense as their older brother."

"Older is correct, when Anna and Nehi are twenty-five I'll let them in on catastrophes such as this, but not now. Though God protect us from another such danger. May we survive this one by His hand! Daniel, go now while the trail might still be warm. Be very careful whom you talk to." Daniel nodded, turned to go, and found his mother's arm through his. He didn't question it and just strode on as she walked beside him.

Marble tiles gave way to squeaking wood as they turned into a little-used servants' stairway and began to snake toward the ground floor.

"Be careful, Dan," Elizabeth murmured, her voice muffled by the ancient wood-paneled walls. "We will all miss your grumpiness until you come back."

"Thanks a lot," Daniel drawled with a sardonic smile. "I might mention, before I leave you all to your impressive optimism, it's very well to talk about the twins not knowing, but you know how inquisitive they are. How do you think they're going to take knowing something is happening, and not knowing what it is?" Daniel said as he held the door and let his mother sweep through into the courtyard ahead of him. Bright sunshine lit up her black hair, and Daniel's gaze ran over the intricate stonework and high pillars of the front of the Judge's house as he followed her into the light. He was leaving this place again. As his feet crunched on the hard gravel, a part of him wondered if it would still be here when he came back. A country without a book would be demolished by the rest of the world. If it became known... In his imagination Daniel saw the white pillars wreathed in flames, heard the screams of his family and friends, watched his home crumble.

"The twins are your father's and my concern, stop worrying." Elizabeth's voice cut through his thoughts, bringing comfort and security as only a good mother can. Daniel looked back at her. She stood beside his oval hoverer, waiting for him, with the same steady gaze he had always known. A sudden wave of love nearly made him turn and go back inside. But he didn't.

"You aren't really considering giving Nehi a laser for his sixteenth birthday, are you?" Daniel asked, strolling toward his vehicle.

"Only a normal Brunhiem. He's very good, Enoch says he is the best shot he's ever seen. Nehi wants a Compton, be glad we have enough sense to say no to that one."

"A Compton? You know those can cause black holes,

right?" Daniel snorted.

"Nehi would look at you with his large eyes at this point in the conversation and say, 'That's only theoretical!' Now Dan, don't fret over it. You have enough to concern you in this sudden disaster. Do you know how you're going to start?"

"In my Burbam '12 naturally," Daniel nodded, and hopped into the driver's seat of the smart little hoverer.

"Only two seats, of course," his mother commented, and Daniel grinned up at her as he pushed the primer and felt the copper coils curled under the oval vehicle begin to heat.

"That way I have just the right excuse to say no to hitchhikers, and have the quiet to use that brilliant brain of mine." Daniel broke off as the hoverer gave a soft beep to show it was ready. He pushed the pump down slowly, relishing the feel of the smooth metal under his fingers. Elizabeth Hillson leaned over and kissed her eldest son on the top of his head, ignoring his annoyed squirm, and stepped back. The steam began to pour from the coil's jets, and the hoverer rose six inches. One quick wave, and Daniel Hillson whooshed off, his mind whirling with what needed done. His mother stood still in the courtyard for another minute, murmuring quiet prayers. Her face was drawn as she turned and began to walk slowly back inside. It was probably a blessing one of her children was out of the country; at least he might survive when the world found out Sojourner's Kingdom had lost their book.

Chapter One: Confusion

"Make haste, O God, to deliver me; make haste to help me, O Lord." Psalm 70:1

A hard, round boot smashed into Paul's middle, driving him over the tiles. His breath choked and pain lanced through him. No reason for it, Paul's mind supplied in a detached way as his body curled and uncurled on itself; pain just for the fun of it. A hand gripped his ankles and dragged him across cold marble. How long had these men had him? It could have been two days or two hours since he had been drugged and kidnapped. He couldn't tell. They hadn't even asked him a question, not through any of it. A groan tried to escape, but it took too much effort to get out as he scraped along. His mind began to numb. It was a relief and he gratefully let his consciousness dim. The sound of hinges creaking and wood scraping over marble filtered through the heavy sack pulled over his head. Paul wished the bag didn't smell so strongly of fish. A hand grabbed a shock of his sandy hair through the bag and yanked him to his knees. Simmons started speaking again. Paul winced as the voice cut through the air, his throat constricting in panic. When that man was near, bad things happened.

"Here he is, boss, as requested. We made sure he was in the mood to listen to you before we brought him."

The trapdoor shoved open with a shower of dust and Anna held back a cough as she hopped out onto the roof. A breeze brushed through her thick black curls. It carried the scent of the stables with it, twisting with the flowers of the public gardens attached to the Judge's House. Anna breathed deep, enjoying even the horsey smell as she let the trapdoor down gently. She didn't want a "bang" echoing back through the tunnels into the hallways of the Judge's House. As far as she knew, only she and her twin used these hidden places, and

A greater flowered tillandsia
Pg. 18

they wanted to keep it that way. Anna stepped quickly up to the edge of the miniscule banister and looked past the park-land trees to where the green grass spread off into the gardens. She spotted him right away.

Nehemiah sat hunched over his notes, studying for their political history class, engrossed in the ideas as always; which opened up a hundred wonderful possibilities for his sister. A soft chuckle slid from Anna as she noticed where he had chosen to study. A greater flowered tillandsia stretched over him, some of its twisted green shoots winding through the air to grip two tall trees. Its bulbous body, forty other twisting limbs, and its single seven-foot flat pink flower, created a perfect pool of shade. It was a good choice as far as comfort went. But a deep cavity resided in the top of the flowered tillandsia, right where the pink bloom sprouted, and it had rained yesterday.

Anna gathered the leather skirts of her dress about her legs, connected its hidden zipper to create a pantsuit, and leapt into the nearest tree. A quick scramble through the pines and hardwoods and she reached Nehemiah's shelter. Anna paused and took stock of her brother. He sat hunched over his notes and hadn't even glanced up. Her nose wrinkled in a frown. This was almost too easy. Oh well. Anna wrapped her hands around the air plant's tangled shoots, where they held it in place six feet in the air, and twisted the shoots violently. The tillandsia flew upside down, and two gallons of flower-scented water cascaded from its bulbous inside.

A roar broke from Nehemiah as he staggered to his feet, cold water (reeking of pinkness) pouring down in a waterfall on his head. His black curls plastered over his eyes and he didn't see his sister drop out of the tree. But he heard her laughter as she sped away. Nehemiah dashed the water and hair out of his eyes and took off after the sound, his boots pounding with the pent up energy of a morning spent studying. Anna heard him coming and veered into the woods, still giggling. But Nehemiah saw the move, guessed where she

headed, and took a different path.

Anna dashed past tall pines and sighing aspens. No under-growth caught at her feet, the foresters did their work well and the Sojourners' woods were cleared and thinned. A glimpse of the road showed through the woods, and Anna quickened her pace. Daniel should be driving down that road at any moment. He had been gone for seven months, with hardly any hologram calls even except hurried, hushed con-ferences with her father. Seven months without his grumpy presence to tease and enjoy. Today if her plan worked, she could lead Nehemiah here and get Daniel to see how wonder-ful he smelled this morning. She topped a rolling hill and the road stretched before her, a line of smoother green trailing through the well-tended forest land. Daniel's little hoverer sped along it, the steam jets leaving a wet trail on the grass. Anna picked up her pace, a happy yell starting up in her throat.

A slim band snaked around her ankle, tightening with a jerk. Anna sprawled forward, damp grass ramming into her forehead. The grip tightened. Her joint popped, and a gasp slid from her as she rolled to her stomach and looked behind her. A cold stone of fear dropped into Anna's stomach. A creeper held her ankle. A bulbous black body lolled four feet away, its fifty dark green vines snaking out in every direction. But they were turning toward her. Feeling their way across the grass, blind tendrils tapping, curling, uncurling, slipping over the ground. A second coil shot around her boot. The grip tight-ened again and Anna yelped as her bones scrunched against each other. She kicked out instinctively. But fear crawled up her throat, tightening her airways. Once a creeper picked something to hold nothing would make it let go, and there was no human strong enough to break its grip. Another strand of vine leapt forward, snaking around her waist, one found a flailing arm, and the rest of the vines began to creep their way forward. Anna gasped out a yell, knowing she was going to be too crushed in about a minute to even scream for help.

Squeezed to death by a plant in her own forest! More vines felt their way toward her as Anna kicked and yelled, heart hammering and throat dry. Six more twined themselves around her middle and her ribs groaned, her breath choked out of her.

The first wave of real panic swept through her.

"Now, now, Simmons," a new voice, mild and friendly, broke into Paul's panic. The tone hit Paul and confused him enough his mind began to numb. "Curb your roughness. He might be a follower of the Sojourner's way, but he is still a fellow human. Take that bag off his head, for heaven's sake. Do you want him to suffocate?" Paul involuntarily shrank back as a hand fumbled at his neck for the cord tying on the bag. The gritty fishiness jerked off and the bright light of an afternoon sun cut into his eyes. It took a moment for his vision to adjust, and a bit longer for his throbbing brain to process what he saw. He knelt on a large porch in a beautiful garden. Green grass rolled into the distance, rising and falling in soft hills, covered in shaped bushes and sprouting flowers. Paul's eye followed the scenery. It was so peaceful. He began to count the bubbling fountains.

Hard knuckles caught him on the cheekbone and he sprawled onto the concrete.

"The boss is talking to you, Christian," the harsh voice of Simmons cut through his spinning mind. "You had better listen."

"Yes, well, I think we can do without that. Help him into a chair and then leave us for a while," the friendly voice said, with a hint of disapproval. Simmons jerked Paul from the ground and plunked him in a chair. A very comfortable leather chair, part of him recognized, hovering on the edge of consciousness. He forced his mind to focus on the man sitting across from him. The stranger positively beamed at him. He was fat. He sat there smiling at Paul as if the analyst was there for tea instead of fighting to stay conscious in his chair.

"As I was saying," he beamed, "we are not members of the Kingdom of Autonomous Man, your country. If we were we would be duty bound to turn you over to Science as a deterrent to the furtherance of mankind. It is so very foolish to be a Christian, you know. But to each his own, I say. If you want to believe in that God, I say go ahead, by all means! I am a citizen of the world, Paul, and I think men should live as brothers. All I wish is for a quiet life the way I want to live it. Unfortunately, for the kind of a life I like to lead, I need money. A great deal of money." The man paused. Paul got the feeling he was supposed to say something. He had the wild urge to recommend a dieting plan and forced down a hysterical giggle.

"If you're looking for a ransom I'm afraid my family couldn't afford anything you would call a great deal of money," Paul rasped, each word like sandpaper dragged through his throat.

"No, no, nothing that crude, my dear fellow, I'm on to a good thing already. I'm only looking for a little information from you, Paul." The leather chair under the man squeaked as he leaned forward and began to rub his chubby, red hands together. "I want to know about the Judges. Just tell me what you know about them."

"The Judges?" said Paul, his confusion mounting. Was he maybe in some kind of feverish nightmare? It seemed almost as disconnected as a dream.

"Yes. Not to do them any harm, you understand, it's just that they have something I'm looking for."

"Aren't the Judges part of the state in the Sojourner's Kingdom?" Paul murmured. He sorted through his aching brain. "Sort of...the oil that keep the state moving smoothly...or something." The smile began to fade from the man's face. Annoyance flitted over him as he leaned back in his chair.

"Yes, Paul, that's who I mean. You are deep in the workings of the International Discipleship Program–"

"You know about the IDP?" Paul gaped.

"Oh, I know a good deal, you would do well to remember it.

IDP; a silly name for the Christian underground. For such a well-connected batch of Christians you really should have a better name. Whoever organized you was a genius, you know that, don't you? There are very few groups who manage to stretch through more than one kingdom, your IDP ought to be proud of their achievement. But I really don't care about that. The point is, being so deep in the dealings of Christ's own you should know something of what I'm looking for in the Sojourner's Kingdom. Tell me about the Judges."

The soft whine of a priming laser cut through Anna's fear. She squirmed her dress' hood over her eyes. A lining of woven lead lay between the soft black leather and the felt of her hood, a shield for any accidental laser rebounds. The hood slid over her long black curls, and the world went dark. The crushing grip suddenly released, dropping limp. Anna slumped on the ground, gasping, filling her bruised lungs, and wondering if her anklebones were as broken as they felt. She groaned as she sat up, shoving her hood off. A tendril of white steam lifted off the bulbous black center of the creeper; now just a pile of smoking ash.

"Anna, you idiot, what did you do that for?" Nehemiah's voice cut through her gasps, and Anna chuckled breathlessly. "Tipping a plant over on me, ruining my notes, and then nearly getting squeezed to death by a creeper!"

"You can't be too mad at me, you killed the plant just to keep me alive," she gasped.

"That wasn't for you," Nehemiah said haughtily. "I didn't want Daniel's homecoming ruined by your playing about with horticulture, and Mom and Dad would insist on crying over your dead body." His assumed superiority melted into a laugh as he squatted beside his sister. "Ann, you have no idea how funny your hair looks right now! I love shooting lasers near you." Anna grinned as her hand went to her hair and she felt it standing up a foot over her head with the static. Then she gave

a dramatic sniff and clasped her hands in front of her in assumed delight.

"Oh, what is that delicious smell in the air? I do love the perfume you've been using."

"Okay, okay, you don't have to gloat," Nehemiah grinned, flicking his wet hair out of his eyes. Anna grabbed his arm and levered herself to her feet. A tall form burst through the trees and two thick arms shot around her and lifted. A yelp flew from her as the arms squeezed her bruised ribs. Daniel Hillson plopped his sister on her feet abruptly and rounded on his little brother.

"Put that thing away Nehi, what are you two doing out in the woods playing with lasers!" Daniel almost yelled. An annoyed pout played over Nehemiah's face. But he slapped the Brunhiem back into its holster. An optical fiber laser with a relatively small battery, the Brunhiem was one of the few lasers compact enough to carry comfortably holstered at the waist. Nehemiah rarely ventured outside without his.

"Don't call me that! And Mom and Dad let me use a laser, so what are you griping about?" Nehemiah grumped.

"The fact I just watched my sister nearly get killed by a plant and then incinerated, that's what!" Daniel spluttered. Anna's bright laughter cut through the clearing.

"You have no idea how much trouble Nehemiah and I get into when no one's watching!" she laughed. Anna stood on tiptoes and planted a fond kiss on her older brother's cheek, then spun back toward the road, her hand wrapped around his wrist, dragging him along as her swift talk filled the air. Daniel found his flustered worry dissipating. Anna had grown even more beautiful in the few months he had been gone, even with her hair standing on end. What a peace-making charmer! Nehemiah began to add to the chatter and Daniel found a smile creeping over his face as he listened. They piled into the hoverer, and Daniel sat blinking in the minuscule passenger seat, wondering how his fifteen-year-old sister had managed to talk him into letting her drive. The vehicle whooshed along the road at a furious pace and Nehi chattered as he perched on the back and pretended it was a seat. Some things didn't change at least, they still talked as much as they always did. Anna jerked the hoverer to a stop so suddenly the steam cut off. The vehicle dropped onto the ground with a metallic bang. A nut jiggled off and rolled down a hill.

"Apparently that isn't how you stop," Anna commented brightly, ignoring Daniel's groan. "You must teach me how it's supposed to stop soon, but now look where I brought you and admit this is a better road to take to get home!" Daniel looked up from where he was studying the side of his hoverer trying to find where the nut had come from. He grudgingly admitted she was right.

The forest dipped sharply, he could see over the tops of the pines and birches and twisted tillandsias, nearly a hundred miles into the country. A network of roads divided farms, copses of woods, and a host of small towns. Off in the distance stood larger towns, their spires and chimneys mingling with more treetops and spiraling shoots of vast hanging tillandsias, with no overcrowding or pushing. A delightful mix of colors; green trees, yellow wheat, white cotton, red brick, blue lakes. Everything peaceful and lovely and orderly. Like an immense, beautiful beehive set in the midst of a rainbow.

And it would all go up in flames if the wrong person learned of their stolen book. Daniel's eyes sought the town closest to them, studying his home. The majestic house dominated the town, set a little ways from the other buildings, and shaded by an impressive oak. If you could call the Corinthian-style building a house. The seat of the Judges, wielders of the sword of justice and protectors of the kingdom. A bit melodramatic, but it was their title. The town stretching around the house looked sprawling and innocent. But Daniel knew where the buried laser-shields lay, and the guards with their scanning systems and weapons. As they watched on the top of the hill, someone would be watching them, someone from the Judge's special guard, the best of the nation's renowned army.

If the wrong people tried to approach, they would be spotted fifty miles out and annihilated. Anna waved and pointed to Daniel. She lifted his hand and waved it back and forth, explaining they probably knew who was on watch, and they ought to be sociable. Nehemiah glanced back at his brother. A dark unease crawled over Daniel's face.

"What's wrong?" he asked. The scowl quickly changed to a smile and Daniel ruffled Nehemiah's hair as he hopped out of the hoverer.

"Nothing, Nehi. Not a thing."

"Don't call me that!" Nehemiah sputtered, pulling away and smoothing his wet hair.

"What? You didn't used to mind. Especially when it fit you and you were about this high," Daniel commented, sticking his hand down by his knee and laughing.

"Oh, don't mind him," Anna said as she followed Daniel down the hill, leaving the half-wrecked hoverer on the road. "Nehemiah is determined everyone's going to treat him with his 'proper dignity.'"

"I suppose you like it when people call you a dear girl and pat you on the head?" said Nehemiah, a blush darkening his olive cheeks as he trotted after his siblings.

"Actually, it usually makes me smile and wonder if I really am a dear girl," Anna laughed. "Come on you two, Mom and Dad want to see Daniel. Dad put off five different appointments tonight in order to spend it with you, and Mom's been worrying you wouldn't get here in time and her chicken and beans would burn."

"We had better hurry then," Daniel said, quickening his pace.

"Not that way!" the twins yelled.

"The river cuts the path in two and you don't see it till you're in the middle of it," Nehemiah explained.

"You mean *you* don't. I saw it first!" Anna giggled. "Come on, Daniel, this way." She dashed off and the two boys followed more slowly.

"I've missed you," Nehemiah said suddenly. "I wish you hadn't stayed away so long."

"I know. But there were things that had to get done," answered Daniel.

"Well, you're back now." An excited grin lit up the boy's face as he looked up at his brother. "Now you can show me that trout fishing hole you've kept hidden so well, and teach me the best ways to get a catch! Dad hates fishing, almost as much as Anna does."

"I know," Daniel said. "All right, it's a deal. The moment I get the time, I'll show you my secrets and let you talk my ear off all day. But what is that smell? Are you...are you wearing perfume?" Nehemiah scowled and ducked his head, but a guffaw from Anna cut off any explanation.

"It's a new habit, doesn't he smell simply divine? But don't let him tell you about it now, it will take too long," Anna called and looked back, hopping on one foot impatiently. "Come on you two, are you going to let a member of the weaker sex beat you back home?" Nehemiah and Daniel let themselves be taunted, breaking into a run, trailing their laughing sister.

"The Judges? The same family's been elected for over a hundred years, I think," Paul mumbled. "The... Hillsons, that's their name. I seem to remember the children are named after prophets... Sir, I come from KAM, Sojourner's Way isn't my country and I don't even remember the Judge's first name." Annoyance flickered over the other man's face; Paul read his future there. He let his gaze drift out to the peaceful garden and prayed for the strength to endure it, surprised that he felt more weariness than agonizing fear. His wife's face rose in his mind; then the fear began to invade. Paul's breath quickened, his lungs constricting as the desperate, begging prayers for a miracle babbled in his brain. He wasn't ready for heaven, not when Mary and the children still needed him!

"Very well," the fat man said, "if you won't speak, I'm afraid

I'm going to have to let Simmons have you again. He has a little house where he likes to take people." The man sighed. A petulant frown cut across his features. "I wish you would tell me, Paul. You seem a nice sort, and I hate to see cruelty done to any creature. Even a follower of the Way. But no matter." The man flicked a hand his direction. The hot bag shoved over Paul's head again and fishy, close darkness and his own rasping breaths speeding in panic filled his world. The string jerked tight around his throat and Paul gagged. A hand closed over his arm, levering him to his feet and shoving him back inside. Paul wondered for the hundredth time what was going on. Why he was here? The Judges? He didn't know anything about them. Mary, now that name he knew. A sob broke from Paul as he thought of how frantic his wife must be now. And Thomas and little Hannah. What would they think of their father who never came back? Oh Lord, grant a miracle, get him home! The hand on his arm shoved, his weak knees buckled, and Paul slammed into the marble tiles. Rough rope shoved over his ankles and drew tight, and tighter, till it cut into his skin. The biting, bruising fingers clamped over his arm again and jerked him to his feet. An arm slid around his waist, and a shudder ran through him as the grip tightened; he was utterly helpless.

A sharp hiss invaded the air, like a vacuum sucking in through a hole too small for it. The sound started in front of Paul, but it whipped through the air till it enclosed him, and brought a sensation of whirling, pulsating wildness with it. The air circulated at a crazed rate all around him, traveling in a circle, and the hiss was swallowed by the sound of the wind current. Darkness spread around him. It wasn't a light being flipped off, and he wasn't pulled into a dark room, it felt like a blanket drawn over the whirling air, a deep black blanket that brought freezing temperatures instead of warmth. Paul stood shivering uncontrollably, his body heat sucked from him as the frozen air whirled and spun and buffeted him. It got into his cuts and burns and made each one feel like a live beast eating its way deeper inside him. A scream ripped through his raw throat. His mind spun out of focus. It wasn't an ordinary loss of consciousness, it was something new with the whirling darkness around him, a sense of weightlessness and spinning.

Hard ground smashed into his feet. Paul sprawled on his back, his captor's grip no match for the force of that fall. Or landing. Or whatever it was. The hissing moved to a higher, more desperate pitch. Then it stopped, it all stopped. Quiet fell, leaving only a hint of the debilitating cold behind. The blackness peeled away, and Paul could feel dim light around him. A calloused pair of hands gripped his bound ankles and dragged him by his legs. It was a different ground. Cold, rough, bumpy, and hard. Bricks. Old, crumbly bricks, that's what the ground felt like as he scraped along it. The air felt different. The light was certainly different. He could tell it was darker here, even through the heavy material. And it was cold. It seemed as if he had changed climates as much as buildings.

"I'm worried, Simmons," a voice spoke up from by Paul's feet.

"Shut up," Simmons ordered.

"You know what I'm worried about?" the voice said. He was either very stupid or very brave to ignore a man like Simmons. "The black raider, that's what."

"I said shut up," Simmons warned.

"He's showed up every time we've tried this before, it's like he has a sixth sense when we've got a member of the Way here. And every time he shows up it means more trouble for us." Paul's legs dropped onto the cold ground and the voice gave a horrible gagging shriek.

"I told you to shut up," Simmons growled. "I want to forget that black raider, got it?"

"Then don't turn around," a deep voice spoke from near Paul's head. Silence fell on the scene. Paul lay hurting, nearly blind and suffocating. But he could feel the tenseness of that silence. It tingled. And then it burst in a sea of action as Paul lay helpless. He heard the soft whine of lasers priming and fir-

ing, and the softer thumps of fists pounding. Feet shuffled around him, over him, and into him. A boot rammed into his side, and he rolled across the rough bricks and slammed against a wall. The sounds went on, people thumping and scuffling and crashing. A distant loud bang drifted through the noise, and a thick curse poisoned the air.

Silence fell. No sound moved outside of the fishy sack. His own blood pulsing in his ear and his painful wheezes were all he could hear. Paul felt his pounding heart creeping into his throat and choking him. Fear had gripped him before, but this silence was maddening!

Something touched his throat.

A rough cry broke from Paul and he pulled away. The thing followed him, and Paul recognized it; a hand, untying the bag. The suffocating string fell away, and the sack gently slid off his head. A black form bent over him. Swathed in soft black leather, Paul could see nothing of the person, they could have been short or tall, man or woman. But two dark eyes shone out of the black leather wrapped around the head of the person, and a deep, twinkling smile crinkled those eyes as they looked into Paul's. They were alone, Paul and the stranger. Paul's heartbeat hammered and he felt a whimper smothering in his throat.

The stranger held up a folk-art, metal cross, dangling on a silver chain. Relief washed through Paul in a wave of nauseous dizziness. That design meant this figure was a brother in Christ, a member of the IDP, the Christian underground. He was being rescued. Oh thank God, he was being rescued! Paul's stomach roiled and he felt sick. The figure put a black gloved finger to his lips to check Paul's relieved babble, the cross disappeared somewhere in his clothing, and he pulled out a knife. The stranger knew how to use the blade, and in an instant Paul's wrist cuffs were off, his feet and arms were free. The figure in black raised him carefully to his feet. Paul slumped, his mind spinning, and every joint and bone and muscle cringing and shrieking at the effort of moving. But the black figure apparently expected his reaction, hefted Paul's arm over his shoulders, and began to walk. The dark eyes met Paul's, and they crinkled in that encouraging smile again. It gave Paul the heart to move, and he found his feet. Partially anyway, he still stumbled along like his daughter at ten months old. He had the urge to start spitting out baby language, and fought the hysteria back down.

They moved along steadily. Where and why Paul had no idea, and didn't try to guess. Why ruin the consistency of such a bizarre, confusing day? To keep his mind off the agony of moving, Paul looked around him as he stumbled along. It was a dark hallway, crumbling with age. Red bricks started at the floor and arched over his head. Paul stopped to look at the bricks closer to try and decide how old they were (and to rest his aching, aching body). Old, very old, almost certainly from before the fall of the last civilizations. The black-clad figure pulled him forward. The long, strange hallway stretched on, and Paul just kept moving, turning corners, stumbling along like a child, leaning on his unknown ally.

Part of the dark hall morphed into another black form. Paul jerked back with a gasping murmur, wondering how many other bizarre things could happen to him today. This other form was bigger than the first, but otherwise they seemed identical. The new figure exchanged burdens with the first stranger, taking Paul's weight and handing over something wrapped in black cloth. The first form faded into the shadows. Paul continued down the hallway helped by his new ally, deciding he didn't even want to ask what it was about. They turned two more corners and stopped, faced by an iron gate. Paul stood leaning heavily against the big figure in black, glad of the rest. But the thought of Simmons somewhere behind them wasn't exactly restful. His skin started to crawl. Paul looked up at his ally, gasping out a question.

"What...what now?"

The figure didn't turn his head, but spoke in a deep, strange voice.

"Wait."

Paul licked his dry, broken lips to try again. A huge roar, of sudden flames and power, rent through the hall and shoved into Paul with a searing heat; an explosion, outside their radius of sight. The bricks trembled, three crashed from the roof, spraying red dust as they smashed into the floor. Paul gasped and clutched at his strange ally as his feet shook out from under him. The iron gate swung open and the dark figure moved Paul swiftly into the deeper darkness through the gate. Another arm reached out and encircled Paul's waist as they passed through. The first black clad figure was with them again. The little group moved swiftly, the two in black almost carrying Paul.

A splotch of pale white sunlight spilled around a brick corner. The first stranger, the one with the nice dark eyes, put a gloved finger to his lips again and slipped ahead out of sight. The others stood still, waiting in the hallway. A long minute ticked by. Paul's senses began to cloud over and his experiences began to merge into a jumbled series of images and sounds. A black gloved hand shot around the corner and a finger crooked in a beckoning movement. Paul's feet scraped over bricks as the stranger carried him forward. As they turned the corner, the first black figure hopped beside him and slid a pair of copper goggles over Paul's eyes, and the world turned blue as he looked out through the dyed lenses. The soft whine of lasers priming came from his two allies. The burly arm around his waist tightened, then their feet began to pound, and they dashed across the uneven bricks. They shot out of the hallway into the sunlit outdoors.

Fire crackled. Men and women ran everywhere, their ugly military-grade clothing dull in the light. Some of them stopped and shifted lasers at him as he was raced through the sunlight. A part of Paul knew he should be afraid. The deadly whine of lasers came from his two black allies and the people fell over. A large Belton hoverer, that's what they were headed for, already hissing, its sleek bronze oval gently rocking back and forth as the steam jets forced it off the ground. The bigger black figure dropped Paul into the hoverer's backseat, and leapt into the front of the vehicle. A black gloved hand landed on Paul's shoulder and shoved him to the floor. He felt the slight up-and-down rock of a hoverer in motion, and the delicious heat of the steam pouring out of the copper coils under the vehicle. The heat seeped into him and he lay still, trying to decide if he was awake or not as the sounds of shouting and crackling and laser-fire mixed with the sensation of moving. It was decided for him. Paul lay unaware of the last frantic moments of his escape from Simmons' little house.

Chapter Two: Between Worlds

"Who would not fear thee, O King of nations?...there is none like unto thee." Jeremiah 10:7

The Judge's apartments were a modest place for such an expansive house, but the family's love transformed it into the most beautiful part of the building. Happy greetings filled the rooms, quick words spilled out around hugs and laughter. The cheerful chaos moved seamlessly to the dinner table, complimented by a delicious chicken with bean and apple stuffing, followed by dessert with a mix of chocolate, berries, more chocolate, and cream designed by Anna for the return of her older brother. Talk flew about the table, led by the voluble twins. New crops, church dealings, friends, the discovery of a gold mine, and various other small dealings poured from them. The older three at the table joined in happily, though the twins could tell they were waiting to talk about something. But it wasn't until after her second cup of tea that Anna could bring herself to drag Nehemiah away and let the grown-ups get on with whatever it was. She sighed, picked up her cup and Nehemiah's before he could pour more, and moved toward the kitchen.

"Come on, Nehemiah, let's get our sleep and allow Mom and Dad to visit with Daniel," she ordered. Anna moved off without waiting to see if he listened, humming gently to herself. But her twin hesitated, studying his father.

"Why can't I know what's happening?" Nehi blurted. "There's something going on I don't understand, and I want to understand it. If I just have the chance, I might be able to help."

"Despite what you think, you're not grown yet. Some things are only suitable for older heads," Titus answered. "I'd rather you remain happy and innocent as long as you can."

"I can handle it, Dad," Nehi drawled, his lips twisting into a wry smile.

33

"Of course you can," Titus said, a sudden brilliant grin splitting his face. "You have a goal, Nehemiah Hillson, a vision, a beautiful sight to look up to from the lowest of valleys. There perched on the hill; what is your vision?"

"Heaven and Jesus, face to face," Nehemiah sighed, very used to this lecture from his father. But a smile mixed with the sigh.

"That's right." Titus's voice grew soft, his eyes distant, as if he could see what he spoke of. "A kingdom with no sickness, no death, no sorrows or troubles at all. There, we will behold our Savior's face, and hear His voice. Will His words be, 'Well done,' or something unspeakably sorrowful? It's a beautiful vision. And secure for us who believe on Christ's blood. Keeping that vision always before you, a sight and remembrance of where you're headed, makes all of life take on meaning. Because we're travelers here and that's our home, every degradation can be endured with rejoicing, every duty becomes a joy, and every day a step closer to the brightest times in our lives. You can handle anything that comes your way in life, because Jesus' blood covers you, He has prepared a place for you beside Him, and that goal is real and certain. Always keep that vision burning in front of you through your sojourn. Keep the vision burning: see all of life through its heaven-tinted glasses!"

"Right, Dad," Nehemiah said, noting the amused smile on Daniel's face and feeling it spreading over his own. Titus Hillson gave this speech often, and it was almost as well-loved and well-worn as the old lace tablecloth. "But that wasn't the point."

"It should be a point in everything."

"Okay, but in this instance, I think it's you dodging the point," Nehemiah said. Titus chuckled and waved his son away.

"Go to bed, Nehemiah. You don't need to be a part of this, and I don't want you troubled with it now."

"But–" began Nehemiah.

"No 'buts,' young man," his mother broke in. "Don't argue with your father. Now go catch up with Anna, as usual she's moving to bed ahead of you." She caught her son in a tight hug, smoothing his hair, and planting a kiss on his black curls. "I love you so much! But...what is that smell? Are you wearing perfume?" Nehemiah stood up abruptly and walked toward his room.

Consciousness drifted back, in sensations first. Stiffness, so stiff Paul felt he couldn't move. He began a lazy stretch on his own comfortable bed. A fiery agony washed over him. His stomach heaved at the pain and his mind dimmed again as a retching cough rent from him. He must have done something to himself, his muddled brain told him, as his vision sparked and he lay gasping in painful breaths...but he couldn't remember what. Two soft arms slid under his head and drew him close, two arms he knew almost as well as his own. That familiar touch steadied him. He opened his eyes to see his wife leaning over him. She was pale, her eyes swollen and reddened, her beautiful face lined with worry.

"What's wrong, Mary?" Paul rasped. His throat burned with the words, and his voice was a gravelly mess. What was wrong with him? Suddenly a wash of horrifying memories swept over him. That nightmare of a day hadn't been a nightmare. It had been real. But then... "How did I get back home?"

"Yesterday I heard a knock on the door," Mary Sireton answered in her practical way. She gave a sharp sniff, of tears pulled back, as her hand ran lovingly over her husband's sandy hair. "When I opened it, there you were. All blood and bruises and dirt, passed out on the doorstep. I was too happy to find you alive to think much about how you got there."

"No hint of who left me?" Paul asked.

"Only this note," Mary said, handing her husband a small, dirty scrap of paper. She laid him back on his pillow and gently kissed his bruised forehead. "The doctor says not to move too much for the next few days."

"Hah! I'll gladly obey that order," Paul said kissing his wife's hand as it lay in his own, his motions slow and painful. "The children all right?"

"Yes, now that you're home and are going to be fine. I'll go and bring them, and then you should sleep," Paul nodded, careful to make it a small motion as every inch of him hurt. As Mary left he sank back and stared at the ceiling. Yesterday. A thrill of fear ran through him. That wasn't long. Surely the people who took him would be back. It wasn't like he was hiding from them, here in his own bed. But then again, he had nowhere to go. And no idea who they were. How could he hide from something when he didn't know what it was? Paul lay and breathed, staring at his ceiling and trying to think. Someone had come and rescued him. Two someones who were incredibly efficient at that sort of thing. And then they had dropped him back home. Surely, if they went to all the trouble to get him out, those Black Raiders wouldn't have just brought him home if there was a question of Simmons coming for him. Maybe the ones who snatched him knew he didn't know anything they wanted and wouldn't risk coming for him again. Paul let his eyes close and lay still, praying his fear out. He had nowhere to run to, and no idea where the danger lay. For now, he would stay and operate under the assumption Simmons and that fat Freddy were no longer a threat to him. Paul opened his eyes and looked at the little note with the single sentence scrawled across it. The words only woke more questions and answered nothing.

"Tell the IDP: Watch out for the Judge."

The old wooden handle dug into Nehemiah's palms and he grunted as he shoved another forkful of muck into the wheelbarrow. Soft, warm horse lips nibbled at his hair, and Nehemiah pushed the muzzle away. Mousey, Anna's favorite bay mare, pulled back with a snort, but pranced over again, blowing warm air at her friend as he leaned down for another forkful. The manure smell thickened the warm air. It made every breath odious. Nehemiah pressed his lips together, his fingers tight around the pitchfork, his eyes focused on the task, and every inch of his brain angry that he was still required to do this.

"I had hoped," Nehemiah muttered through clenched teeth to Mousey, "when Daniel came back people would start taking me seriously." The horse nibbled his hair again and Nehemiah shoved her back. "Stop looking at me like that, no, I don't know what that should look like!" he snapped. "Studies I can handle, and Mickelson's defense classes are actually fun. But this!" He grabbed the pitchfork and went at it harder. It took the rest of the hour to finish the chore. The morning sun was brilliant as he finally emerged, still rubbing his hands on his pants to make sure he had gotten them clean. He looked up and saw Daniel across the courtyard, putting his things in the family's old '27 Montrall. Nehemiah's steps quickened, turning into a run.

"Daniel, why are you loading the old hoverer?" he asked, his voice tight.

"Due to Anna's driving skill, mine is still broken," Daniel growled.

"That's not what I mean, and you know it! You aren't leaving are you?" Nehemiah prodded. Daniel pointedly didn't look at him. "But you just got back!"

"It can't be helped, Nehi–"

"Don't call me that!"

"–someone has to go, and Dad's needed here."

"Master Samuel doesn't think you should leave," Nehemiah said. Daniel stiffened, his eyes narrowing as he stared at his brother.

"Have you been listening outside our door at night, Nehi?" Daniel asked. Nehemiah was too insulted by the question to take offense at the nickname.

"No, I have not! It was after one of our history classes, he was talking to Mom, finishing a topic that had been going on the night before. What have you four been talking about so late at night in our kitchen, anyway? Every night since you came back. And why can't I know? And why are you going away again so soon?" The last came in almost a wail, and Daniel forced a smile.

"I'll be back. You survived over half a year with me gone, remember? After all, it's not the end of the world, nothing is going to change." Daniel slapped his brother's back in a chummy goodbye. Anna came out the main door and Daniel waved to her, hopped into the old hoverer, and pushed the igniter. The coils curled under the oval vehicle began to heat.

"God go with you, Daniel. Wherever you go!" Anna called as she waved, her beaming smile conspicuously missing.

"Goodbye, you two! I'll be back," Daniel called, and shoved the pump down. Water shot into the hot coils, and the vehicle rose a half foot off the ground. Daniel waved again as he rotated the vehicle and pushed the stick down. The jets pointed backward and the hoverer shot off, trailing a slim cloud of white steam behind it. Nehemiah walked slowly up the steps and stood under the Corinthian columns beside Anna. For once both of them were silent, watching the steam trail disappear over their horizon.

"I wish I knew what it was all about," Nehemiah finally said.

"I wish he didn't have to go, whatever it's all about," Anna said.

"I wish he wouldn't call me Nehi."

"Well, if it's that kind of wishes, I wish I could grow bread in the garden instead of having to bake it."

"Then I wish the horses would become stable trained."

"And the garden fountains would start bubbling Earl Grey instead of water."

"And the stars would really be close enough to touch on a summer's evening."

"And that we could slide down a rainbow's stripes, like a slide!"

"I also wish I could make my harp play by itself, so I could be camping during music lessons."

"Oh, music lessons, we're late! Race! I'll beat you by a mile," Anna declared, adding a poke to her twin's chest for emphasis. Nehemiah sprinted off instead of answering. A laugh burst from Anna, her boots pounding over the marble steps and into the gravel walkway, darting after Nehemiah. The twins raced on, letting their older brother travel farther along his way as they went down theirs.

Chapter Three: Disintegration

"Who shall separate us from the love of Christ? Shall tribulation, or distress, or persecution, or famine, or nakedness, or peril, or sword? ... Nor height, nor depth, nor any other creature, shall be able to separate us from the love of God, which is in Christ Jesus our Lord." Romans 8:35, 39

T he stars are a better picture of God's glory than the sun,"
Nehemiah said, and shifted to pull a twig out from under
his back. He slumped deeper into his sleeping bag and listened
to the sounds of the forest. Aspens moved in the gentle au-
tumn breeze, while tall pines stood around them in silent
grandeur. Night birds chirped, crickets sang. The breeze
stirred a branch until it began to creak. Over it all the stars
shone with their unvarying luster. There were more stars out
than seemed possible in the fall sky. Nehemiah couldn't take
his eyes off them.

"But the sun is so bright, and the night is so dark," Anna
yawned. She blinked, slid her pencil into its place beside her
drawing of the sun, and shut the leather case. A tired smile lit
her face as she slipped it into the pocket of her dress. Her
mother had passed her the leather case for her birthday, with
its hard plastic white pad for placing drawing papers on, and
it was Anna's most loved possession. If she had a moment to
sit still she had a moment to draw, and the leather case lived
out of her pocket almost as much as in it. She lay down, pulled
her blanket higher and stifled a yawn. "'The people which sat
in darkness saw great light; and to them which sat in the region and shadow of death light is sprung up.[1]' Now the sun's a
great light, it's a good picture of Jesus. But the stars aren't
even a light, not really."

---

[1] Matthew 4:16

"'Praise ye him, sun and moon: praise him, all ye stars of light.[2]' They are too a light!"

"All right, I'll concede that point. You know what I think of the stars, Nehemiah?"

"What?"

"I think they're the heralds of sleep, and I'm going to listen to them. Goodnight!"

"Goodnight, Anna, sleep in Jesus' peace," Nehemiah murmured. He couldn't bring himself to close his eyes. The night was cool and still. The stars almost sang in their beauty. He loved their bright pricks, partially because he couldn't define them. There would always be something new to learn about the astral regions. While beyond them... Beyond those shining, inaccessible balls of silver fire rested his heavenly home where his Savior ruled and waited to greet Nehemiah face to face. Those twinkling lights that broke through the deep blackness sang a silent, mysterious song of hope.

A piece of wood shifted in the ring of rocks where their fire had roared an hour before, and ashes spurted into the night. The scent drifted to Nehemiah, mingling with the dirt of the forest floor and the pine trees. He absently wished someone would create a candle that could make his room at home smell like that. A cricket chirped, and a nightingale answered. The humming drone of a fist-sized sphinx moth buzzed by just behind his head. The trees rustled. It was so peaceful, so still, and so eloquent. Nehemiah began to hum one of his favorite hymns, feeling he had to join in with the forest's night song, to help it sing God's praise.

A series of deep, throbbing booms broke through the quiet. Nehemiah flipped to his stomach and stared into the trees, toward the sound. It came from town.

Boom! There it was again. It sounded like when the gold miners had blasted through a wall to get at a new vein. The sharp whine of Brunhiem lasers drifted to him, at a pitch that

2 Psalm 148:3

was more felt than heard, vibrating in his mind; that sound reaching all the way out here meant a host of lasers firing at once. That many Brunhiems had never had a reason to fire together, not in his lifetime.

Nehemiah sat up, staring through the trees, dread stealing over his heart as the whine went on, rising and falling as individual lasers joined in or dropped out. More booming started up. A haze covered the stars in that direction. Smoke, drifting up into the sky. Dim, yellow light began to shimmer far away, above the tree tops. The light grew, and shifted. The way only firelight moves. Nehemiah stared, not daring to comprehend what he was seeing.

Fingers curled around his arm. Nehemiah spun, his throat tight. Anna crouched beside him, the shifting, yellow glow from the east lighting her face. Her deep black eyes were wide and staring, her mouth trembling. Nehemiah looked at the frightened face of his sister and forced himself to be brave.

"Anna, we have to get back to Mom and Dad," he murmured. His voice sounded small and frightened as it mixed with the sounds coming from town. Anna nodded and the two stood up. They began to walk through the wood, leaving their gear. A few steps, and it turned to a trot. A few more and they ran. The twins dashed down the soft dirt paths, racing toward the sounds. As they ran, Nehemiah wondered numbly if they should head toward the trouble. The faces of his parents rose into his mind and he kept them racing toward town. They had to find their family.

The whines grew louder, till the noise pierced through their brains and kept up a ceaseless ringing in their ears. The yellow light grew, and yells, screams, and crackling fire mixed with the whining lasers. As they neared the road the laser fire slowed down. Soon the sounds of each separate whine cut through the air again. The road came in sight and the twins stopped, breathless and gaping. By the light of the burning town they watched the smooth green of the road. People filled it, all of them running. They ran with the look of frightened

deer with the dogs on their heels. Jones the miller with his family, looking back over his shoulder and carrying his three-year-old as he helped his sick wife to a better pace. Deborah, the widow Anna took food to every week, moving along as fast as her old legs could take her, her cane jabbing the road with such a speed it was a wonder it didn't snap. Micah and Mary; Anna had sung at their wedding last weekend. Micah's arms were around his wife's shoulders as he hurried her sobbing form down the road. Nehemiah pulled his gaze away from the hundreds of packed figures, most of them faces of friends. There was something else down the road toward town, at the back of the line of frantic people. The whining and screaming grew louder there. Much louder. His clammy hand found Anna's and he began to pull her back under the shadows of the trees, rethinking his plan. They would have to try something else.

"Nehi, it's Samuel," Anna said. Nehemiah looked back and saw their old friend coming along the road. Samuel Thomas pushed in and out of the groups, picking up fallen children and encouraging the despairing as he went. His eyes raked the forest on the side of the road, his lips moving as he shouted for someone. The twins couldn't hear his words for the mass of noise coming from the crowd below. But they knew he was calling for them. Anna pulled forward, out of the shadows of the trees till the yellow flickering light played over her, yelling an answer. Nehemiah followed reluctantly. Samuel saw them, and a wave of relief washed over his tight face. He looked forty years older than he had yesterday. Samuel began to stumble toward them, through the jumble of people, and the twins slid down the steep green hill to meet him. He waved them desperately back. Anna's heels dug into the hill, and she turned and scrambled back up. Nehemiah's boots cut two deep furrows as he slid down, reaching for his old friend. Samuel's shaking, thin fingers locked into his and Nehemiah dug his heels into the hill, helping Samuel up. The tree leaves mottled the moonlight around them as the three stumbled off the hill into the forest.

"Back, farther into the trees!" Samuel gasped. Nehemiah and Anna plunged gratefully under the dark pines and cool aspens, out of sight of the firelit masses on the road. They stumbled into a clearing and the twins spun to face their friend, gasping out questions till three voices mixed and muddled each other. Samuel grabbed the twins by the shoulders and shook them, hard.

"We don't have time for this!" he hissed, his wrinkled face white and haggard. "Have you spoken to anyone tonight?"

"No, you're the first we've seen–"

"Since yesterday," the twins answered, interrupting each other out of habit.

"Tell no one you are the Judge's children, do you understand me? Don't mention you're a Hillson," Samuel said, his voice trembling.

"What's happened?" Nehemiah burst out.

"Disintegration. Just as your father and I feared."

"But– why? Who? How so suddenly?" Nehemiah gaped, his mind spinning, but Anna interrupted.

"Mom and Dad, Samuel, where are they?"

"Dead. They're both dead," Samuel answered, his voice breaking. Silence fell like a thunderclap.

"What?" Anna choked, her voice barely audible.

"Yes, I am so sorry my dear friends!" Samuel gasped, more a sob than words. "Both dead, I was there, both..."

"Why? Why now?" Nehemiah asked again, his dark eyes filling with tears that he didn't even notice, his stomach churning, his pulse humming in his ears. He could feel Anna's uncontrolled sobbing, a dry, panicked gasping for breath.

"Our book–" Samuel began, but was interrupted. Five figures stepped out of the trees in a line, men and women dressed alike in blue uniforms the twins had never seen. Dull black carbon lasers swung from straps over their shoulders. The guns were massive, employing a gas lasing medium requiring a large battery.

"Hands on your heads, now!" barked a squat, thick-jawed man, his blue uniform rumpled and a week's stubble on his chin. Samuel's hands rose and dropped on his silver hair; his face was drawn and eyes bloodshot as he nodded to the twins to do the same. "More stragglers, trying to slip away through the woods. Take them in, Huxley." A tall soldier stepped forward and prodded Nehemiah in the ribs with his rifle. It already whined, the sound coming from the Pylum battery absorbing the heat from the stored energy. Light played about the mouth of the weapon, the laser beam just waiting to be fired.

"Back toward town, boy, come on," he said. Nehemiah's eyes burned. His face flushed, and Anna could tell what ran like fire through his mind.

"Don't!" Anna hissed at him under her breath. Nehemiah's hands came off his head in a blur. His left arm hit the side of the laser rifle, driving it away from his body, his hand coming up on the inside of the stock so the muzzle lay trapped in the crook of his arm. A whine filled the clearing as Huxley instinctively hit the trigger, and a bright white light briefly lit up the darkness as a hole burned in a pine. Nehemiah slammed his left hand down, pushing with all his strength as he stepped forward, his right fist smashing into Huxley's jaw. The soldier stumbled, the gun came away, and Nehemiah flipped it into his control.

It took two seconds. But it was a fourth of a second too slow. One of the other soldiers stepped in and swung his laser like a battering ram as it hung on its shoulder sling, cracking the butt into Nehemiah's head. The boy crumpled and lay senseless on the rotted leaves of the forest floor. In the sudden quiet Anna heard sap sizzling in the hole burned in the pine, mixing with Huxley's groans as he slowly straightened back up. Nehemiah lay still and silent.

"Just because they're superstitious doesn't mean they're dumb, Huxley," the squat one sneered. "Don't get so close next time. You two," he said pointing to Anna and Samuel, "pick him up and move." Samuel's blue eyes locked onto Anna's, the girl's dull with shock. He nodded, and stepped forward, never taking his eyes from her. She followed him. Anna slipped an arm underneath Nehemiah's shoulders and lifted. His weight dragged at her, but he was manageable when Samuel took his other side. They moved toward the town, Huxley in the back prodding them to a stumbling jog through the dark woods, dragging Nehemiah between them. Anna's mind whirled and she didn't think. She couldn't think, numbness clung to her like ice over a seething pond. It was all happening too quickly, and was too horrible. Her country was dying. Her parents were dead!

A sob escaped Anna's hot throat and her arms suddenly felt so weak, as a messy torrent of tears poured out. She paused as she nearly dropped Nehemiah, and found an automatic prayer flying from her, a plea that he would be all right. As soon as her prayer began, Anna found her heart pouring out to her Savior. She couldn't understand the babble of thoughts that flowed from her to the foot of God's throne as she stumbled through the darkness dragging her brother through a dying land. But she clung to Him, and felt Him clinging back. Her feet kept moving, the tears for her parents flowing steadily. They were almost to town when Nehemiah began to stir and groan. Anna swallowed, gulping in air, and hefted him a little higher.

"Shh, be still Nehemiah. Jesus is with us and we'll be fine. Neither height nor depth can separate us from Him, remember?" Anna murmured, pushing his hair away from his eyes, avoiding the damp lump where he had been hit. He stopped groaning. His feet began to move, slowly, clumsily. Nehemiah started to take his own weight back as they came out of the forest into the town. Charred skeletons of buildings smoldered, poisoning the air with smoke until every breath tickled their throats and tasted foul. Where buildings still stood, people huddled together, held in place by soldiers. Strange rifles and lasers, and even projectile firearms, glinted in the sol-

diers' grasp as firelight danced. Cinders and ashes flew up with each step.

Anna stumbled down the most familiar path she knew; they were headed home. But as she turned into the courtyard, it didn't look like home. Black patches smoked on the beautiful house. One Corinthian column had been shorn through and lay in a smoking heap. The outlying buildings were piles of charred wood, and most of the trees were gone or burning. Soldiers in all types of uniforms moved in and out, busy, official, and triumphant. Huxley marched the little group up the steps, into the house, and toward the great hall. Anna stopped outside the massive door to the hall, her eye tracing the intricate wood carvings. The door swung open and Huxley's rifle jabbed into her back. Anna stepped off the red carpet and just walked. Her footsteps sounded hard on the swirls of black and gold marble as her eyes fixed on the far wall behind the vast table, on the fresco of Moses sitting in judgment before the tribes of Israel. In this room her father had sat, meeting visiting dignitaries and watching over the state. *Had.* The word seared through her. Anna felt tears flowing again as her gaze darted to the immense oaken table. There were strangers in the seats. Huxley stopped them just before the first chair, stepped forward, and saluted, his eye on a woman wearing the same kind of blue uniform he wore.

"Three more, sister, trying to get out of their duties to the new state. This one," he pointed at Nehemiah, "objected with force."

"If you please," Anna spoke up, her voice small, "we were surprised, and he did no harm."

"So...what are they doing here, soldier?" spoke up a young man slumped lazily in his chair.

"I was told to report to my sister directly," answered Huxley.

"Yes, well done brother," the stiff woman barked, flicking a piece of ash off her sky blue jacket. "Hand them over to the Director, she will tell you where to put them."

"I will not be put anywhere by you!" Nehemiah burst out. His shaking voice resounded around the hall. "That table has been the place of true justice and peace till today. Now you make it a place of cruelty and evil. God's justice will not be mocked, He sits in the heavens and laughs at your councils!" Nehemiah shifted his weight, gathering his breath to go on, his mind sick and spinning. The group at the table stared at him in surprise. Anna saw Huxley beginning to finger his rifle. Her stomach tightened, flipping on itself. She stepped in front of her brother, laying a hand warningly on his arm.

"He is still very shocked, we all are, by your swift control," Anna said. "I hope you will take his years into account."

"Yes, they are perfect for good labor," sniffed the stiff woman.

"If he will keep his tongue still. Otherwise he may become an inciter," a thin, dark man spoke up, studying Nehemiah with passive interest. "I think he ought to be destroyed, for the sake of the delicate balance of morale here." Several heads nodded, and Anna felt panic clamping down on her chest. She couldn't lose her brother too, she couldn't! A warm, almost cheerful voice broke in.

"Oh, I don't think we should do that. I mean, it's not like he has genetic deficiencies, and he's a fine looking specimen, nearing manhood. Besides, I would hate to see his pretty sister cry." Anna looked for the speaker and found a fat, red-haired man smiling at her in a friendly way. She tried to smile her thanks back, but couldn't. Dislike and a vague fear played down her spine. "Why don't you put him in a corner somewhere and decide what to do later when we've all had some sleep? I don't know about you, but I'm very tired."

"Yes," said the man slumped in the chair. "Sleep sounds good. Put the boy on hold, let the old man go to the Directors. As for the girl, she seems willing enough, why not let her help make the other..." He paused, searching for a word.

"Slaves?" offered a tall, stiff, muscular man, his blue eyes running up and down Nehemiah; Nehi's skin crawled. "Cap-

tives? Prisoners?"

"I was trying to think of a less offensive word. Anyway, she might make them more willing," the lazy one answered. Huxley's rifle slammed into Anna's shoulder blade and she spun around with a little gasp. The rifle prodded again, and her feet stumbled into a walk. She looked back over her shoulder as she was shoved out by Huxley. Her eyes met Nehemiah's as a soldier jerked a rope around his wrists, dragging him to a corner. His face was tight, smudged by tears and dirt, eyes red and snapping in fear.

Huxley's bulky laser prodded her back, shoving her along to a new life. She walked, sobs shaking her so hard she staggered.

Anna stepped off the wooden stairs into the courtyard that was littered with debris, ashes, and huddled, still masses she couldn't bear to even look at and shied away from comprehending. The ancient oak tree smoked, ashes raining on their heads from its network of blackened branches. Huxley's rifle dug into her back, and Anna walked on, to the vast cellars behind the house. A large crowd of Sojourners bunched at the entrance to the cellars, held in place by uniformed soldiers. Huxley shoved his way to the entrance, taking Anna with him. A young woman stood there in a uniform of red and blue, a list in her hand and stress crinkling her pretty face.

"This one's to help with the captives, Joan," Huxley growled, shoving his rifle butt into Anna's shoulder. She stumbled in front of the woman, shoulder blade aching.

"Oh good. Terra! Here's someone to take over cell three," Joan called into the dark opening of the cellars, her hand moving out automatically to clamp onto Anna's arm. "Down the stairs, turn right," she ordered Anna, pushing her through the door. Anna walked down the stairs. She had been down them thousands of times to fetch ingredients or check stores, but there was nothing familiar or comforting about it tonight. She

Disintegration
Romans 8:35

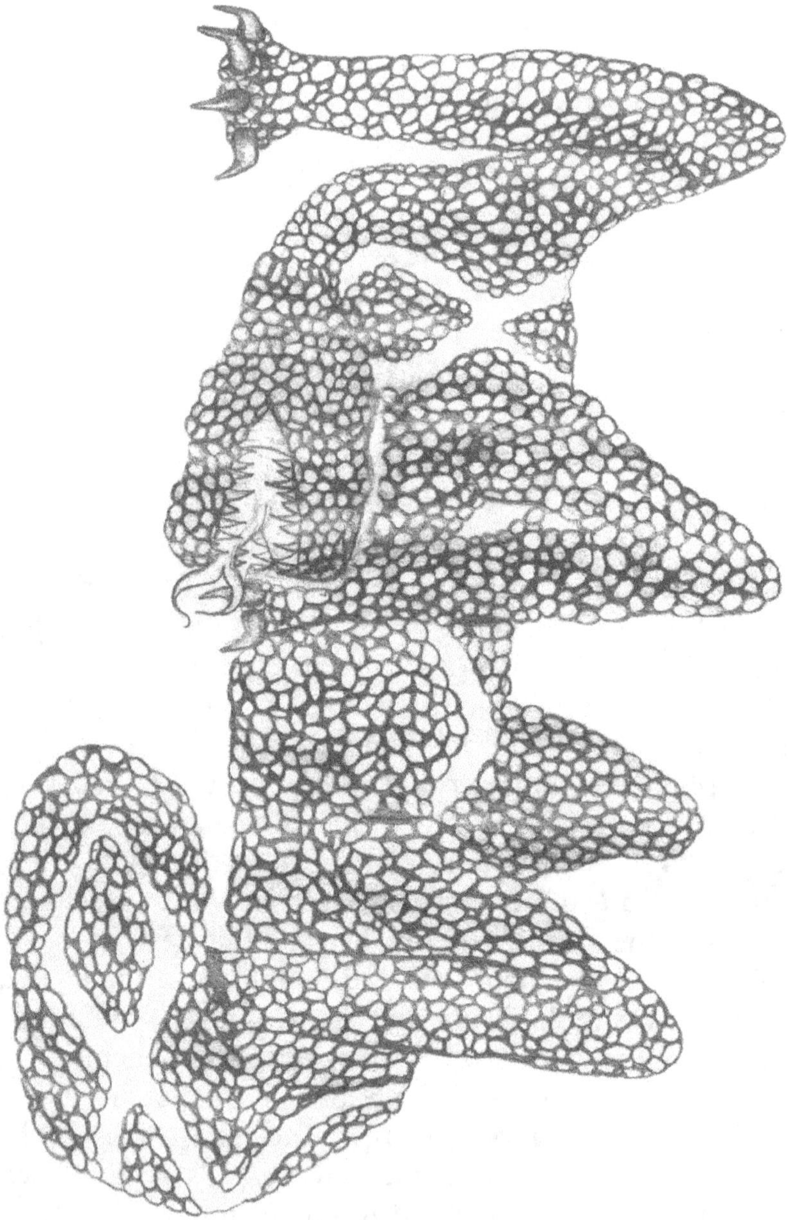

A stumpy tail
Pg. 146

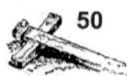

reached the bottom, turned right, and was cornered by a middle-aged man with large whiskers. He wore a yellow uniform with odd patches and pockets, and Anna numbly wondered what they were all for.

"Here," Terra said, shoving a bowl full of warm water and a wad of bandages at her. A bitter medicinal scent wafted up from the bowl, curling around Anna's face. The soldier spun on his heel and led her swiftly down the hall, stopping at a door marked "Legumes." Terra inserted a key in the lock, but paused. His bright brown eyes turned to her, and softened. "This is where some of the recoverable wounded have been placed...do you want a different task?"

Yes, I want to go to my brother, Anna thought. Stifled crying drifted through the door. Her brain kicked into gear again, a little. Whoever was in that room was probably her brother in Christ too.

"No," Anna murmured. "Thank you. I'll look after them." The man with the whiskers nodded and opened the door. Anna stepped out of the bright hall into the dim, close air of the little room, hot with the scent of humanity. The sharp click of the lock snapped behind her. Men, women, a few children, lined the walls and splayed over the ground; packed into the room like sacks of potatoes. Some sobbed, some whimpered. Most stared at nothing, silent and glassy-eyed. Anna wondered dully if she had enough bandages. A young woman looked up at her out of a pinched, wild face, her arm pressed against her side. Anna looked at her, and then at all the other despairing faces around her.

They couldn't give into despair. If they gave in, Sojourner's Way was doomed. And this country was the only light the world had. The quiet knowledge that she must be these people's strength began to weave through her mind, permeating the numb sorrow that kept her from the full realization of her loss. *Lord, don't desert your people now. Let me be their strength!* Anna prayed silently, and suddenly found she could smile at the woman. She held up the bandages.

"Hello," she said. "I'm here to help."

"Anna?" a weak voice rasped, and Anna knew it.

"Peter?" she asked. A hand lifted shakily near the back and she moved toward it, pushing past people in the crowded, stinking room, till suddenly there he was, almost under her boots; Peter Lovine, the youngest member of the Judge's guards. He splayed on the wooden floor, his head bandaged with an old shirt, his skin mottled with burnt blackened patches. One hand lifted toward her, skin burnt raw, shaking with the effort.

"Anna, I'm so sorry!" he grated, as she took his hand and knelt beside him. "We tried, we tried so hard. But there were so many, and it was so sudden. One minute the night was calm and there was no one, then suddenly they were everywhere! It was like the hand of God dropped them in our midst, I blinked and suddenly there was an army inside the town. They came for your parents. I was there." His soft eyes filled, and she knew tears were spilling down her face again. "I tried, Anna, really I tried. But we had no warning, no sighting beforehand, we–"

"Shh, say no more, Peter," Anna said, wiping a hand quickly over her eyes and gently putting his hand down. She reached for the dirty bandage wrapped around his head. "I know you did your best, and of course I don't blame you. Say no more of it." She looked into his eyes and he noted something more than sorrow and pity in her face...a caution, and even fear. "Do you understand, Peter? Say no more of my parents."

"I understand," he murmured as she bent herself to the task of re-bandaging his wound. "Nehemiah?"

"I don't know," she said dully. "I don't know what's happened to him. At least Daniel is still gone, out of the country during this... You lie still and don't worry about it. Sleep if you can." Anna laid his head down gently on the wooden planks and stood up with her bowl and remaining bandages. Her eyes rested on the young woman she had first seen.

"Move your arm, dear, and let's see what we can do for

you," Anna told her. Anna began to work at relieving those in the room. Her heart was numbed, but her hands were busy, and it helped. As she worked, she remembered what she had whispered to Nehemiah.

"Jesus is with us, and we'll be fine. Neither height nor depth can separate us, remember?" she began to tell each person she went to. The more she said it, the more she knew it was true. Realization of her loss was pushed away. But Jesus' hope she knew. By the time she was on her third roll of bandages and her fifth bowl of medicinal water, she sung a hymn as she worked. Jesus held her and Nehemiah, and He still held her parents. The vision her father painted for them was more than untarnished, it was sweeter and more vivid after tonight.

Nothing could take their hope away.

Chapter Four: Another Way Out

"And though the Lord give you the bread of adversity, and the water of affliction, yet shall not thy teachers be removed into a corner any more, but thy eyes shall see thy teachers: and thine ears shall hear a word behind thee, saying, This is the way, walk ye in it, when ye turn to the right hand, and when ye turn to the left." Isaiah 30:20-21

In here," Joan ordered, her keys clanking as she dragged open the squeaking door. Anna walked through, swaying on her feet. Four walls, concrete floor, one hanging light dim with the dust of years; her eyes took it in automatically. The door slammed shut behind her, the lock clicked home. A faint sweet smell of apple cider permeated the place. Anna stood and swayed, grateful for the silence and the solitude. Her stiff arms moved, fumbling with the gray blanket as her knees almost buckled. The floor was cold and hard. But she only felt it for a moment, pulling the blanket over herself with a shaking hand. Darkness, blessed, blank blackness closed down her body and she slept.

The bang of the door slamming into the wall shot through her and Anna jerked up, her heart racing. Her vision was fuzzy, and she blinked as she dragged her feet under her. Something came sailing toward her face and Anna caught it automatically as her brain tried to wake up. A clipboard. She held a clipboard with a map of the cellars staring up at her, the rooms labeled things like, "Surgery," "Cell Block 9," "Mess," "Death Row." Anna closed her eyes, drew in a deep breath, and opened them. Joan was talking. This time Anna understood her.

"Finish it fast," came Joan's quick, stressed voice. She stood holding open the heavy door to Anna's tiny cell, her eyes fastened on her own clipboard. "Then you bring meals to Cell Block 2. One meal a day, it should only take you two trips for

each block. Then report to me."

"What was the first one?" Anna blinked, sliding out the door beside the soldier, her voice still muddled and slurred. She wondered how many hours she had slept. It hadn't been enough, that was certain. Joan glared at her. Anna's face moved into an apologetic smile, almost from habit. Joan's fury melted into normal annoyance, her hand coming off the door and letting it slam home. The soldier began to pace up the hall, Anna jogging behind her, and Joan started her instructions over again.

So the day begins, Anna thought, trying to remember all the orders pushed on her.

Every day began that way. Day followed exhausting day, and Anna survived. The four gray walls and concrete floor became what home she could claim. No breath of fresh air ever reached her. Anna worked from the moment Joan banged on her cell door to wake her to the moment she dropped back on her blanket in the early morning hours. The extreme busyness was a blessing and curse. It kept her from having to wonder where her brothers were, or having to think about how thoroughly her life had changed and how desolate existence had become. But it would not let her grieve. Anna knew there would come a moment when realization would hit, and these days climbing into months would become a horror and not a blessing.

"He is a handsome specimen," Sonja, representative from the Gaia, cooed. Nehemiah could have spit at her. If he hadn't been so parched; he wasn't sure he had the ability after a night grieving alone, sick and sore in a corner.

"But too quick tongued," the rigid soldier lady from the People's Kingdom barked. She barked everything.

"Why are we spending time on this one slave?" asked Henderson, the Story Land rep. He lounged in his chair. Nehemiah wondered if he even had a backbone to sit up straight.

"Give him to me." The voice was deep, rich, and hard. Nehemiah's spine crawled as his eyes met the speaker's. The corner of Hadi Abid's mouth twisted up. But it wasn't a nice smile. "I will teach him or keep him where he can do no harm." The others at the table glanced at each other. Henderson shrugged. His arm lolled forward, gripped the gavel and gave it a nonchalant tap on the hardwood.

"This boy is designated the personal assistant of Abid, the leader of the soldiers from the Kingdom of the Prophet's Peace. Enjoy, Abid," Henderson yawned. Abid stood and walked over to claim his new "assistant." His fingers bit into Nehemiah's arm with bruising force. Abid shoved Nehemiah forward by his bound arms, and there was no fighting that grip. This man was strong. He pulled Nehemiah out through the side door, into the servant's entrance to the great hall. No one was near them. Hot breath landed on Nehemiah's ear and the fingers bit harder.

"You are my slave now," Hadi Abid murmured in the boy's ear, shoving him up the steps. "As long as you remain an enemy of the Prophet and not a follower of Allah's laws you will stay my slave. And I do not like enemies of the Prophet, boy." He jerked Nehemiah off the stairs and his teeth bit into his lip to swallow a yelp. A drop of blood fell from his bound wrists. Abid shoved Nehi to his knees as the optic scanner shone from the first door on the left and ran over his face. Numbly, to distract himself from his growing panic, Nehemiah calculated how fast the intruders had moved to have already reset the scanners; their technicians were good. The door clicked open. Nehemiah glimpsed white sunlight, tile, blue frescoes, everything neat and tidy and perfectly orderly.

The grip on his arm jerked, flinging him forward. His shoulder crunched as he landed, his right ribs groaned, and he rolled. Dizzily, Nehi looked up, searching for Abid. The tall man closed the door behind them, shutting out the world; shutting out everyone but Hadi Abid, and his slave. He strolled to a small white door, that half-smile quirked over his face again as he watched Nehemiah squirming to get to his knees. Each squirm jerked his bleeding wrists. Nehemiah stopped moving and lay watching Abid. The man flicked the door open. A stench of blood and refuse flew out and Nehi gagged, his eyes widening. A wardrobe closet; no, now a cell. Mirrors lay stacked waiting to line the walls, shackles waiting to be hung, a shiny new rack lined with tools, that horrible smell... Abid's hand went to a hook by the door and he pulled off a bullwhip, unwinding it with an expert's easy skill. He stepped back and flicked the closet door closed again. His boots thumped over the shiny white tile, coming toward Nehemiah as the boy lay helpless.

Fear coiled in Nehi's stomach.

"Anna!" Terra called. Anna slammed her boots onto the concrete, forcing herself to a stop, the message from Joan fluttering in her belt. Terra's gray whiskers had grown more magnificent in the two months since Anna's parents' death (that was how she counted time now). A table with a still figure covered in a white sheet wheeled in front of the doctor. One wheel squeaked as it moved. Anna stood and blinked at the covered shape. Dead...like her parents...the hole inside her ached again, burning till she felt a trail of tears down her cheek. If Terra noticed he didn't comment.

"Didn't make it through surgery," the doctor grunted, shoving the table farther down the musty hall. "Be a good girl and get the doors for me." Anna obediently turned and walked in front of the table down the passageway, farther down than she had been since the cellars had become a prison. *"He will swallow up death in victory; and the Lord God will wipe away tears from off all faces...*[3]*"* The verse flew through Anna's mind, one of the thousands her parents made her learn. After

[3] Isaiah 25:8

months down here, Anna finally understood why they had insisted on it. God's promises, like unchanging, steady rocks, were the only thing that made life bearable. He was always there, bringing comfort, and purpose, and even joy. Anna's chin lifted again, strength flowing from the words of the verse into her bones and marrow, and Anna let go again. It wasn't all right; it would never be all right until she met them again in heaven where all tears were wiped away. But the promises were true. And that was enough.

The darkness grew, until it surrounded them and the only thing Anna could see clearly was the white sheet over the still figure. But the air grew fresher, sweeter. Anna spun around another corner and jerked to a stop just before she banged into an iron wall. She took a step back and looked again. It wasn't a wall. It was a door.

"Here's the key," Terra said, handing Anna a massive iron key. It matched the ugly door and took both hands to turn. Anna gripped the metal latch, her muscles straining as she pulled it open. Terra wheeled the table in. Anna followed, her curiosity at a height it hadn't reached since the night she had been separated from Nehemiah. Darkness filled the small, square room. But there was no staleness here and Anna breathed deeply. Terra moved to one side of the room and pushed open an iron chute marked, "Debris." He sent his burden through the chute and closed the flap with a bang.

"They're picked up by others outside," Terra said, answering Anna's unspoken question.

"What about the one marked, 'Up'?" asked Anna.

"It's an elevator, connected to the hallway that leads to the kitchens. Stores go in and out of there sometimes. But not often, because the idiots who installed it forgot how slow elevators move, and it's easier to just walk it down the stairs." He cocked his head, studying her in silence. The seconds ticked on and Terra watched her, chewing a corner of his mustache.

"What?" Anna finally asked.

"It's a strange thing, you're not like some of the others that

come through here. So full of despair or rage that there's little left of humanity to them. You're...stable. Even when everything's been taken from you."

"'...and, lo, I am with you alway, even unto the end of the world[4].' God doesn't change, and He never left me. He's my purpose and support in life so my foundation has never moved."

"Huh." The old doctor stood still for another moment, thinking. Then he snapped back to life, shoving the table forward and not looking at her. "Go on, hop to it girl, we both have work to do." Anna shoved the giant door open again. Terra began to push the table back through the hallways, grumbling about the distance and the bother of these dour deliveries. Anna said nothing as they walked. An idea formed in her mind and she tried to decide the best way to turn it from an idea into an action. Memories of "Death Row" played through her. The almost tangible despair. Quiet sobs. The sickening stench.

"Terra, I can make these runs for you," she said as they got closer to his surgery. He stopped pushing the table and looked at her, one eye squinting, his mouth in a frown. "I don't have much time, but your time is more important than mine. I know I could do these disposals for you."

"Why are you offering?" Terra asked, stroking his whiskers.

"These are my brothers and sisters in Christ you're helping when you ply your trade. I don't want them to suffer because you have to do a chore I could do instead." Anna hoped she didn't show it wasn't the whole truth as Terra watched her. She had never been good at subterfuge.

"I'll run the idea past Joan and see what she thinks," answered Terra. "Go on, back to your tasks." Anna ran down the passage to deliver her message and collect the west wing's evening meals. Peter waited for her in the west wing. He was

[4] Matthew 28:20b

still here, his wounds had taken time to heal. Now the young guard was back to his virile strength, but he still hadn't been designated. There was some complication with his situation. Every other "complication" Anna had seen ended in the person being declared "unusable", or, translated out of the conquerors' jargon, only fit for execution. Anna prayed it would not happen to Peter. She always saved his meal until last in the hopes she could spare a few minutes there. Tonight as she unlocked the oak door to his small cell, and stepped through onto the cold stone floor, there was something different in the way he took his thin tomato soup. Especially in the way he didn't lift his head. But the conversation started the way it always did.

"Any news about Nehemiah?" Peter asked.

"No," Anna said, her voice flat. Every moment she could think, her prayers flew to heaven for her twin, his tight, frightened face hovering in her mind. Daniel was so competent, so sure, so grumpy, she could hardly imagine him in trouble; besides he was gone when the crash came, he would be too smart to be caught now. But Nehi... Anna pushed it away again, ignored the way her stomach tightened and how most of her didn't actually want to know the answer, and asked the question she had to. "Is everything all right, Peter?"

"I've been declared," he said quietly. "I'm going home tomorrow. To my real home, you understand."

"Yes, I understand," Anna answered. Her heart sank into her stomach and burned. But her half-formed idea flared up into a full-fledged plan. "Peter, do you know where you could go if you suddenly found yourself free?"

"I would leave the country," Peter shrugged, assuming the topic was one of Anna's random conversations. An excited spark flamed up in his soft eyes. "I've heard of a group of Christians out there, in the other kingdoms of this world. They work underneath the countries to help the lost come to the Shepherd. I would find them and help. This world is a big place, Anna, and there are so many souls in it who don't know

their Creator!" He slumped back against the stone wall, and the spark left his face. "But I forgot for a moment, Jesus is calling me home tomorrow. Oh well, someone else will have to fight for Him down here."

"Don't be so sure," Anna said. She picked up his bowl of tomato soup and poured half the contents over his head. Peter sputtered, jerking up in shock. Anna put a hand to his mouth. "Shh. Dead people don't talk. You're dead now."

"What?" he spluttered, tomato soup flying with the word.

"You're dead. Dead people don't ask questions, and they don't sit looking bewildered. Come on, be a polite corpse and lay down for me," Anna said, amusement playing through her. She got Peter on the ground with his limbs laid out and the rest of the soup splattered in the right places. Anna stepped back and surveyed her handiwork. Yes, if Terra didn't come too close and if he only handled the parts without the soup...

"Now whatever you do, remember to act like every well-behaved corpse, Peter," Anna said over her shoulder as she ducked out the door. This was mad! Tomato soup and an iron key, those two didn't mix!

The suite's door swung back and Shareef bent into a polite bow for his superior, his red hair flopping. Abid waved him in, not returning the salute. The young man stepped inside, his boots clacking on the pristine white and blue tiles, his eyes darting around the gleaming apartment. Abid sank into a chair at the table and studied him.

"You are younger than I expected," he said.

"You are taller than I had heard," Shareef commented, a twinkle coming into his green eyes at the man's rude greeting. Abid shrugged and handed a paper to the young man.

"I hear you are able to acquire anything. Your skill as an army supplier is becoming legendary," Abid said.

"I have kept up with my late father's acquaintances," Shareef murmured. He eyed the list and his freckled face began to wrinkle in distaste. Hadi Al Abid's eyes narrowed as he watched. The supplier spun the paper around and tapped an item. "The Black Box will not be covered by government funds, it is considered for private use only. And it is immensely expensive."

"I know."

"I do not see why you need such a...tool." Shareef did not bother to hide his disgust. Abid turned almost lazily and snapped, the sharp sound echoing off the walls of the still apartment. A shuffling step came, exhaustion dragging at heavy limbs. A ragged, emaciated boy stepped into the gleaming room. His head was hunched, shoulders pulled in, olive skin sagging and torn on his pinched, fear riddled face. Abid's finger crooked. The boy dropped to his knees, eyes fastened on the tiles. Whip cuts covering his back gapped and oozed as he moved. A jaw muscle twitched as he sat hunched, his hands on his knees, a wet rag clutched in one hand slowly dripping soapy water onto the tile. He stayed there, unnaturally still, as Abid turned back to Shareef.

"He tried to run. And he is stubborn about his cross," the man shrugged. "It will amuse me."

"You are a beast," Shareef hissed. The boy's eyes shifted, though nothing else moved. Abid smiled, but it wasn't a nice one. Shareef didn't care, he swept on, knowing this was an informal meeting and he couldn't be reprimanded for his words. "I have heard of your amusements. I tried not to believe it until now. It sickens me to know this is the man who leads our army here!"

"You are the one denying your holy Karan," Abid said.

"The portions you speak of allow for the severe treatment of the unbelievers. The book does not praise your deeds." A harsh laugh barked from Abid, and color flooded Shareef's face. "I am not the only one who holds this view of the holy book, and you know it!"

"You and your mincing kind try and fit the Karan into your ways," Abid sneered. "But you have not studied it as I have."

"You have not the common humanity I have!" Shareef almost spat. Abid came to his feet in a swift fluid motion. The boy cowered back, biting his broken lip, but neither man noticed him. As his heart pounded with the fear again, Nehemiah tried to make his thoughts go to God, to get his fogged mind to pray. But with the brokenness of his body and spirit, something broke in his soul. His prayers began to falter. When he forced his grasping thoughts to turn to God, all he found was what felt like a door slammed in his face.

"I am chosen by the Wazir as leader here, and you are nothing," Abid stated, his tone dangerously low. "Use such words with me again and I will break you. Perhaps you will find a taste of the Box yourself if you do not mend."

"You would turn your tortures to even those of the true faith. I expect no more from your kind," Shareef snarled and spun on his heel. His hand trembled as he pulled open the door and marched out, slamming the door behind him.

The image of the cowering, broken young man seared his mind.

Anna pushed her doubts away and her feet flew over the concrete halls, speeding to Terra's surgery. She dug her fingers into the wooden doorpost, using it to swing into the surgery, her lungs burning.

"I've found the first of my deliveries," Anna gasped. The doctor stood up, his desk seeming minuscule as he towered over it, his expression surprised but not suspicious. Anna didn't know it, but her anxiety looked like fright over a discovered body. Terra grabbed his bag but (the tomato soup on her mind) Anna quickly spoke up.

"You won't need it, I've seen enough of your cases to know that." To her surprise, the doctor nodded, and began to wheel the table out. Soon they were at the little room where Peter lay sprawled. Terra looked through the door. He looked at Anna, then through the door again.

"This is that young guard you tend to talk to, isn't it?" he said. Anna nodded trying to show great grief. "He was just marked as unusable, wasn't he?" asked Terra. Anna nodded again, trying not to show her rising fear that Terra knew exactly what she was up to. The doctor looked at Anna and then through the door again. He stroked his whiskers for a moment. "Yes, well, this afternoon Joan gave me permission to let you run these errands for me. I think he looks dead enough. Here's the key. Now you bring it back to me, tonight?" He stared at her, his eyes boring into hers, his calloused hand holding onto the key as Anna's wrapped around it.

"I promise, Terra, I'll bring it back to you tonight," Anna said. Reluctantly the old doctor's fingers loosened, dropping the key into Anna's hand. He spun on his heel and walked down the passageway. He didn't even bother to feel for a pulse. Anna's breath fluttered out of her in a thankful prayer, dizzy with the relief.

"Thank you, Terra," she called softly after the retreating figure.

"You just bring that key back," the doctor muttered over his shoulder, and hurried on to his surgery. Anna opened the door wider, wheeled the table into the room, and lowered it. Then she realized a weak point of her plan. She couldn't move Peter. In the end, he shifted himself onto the table. Anna pulled the cloth over him and began to roll the corpse out of the room. The large iron key clanked against the table as she trotted through the halls, her heartbeat pattering. Anna wished Peter didn't have to breathe so much as she watched the cover over his chest shift up and down rhythmically. It seemed like a hot, musty eternity to that massive door. But she made it. Such ugly metal had never been so welcome to Anna, and the heavy iron seemed as light as pumice in her adrenalin rush. The table squeaked and jumped as she jerked it into the room, and Peter started under the cover as the iron door clanged in place behind them.

"Peter, come forth!" Anna called, mimicking her Savior.

The cover shot off and Peter leapt from the table. Anna giggled at his confused expression and soupy hair.

"The lift is marked 'Up.' It takes you to the hallway connected to the kitchen, there's a door leading straight to the gardens just before you get into the kitchen. At this time of night it ought to be safe enough if you're careful. Go in peace, and go quickly!" Anna said, and gripped the table to wheel it out. Peter grabbed her arm, pulling her to a stop.

"Why go back? Come with me and we'll find the Christian underground together," he said, his voice low and earnest, his expression begging her to listen. Anna shook her head and held up the iron key.

"I promised to return it to Terra. Besides," she added quickly as she saw him about to object, "I can serve our Savior very well here. There are many more 'unusables' like you. Go now, Peter, and hurry!" Peter did go, and a moment later Anna wheeled the empty table back to the surgery, careful to wipe the tomato soup stains off before she turned it and the key back to Terra.

Anna was so pleased with her delivery that night she couldn't go to sleep. It made her feel alive, and broke her a little out of the dull shock. Life...real life, not just existence, might go on still. She stayed awake for almost ten minutes, praying for Nehemiah and trying to draw a picture in her little leather notebook of Peter's expression when she poured the soup on his head.

Two months after Nehemiah's enslavement, he lay sobbing for the breath to stay alive after another session of his master trying to make him convert, knowing his father was dead and his mother would not come to soothe the hurts. Abid kicked him into the cupboard where he was locked when not in use, then paused with his hand on the seamless door, listening to his slave's gasps. Abid began to speak, his cold voice almost alive in the knowledge he was dealing damage in places none of his other instruments could penetrate. Nehi's master told him Anna was dead, describing the horrors of her enslavement and the way he had seen her body with an exactitude that erased all doubts over whether he spoke the truth. And if Daniel could have come to him, Nehemiah knew his strong older brother would have already been there. The door slammed shut, cutting off all light, all sound except his own sobbing.

Through the next weeks and months, the iron key clanged against Anna's legs and the white cover shifted up and down rhythmically, almost daily. Sometimes more than once daily. By the grace of God and the pointed ignorance of Terra, she saved lives that would have been offered at the idol of the state and 'usefulness.' But after another two months had ticked into reality and on into the past, it became more difficult. A second wing was added to the cellars to accommodate more prisoners for designation. With the added prisoners came new soldiers, and with the new soldiers came new dangers. Terra grew more and more reluctant to hand over the great iron key, and her legs began to feel weak with exhaustion at the extra runs to the far-placed room. Anna knew she couldn't keep up her deception much longer. She needed a different method, or she would have to give it up. But then a new circumstance intervened.

Samuel was brought into "Death Row." Oh, they had renamed it something else officially. But unofficially, that's what everyone still knew it as. The section was no longer under her domain, the new soldiers had taken it over. But Anna contrived a few minutes to go in and speak with her old friend the second night he was there.

"I can't give you much time," Charles, the soldier in charge of the new wing told her as he opened the cell. "In fact I'm not supposed to give you any time. If it weren't for those big dark eyes of yours..." He closed the door on her, still muttering un-

der his breath. Darkness closed in, smelling of decay and damp and dead things and despair. For a moment Anna couldn't see anything. The white sparks in her eyes cleared as they adjusted, and she noticed a huddled figure sitting on a cot to her right.

"Samuel?" Anna said quietly. He lifted his head, and she saw a bruised face, sagging with emaciation and wrinkled with age. But a smile of pure joy turned his blue eyes bright again.

"Anna! I don't believe my old eyes, Anna!" he held open his arms, ragged sleeves ripped and filthy. Anna flew to him, burying her head on his shoulder, big blubbering, messy sobs breaking from her as she clung to him. For a moment they just held each other, Samuel murmuring what comforts he could find to give the girl. But Anna's question was too pressing to allow her to give in to sorrow long. She pulled away, swiping a shaky hand over her eyes, and even managed a smile to show her old friend she really was all right.

"Do you know what's happened to Nehemiah?" Anna asked. "He hasn't been through here and I've had no news of him at all! Can you give me any?"

"No, dear girl. I have no news about your brother."

"Daniel–"

"No, I have nothing to tell you about either brother. Well, that's not strictly true..." Anna stared at him and he went on. "You can keep your own counsel, can't you?"

"Of course I can, what do you think I've been doing?" Anna almost snapped, dashing a hand over her eyes again. "No one knows who I am. At least none of the newcomers, and no Sojourner who recognizes me from the old days is going to give me away."

"Yes, of course. If you had told anyone, they would have had you out of here."

"Why? The country is dead, it doesn't matter that we're the old Judge's children, no one should care."

"I... Anna, I'm going to give you a short lesson in political history. Very recent history, so sit still and listen." Anna pulled her knees up to her chin, drew the skirts of her worn, filthy leather dress around her, and regarded her old friend expectantly. "A year ago now, a most dreadful thing happened in this country. Our book was stolen. Stolen right out of the midst of our guards. You know what happens to countries that don't have a book. They are disintegrated. Out of principle."

"Didn't we have a copy, a spare, or something we could use?"

"What? Dare to copy a book?" Samuel asked, shocked. "Don't ask silly questions, child, no one copies books." Anna wasn't so sure it was a silly question and felt the answer was rather silly itself, but she held her peace.

"We kept the knowledge to only an elite few. The head of the guards, your father and mother, Daniel, and myself, and went on with life hoping it wouldn't be discovered. But we knew such a catastrophe couldn't be kept silent forever. Daniel went out to make whatever discreet inquiries he thought useful, but I didn't have much hope in that. After months rooting for facts and traveling, he finally came back with news. He brought a letter that had been delivered to him. It was an anonymous letter stating that if we paid an exorbitant sum, we would be given our book back. Think on it, the letter said. Daniel had thought on it, and was busy finding the money when a new letter reached him. The terms had changed. Whoever had our book no longer wanted money, now they wanted...oh, let me see if I can remember the exact words: *'The treasure known to be held by the Hillson Judges, this alone can buy your book and your kingdom back.'* Yes, that's how the letter put it. Daniel came home immediately, but none of us knew what it was talking about. Not Titus, or Elizabeth, or Daniel, and if anyone knew what treasure they were holding, they should. I don't suppose you...?"

"I've never heard of any treasure," Anna said, shaking her head.

"Well, only a few weeks later the third letter came, an an-

gry one, demanding the treasure immediately, Daniel went off on a last desperate attempt to save the situation, and the invasion came. Then this disintegration. Somehow the world found out about our missing book and everything fell apart. I was there when they came for your parents. We were in your kitchen discussing things when it hit. We didn't even know why the guards were firing their weapons when the door burst open and the strangers were there. Non-uniformed, angry, nasty, they started demanding the treasure, shouting questions, and...they weren't nice people, Anna. Only a few minutes of it and they grew too excited, too angry and chaotic, and your parents were dead. I made it out in the confusion afterwards." Samuel paused, watching the tears roll down Anna's face again. She didn't try to hold them back and it struck him this wasn't a child crying. Her calm sorrow spoke of an older, more knowledgeable grieving. She would understand he wasn't just creating bugbears to frighten her. "No one notices an old slave if he keeps his head down and does what he's told. I've been listening to conversations these past months, Anna, and those nasty people are still out there and looking for you and your brothers."

"What! Why? We don't know anything. We don't even own anything anymore! There's nothing we can offer them."

"They don't know that. And they aren't the sort who listen politely while you explain. I haven't been able to learn any more than I just told you, all I know is someone is looking for you. Keep your family name quiet. No one who might recognize you from the old days would give you away on purpose, that I'm certain of. Goodness knows none of us have a reason to help the intruders." Samuel leaned back with a sigh, glancing around the cell, weariness sagging on his face. "Practically all the nations of the world are here, you know. That's why you see so many different uniforms. The Kingdom of the Prophet's Peace, the People's Kingdom, the Battle Kingdom, the Kingdom of Autonomous Man, Kallipolis, The Kingdom of Gaia, The Kingdom of the Wise, even Story Land has a presence here. All of them hate our country because it so firmly holds forth the truth."

"'If the world hate you, ye know that it hated me before it hated you.[5]'" Anna quoted Jesus, nodding. A loud rap sounded on the door. "Oh, I have to go now, Samuel, I'm not supposed to be here." She leaned forward and whispered in his ear. "I'll be back tonight; be ready."

[5] John 15:18

Chapter Five: A Crack of Hope

"For I the LORD thy God will hold thy right hand, saying unto thee, Fear not; I will help thee." Isaiah 41:13

Nehemiah sank slowly into despair. He began to beg for death. Abid just laughed. Quietly, like a burning worm wiggling into his mind, the question of "why" closed around his heart. It had been there since the beginning, since he had spoken it to Samuel. But he had fought it, keeping away the doubts and despair it carried, praying on even when he felt no answer, believing even when the heavens were closed and he could not feel God's presence. But gradually it became stronger than him. Why was God requiring this of him, day after wrenching day, why couldn't it end? Why did it have to start? Why was someone like Simmons even alive, Abid's horrible friend with the light-killing room upstairs where the worst nightmares were birthed? The questions were half formed, nebulous doubts that circled in his subconscious. Every ounce of strength in him went to surviving another day and he had none to spare for thinking. But the nebulous black cloud grew stronger and clouded over even what little comfort he drew from the verses quoted silently in the darkness, the prayers sobbed out in the night.

Abid held dinners in his rooms occasionally and there were a few regulars who came and knew of the ragged slave clinging to life and a cross. There were others who came sometimes, for orders from their leader. But they never stayed, and the disgust, outrage, and pity on their faces spoke a blessed truth to Nehemiah; not all Muslims were like Abid. And not every cruel man was Islamic. The vilest of the lot, the lithe Simmons, believed in his own lust for cruelty and nothing else.

One of the regulars was a young man named Atif, only a few years older than Nehi. Sometimes Abid would have his starved slave serve at the table, and Atif's tall build, light col-

oring, and his large, deep brown eyes reminded Nehemiah of Peter. It gave a strange comfort to Nehi to have the young man at the table, a sort of bittersweet wash of memories; for pleasant memories were very hard to hold to in Abid's back rooms. Three months after his enslavement, one of the dinners turned to talk of the slave. Talk turned heated, then it became action. Atif helped hold the writhing slave down while the others plied their skills in an attempt to break through the stubbornness, and Abid looked on and chuckled. The blackness and the nebulous cloud of "why" closed deeper over Nehi than he had ever felt it. Despair began to shut his mind down.

A week later he was nearly overcome by it, though he didn't recognize the fact. He recognized very few things around him. His master's voice had the power to animate him, but few other things did. In a rare moment, he had everything perfect in the suite, and no tasks to finish before *he* came to inspect. Nehemiah crouched on his heels in a corner, his eyes focused hungrily on the stuccoed wall, obsessively picking out patterns and shapes, as ketosis chewed at his insides and his swollen, pulsing hand sat cradled in his lap. The door to the room clicked open and Nehi pulled back instinctively, a tremble running through him and his eyes latching onto the floor tiles. A slave must not look up. Footsteps came closer and Nehemiah's lips tightened to a thin line as he pulled farther into the corner, too tired and terrified to notice that the steps were stealthy. They padded over the floor almost silently, someone moving on the tips of his feet, slipping over the hard tiles instead of striding over them. The soft sound stopped just in front of the cowering slave. Nothing moved and the seconds ticked by. Nehemiah stared riveted at the floor, his breath wheezing out of him in panic, feeling the stare of this someone focused on the back of his bowed head. The seconds stretched into a minute. Fingers tucked under Nehemiah's chin and lifted, forcing his neck to move. Nehi looked up compulsively, unable to command himself to do anything else under a clear order like that.

Atif knelt on the tiles in front of him. The Muslim's eyes were bloodshot, his pale face three shades paler than when Nehemiah had seen it last.

"Tell me why you endure it," Atif hissed. Nehi stared at him, his sluggish, panic-fogged brain unable to cope with the situation. "Tell me why you love a wooden cross that only brings you torment. Tell me why you will not confess Allah!" Nehemiah's exhausted brain caught onto two words; confess and love. His voice came in a whisper, cracked and hoarse, almost a croak. But it came.

"'Whosoever shall confess that Jesus is the Son of God, God dwelleth in him, and he in God... There is no fear in love; but perfect love casteth out fear: because fear hath torment. He that feareth is not made perfect in love. We love him, because he first loved us.[6]'"

The hand let go. Atif sat back on his heels, his reddened eyes staring into the slave's. Nehemiah's mind cleared with the verses. The black cloud around his heart broke a tiny crack, as a shaft of hope pierced through. It was hope focused on someone else, there was nothing in it for him. Nothing but an answer to a question.

"I love Him," Nehemiah croaked. His throat burned and his voice sounded unnatural, breaking and husky. But he went on doggedly. "And He loves me. This world only lasts for a brief few years. Love lasts forever. You don't have that." Atif winced and made to rise. Nehi's hand shifted out of his lap. It was bloodied and swollen out of recognition. A shudder ran through the Muslim as it landed on his bent knee, his gaze focusing on the mangled skin as his face contorted. "Confess Him," Nehemiah murmured. "He will take you, and love you too. Jesus died for you. That's why you're here now, in front of me, and you know it." Atif looked up, his face wild and flushed. For an instant the panic returned as Nehemiah felt the pent-up strength curling in Atif, and sensed (with the fear of the

[6] 1 John 4:15, 18, 19

73

abused) what ran through the young man was only a brief second from becoming a wild beating to the slave. But the second passed.

"I believe." Atif's voice trembled, wetness clogging it. "No one holds to a lie like you have held to this."

"Believe what?" Nehemiah pressed. A smile flitted over his broken face, a thing that hadn't been seen there since *he* took over.

"I believe that Jesus is God. That He died for me," Atif answered, his voice a whisper, almost inaudible. His hands went over his face, his words rising to a panicked hiss. "Jesus, I am yours!"

In a sudden flash that was not from himself the rest of the passage Nehi had quoted flitted into his mind like an unwanted guest. *"If a man say, I love God, and hateth his brother, he is a liar: for he that loveth not his brother whom he hath seen, how can he love God whom he hath not seen?"* Nehi recoiled as if punched. But only for an instant. His bloodied hand went out again. It rested on the back of Atif's neck and drew his face close till the men's foreheads touched. Nehemiah could feel the other shaking.

"I forgive you, brother," Nehemiah murmured, and he meant it. He let go and Atif fell back, shaking and one hand planted on the tile, holding himself up. "Go, now. There are cameras and sensors everywhere. They'll know in a few hours. Get over the border while you can."

"I will take you with me," Atif hissed.

"You can't," Nehi answered flatly, the thin band around his neck heavy and suddenly choking. They both knew it was true. Abid was much too careful of his slave to allow him any means of escape. Certainly not from these sensor-filled rooms, reacting to the control-collar. Abid knew every heartbeat of his slave in these rooms, every twitch of his nervous system. "Go, now. Go to serve, and to love. Hurry." Atif staggered to his feet,

[7] 1 John 4:20

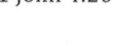

still shaking, his face working as he stared at the slave crouched in a corner. "Not like that," Nehemiah said, a smile breaking over his face for a second time in one day. "Get ahold of yourself. And get out of here."

"I'll come back for you," Atif whispered.

"Maybe I won't need it." Nehemiah felt the hope he spoke when he said it. The crack widened in the black cloud. Atif glanced over his shoulder as he slid out the door. His pale face nearly shone as their eyes met. Joy gleamed there, and it transformed the young man. The black cloud broke and began to dissipate into a quiet peace. For a long dizzy moment Nehemiah blinked, and Atif was gone. Nehi's head lolled and he let it lean against the stuccoed wall. The slave mustn't sleep. *He* had forbidden it. But...but peace was his, as Nehemiah hadn't known it in a long time. God moved in mysterious ways, and at least one answer to "why" rested in Nehemiah's heart and mind now. A new soul lay safely in his Savior's hands. He crouched and prayed, and his prayers had a solidity to them he hadn't felt in ages.

Two stories above Nehemiah, another man sat watching the slave crouching in a corner. His eyes stayed on the tiny screen illuminating his face in a green glow. Naqi Noorzai reached out a trembling hand and moved the footage back, shifting through the rooms till Atif picked his way through the outer door and slipped in to find an answer. The techy's hands flew across his keyboard, selecting a time the week before when the battered slave had knelt in the same corner, grateful to be ignored for an hour, to have a brief moment just to stop, to not be scrubbing and shining with each movement making his wounds gape. Naqi had set up the sensors and cameras in Hadi Al Abid's rooms. He knew how to erase a tape. A moment, and there was no trace left of Atif's visit on the security footage.

Naqi shoved the gadget off, swept it into his shabby black

bag, slung it over his shoulder, and stood up.

"I need coffee," he muttered to the other man manning the booth. His hand shook as he gripped the latch and pushed into the bright white hallway. But he shifted the bag higher and took off at a trot. He needed to talk to Atif.

He needed to know the slave's answer.

Everything with Samuel's rescue went fine, especially the five minutes conversation Anna was able to snatch with him before she shooed her old friend up the lift. A smile, wet but brilliant, still hung on her face as she locked the door and turned to push the table back to Terra.

A new soldier stood staring at Anna, blocking the table. A woman in a Story Land uniform, eyes hard and face set like a stone statue. Anna swallowed. She shifted her hold on the table and made to move around her, one wheel squeaking in the quiet hall. The soldier's hand shot out, gripping the table and whipping it from between them. It bounced across the hall and banged into the wall with a clang that rang in Anna's ears.

"You are found out, child of the Way," the soldier growled. A sick lump formed in Anna's stomach. "How many of those marked as unusable have you let go? I suppose all that will come out later. Right now I'm to take you upstairs for your trial." The soldier slung her rifle off her shoulder, the crystal lens of the Brunhiem glinting in the artificial light. The sharp whine of the laser priming, building up energy, filled the air. The soldier waved the rifle at Anna. "Come on, upstairs."

Upstairs. Anna hadn't been out of these cellars in four months. Despite knowing certain death waited for her there, a thrill of pleased excitement coursed through her as she moved through the halls toward the door out. The soldier pushed her ahead, her rifle nudging Anna's back uncomfortably. They moved through the hallways toward the stairway. Anna's heart beat gradually faster and faster. They came to the door leading to the stairway, and Anna reached for the handle. The

guard was saying something, but she couldn't hear it through the pulse ringing in her ears. Every rust mark and ding on the door was clear to her eyes. The old metal handle felt exquisite as her hands closed around it. Anna pulled open the door to the stairwell.

A tiny breeze caressed her dirty face. The rifle muzzle dug into her spine and Anna started up the stairway. Life waited there, if only for a brief moment before it was snuffed out to send her hurtling into eternity. Anna's footsteps rang as she walked up the stairs, and as she reached the end the rifle muzzle jammed into her back. She stumbled and nearly fell into the stairwell at the top. But she hardly noticed it and didn't feel the pain of the growing bruises. The door stood open. There was a real breeze here, cold and fresh. Anna lifted her arms almost unconsciously as she moved forward to the guard's prodding and spun in a little delighted circle.

The stars still twinkled, the night shone silver, the beauty of the outside still here! The invaders hadn't been able to kill it. She was outside again! Anna gazed into the night sky, shining with the stars Nehemiah loved so much, and realized she was praying for him again. But this prayer had more hope than she had been able to conjure up since her parents' deaths. She was outside. Perhaps Nehemiah waited for her, well and happy. Anything could be possible here.

The wind had breathed hope into her, and Anna was awake again.

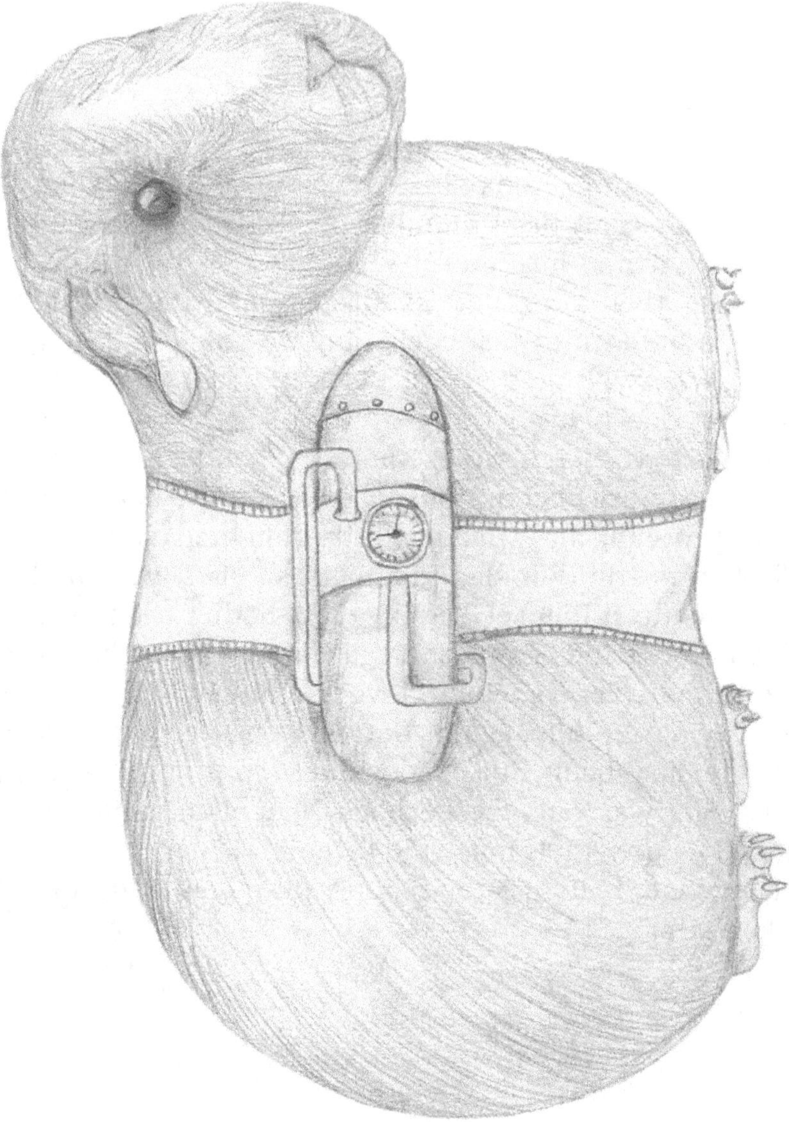

Prissy
Pg. 81

Chapter Six: The Ravens

"He delivered me from my strong enemy, and from them which hated me: for they were too strong for me." Psalm 18:17

Four months after Abid took over, Nehemiah waited on his master at dinner in the great hall, at the table where he and Anna and Samuel had found themselves the first night of the invasion. At first his master rarely took him to the communal table, but lately Abid had fewer concerns over removing the control-collar and bringing his slave out of the secure rooms. This one wasn't going anywhere. He was broken. Nehi stood still, looking meekly at his toes. He heard the door open and someone approaching, but had forgotten the possibility of lifting his eyes to see who it was.

"A traveling musician, brothers," said the newcomer. From her peculiar use of 'brother' Nehemiah knew she was a soldier of the People's Kingdom. "They wish to know if you want to be entertained at meal."

"By all means," Henderson yawned. "A little entertainment would go perfectly with this delicious salad." The soldier retreated. Nehemiah heard the door creak open farther and a collection of loud noises greeted his ears. Creaking and groaning, like wood moving more than it should, and a hiss of steam escaping. It mixed with the shuffling of a large creature. Swirling in the cloud of noise came a sort of snuffling, wheezing, squeaking sound. A spark almost strong enough to be recognized as curiosity spurted to life in him. A deep voice boomed around the hall, and Nehemiah's fragile nerves sparked. He leapt an inch, trembling, his breath panting out of him in short gasps.

"Greetings all, we thank you for this opportunity to entertain you!" the voice boomed. Nothing horrible followed the sudden noise and Nehemiah's heartbeat began to slow a little, and his mind was able to focus on the voice. It had something different to it, a quality that Nehemiah couldn't place. "We are the Ravens, traveling musicians with no home to our name but wherever we choose under the stars. Sit back, and prepare for your senses to be amazed and delighted!" Near the end of the booming speech, more strange noises drifted to Nehemiah; the clanking of metal and wood and a few preliminary toots on an instrument that sounded like a nasal whistle. Silence fell in the room, as everyone waited.

A note sounded from the middle of the hall. Its beauty reached out and slid into Nehemiah's soul; and slid his brain into gear as he tried to identify the instrument. It had a strange tangy quality. Quiet, gentle, he had to strain to hear it, forcing him to give all of himself to listen. The note grew, filling the hall with its volume. The single note erupted into a beautiful, enchanting melody. Another whistle joined in and blended with it, then another, creating a haunting air that danced and sang and mourned all at once. Nehemiah lifted his head, though his eyes stayed down. Music used to be a large part of his life. He and dear Anna had shown a flare for it. He had been allowed no music since *him*. This was so beautiful and moving it wrenched his heart. But it was wrenched in a joyful expectancy, a direction he had hardly felt since *he* had taken over. The music paused and Nehemiah waited, his mouth parted, breath held still in his lungs. The hall exploded with a remarkable rhythm. The strange whistling music joined with the vibrant, pounding beat, rebounding off the walls. Every mouth involuntarily dropped open and stayed that way. Nehemiah lifted his head farther and looked out through lowered lids.

A large wagon rested in the hall, not mechanized like Nehemiah had seen before, but animal drawn...at least...metal tubes could just be seen twisted under it, and a few wisps of steam trailed out, so it must be a hoverer of some sort. It looked like a sturdy shack with a bench on the top front. A gorgeous mural of ravens in a forest at night splayed over its large side. Attached to the front of the wagon was a huge hairy beast who looked almost entirely cylindrical. Little pink feet

stuck out of it, ridiculously small for its size, and the front of the cylinder sloped down to form a nose and face. It had large, brown eyes and a mouth with what looked like rabbit teeth. On top of the wagon stood another large figure, a man of immense form with his hands on his hips. His nose was blunt, as if someone had slapped a lump of dough on his face. His ears were large and the tops seemed to have grown so high they couldn't support themselves and fell forward, creating a sort of flap. He was hairy. Very hairy. The music rose in pitch and the rhythm grew in excitement, and Nehemiah looked toward the sound. His mouth dropped open along with all the others in the room.

Only one person created the beautiful, strange music. A black-clothed musician danced with blurring speed in the midst of the hall, a pile of metal and wood scraps splayed around him. As he danced the musician's feet hit the things laid out or scraped across the gravel, sending the rhythm dancing through the hall. The little wiry form spun and kicked, flipped and twisted, his hair whipping around his head in a blond-colored halo. Every movement was precise and elegant, perfect and sure. He held a set of whistles tied together, double reeds poking from the top, different sizes speaking of different octaves, playing sometimes one, sometimes all of them. He blended and harmonized as he danced in the midst of the metal and wood. The music seemed alive under that pulsing, strange rhythm, the driving energy giving the melody wings. Nehemiah stood fascinated. He forgot even to fear that his master would notice his interest, he forgot everything but the music. He stared and wondered with the rest of the hall.

The musician did one last twirl, his soft black boots smashing into the correct pieces. His blurred form materialized in a kneeling, boy...no, maybe it was a man...or a boy? Whichever it was, he looked almost half Nehemiah's size. The musician knelt on one knee behind his rhythm makers. The same single note where he began rang through the hall. The note softened, died, and silence fell. A moment passed in the room, as everyone drew in a wondering breath.

The hall erupted with applause. The little musician's head lifted and his gaze swept the occupants of the room as he slid to his feet. The amazed applause went on and he took an easy bow, his pale face calm. The musician's eyes locked onto Nehemiah's; those eyes were green, calculating, remarkably intelligent. They were beautiful. Nehi quickly dropped his gaze back to his feet, heart beating wildly in the knowledge he had been disobeying to watch. If *he* should notice! Those bright green eyes woke him from his musical trance and back into the hard reality of life.

"My friends," the strange man on top the wagon boomed, "you have just heard the sounds of–"

The large door to the hall banged into the wall, shutting off his words. Nehemiah heard two people approaching the table. He tightened his jaw and stared harder at his toes. Two people approaching while they were at dinner, one with the smart step of a soldier and one with an ordinary step, meant a Sojourner being brought for judgment. Nehemiah had seen many cases in the past four months and all of them had ended in an evil fate for the member of the Way. The two sets of steps stopped in front of the table.

It was then Nehemiah's heart leapt into his throat and tumbled to his toes. A wave of nausea, of heart-rending hope and dread, swept over him. He would have sunk to the floor if he dared. He heard a voice he loved so much more than his own, that he had believed he would never hear in this world again.

Anna whispered his name.

Nehemiah's head shot up, not caring if his master noticed. Anna stood there with a female soldier in the yellow uniform of Story Land. Alive! She was alive! And now here, in judgment to be killed again. She stared at him. Her sweet face almost shone, joy and concern so beautifully mixed. So pale. She looked like a woman. So beautiful and steady, unafraid, and uncaring of herself. The spark that had started with curiosity

and been kept alive by the beauty of the music, sprung into a small, real flame. His sister was alive, and she needed him. She wasn't even listening to her own sentencing. Well, he listened. She had been helping the condemned escape. Well done, Ann, that was showing Jesus love for His people. But she was caught now, and sentenced to die. Oh, they had many fancy words for it, but that's what they meant. Nehemiah looked at his sister. Anna was alive. She stood there, so glad to see him, a grin split her skinny face, and she didn't notice or didn't care that she was about to be executed. At the sight of that familiar, happy smile the flame crackled into fiery life in Nehemiah, growing into a roar of vitality and strength. No. No! He could not let Anna die, not again. He was her only protector now. Daniel was gone or dead, his father was dead, his mother was dead. But she wasn't. Not yet. Nehemiah began to look about the room, careful not to catch the attention of his master. That wouldn't do, not now. Not when he had to get Anna out.

The two soldiers standing by the door held red Krackmens; dye lasers utilizing rhodamine. Their accuracy was legendary, but they took a full seven seconds to prime. The soldier beside Anna held a Brunhiem (taken from the Judge's guards), and there was the simple projectile pistol his master always carried. Abid preferred it as a bullet dealt more agony to those it killed than an incinerating laser, and the clips could be switched for non-lethal projectiles that incapacitated. Those were the only arms in the room. Nehemiah let his gaze fall on the pistol by his master's side. It had live bullets loaded now, he knew. It lay near his hand. Very near. The soldier by Anna prodded her, moving her toward the door. He had to do something now.

Nehemiah swallowed his terror, willing himself not to think of how long he would be left in Simmons' room for this, hooked his toe around his master's chair, and jerked his leg back. The pistol stock was cold as his fingers wrapped around it, his thumb fumbling for the hammer. As he grabbed the pistol, Nehi vaulted onto the table, knocking off plates, bowls, and cups, to shatter on the ground. His feet hit the marble beside Anna as his master banged into the ground on the other side of the table.

The instant Nehemiah moved, Anna's hand shot back and latched onto the black laser prodding into her spine. She dashed it up into the guard's chin, spun in a tight circle, and jerked the weapon into her control as the soldier staggered. She still knew Nehemiah well enough to know what he was thinking, and she was ready.

Nehemiah landed running beside her, and she dashed beside him. Two quick shots spun out of the pistol, the bullets creasing the guards' scalps. The two soldiers sunk gently to the ground as the twins rushed by them. Nehemiah's hand shook uncontrollably as he gripped the cold metal handle of the door, watching Anna grab the left door in his peripheral vision. He could feel his master's heavy tread pounding behind him. The twins spun out of the hall, using the doors for leverage, jerking them closed together. The heavy metal clanged shut. Two sharp thumps came almost in the same instant, as Abid and the large leader of the Battle Kingdom slammed into the other side. Anna shoved the Brunhiem laser between the door handles as Nehemiah held his pistol in both hands, eyes scraping up and down the hallway, waiting for the soldiers who would run toward the shots.

"Well this is a fine jam," Anna commented as she shoved the laser in harder.

"Let's hope it's tight," Nehemiah gasped, his voice hoarse. They took off, feet slamming into the tiles and ruined carpets. Speed was everything, and they headed for the nearest exit; the main door. The twins pelted on, rushing through the elegant domed entry hall, their own fear pounding too hard in their ears to hear the murmur of interest from those who noticed. Nehi strong-armed the postern door open, feeling it slam into a heavy body. The night air washed over them as they leapt over the steps, feet thudding into the charred ground. They were almost out of the courtyard before the

startled guards at the door gathered their wits enough to fire at them. The whine of lasers cut through the night, and Anna automatically raised her hood as they dashed along. Dirt spurted up in little volcanoes of white light around their rushing feet. Nehemiah gripped the corner of the old Miller's hut, and he spun them onto the streets toward town. A dark maze of quaint winding roads opened before their feet. But the twins knew every cobblestone. They raced down the main road, ducked into an alleyway, through a bakery, and through another alleyway. Anna paused against the charred side of a house.

"Where to?" she asked.

"Woods," Nehemiah gasped, one arm snaking around his side. He looked so thin and hurt and weary, Anna noted miserably. They moved off, hands clasped, a silent pact to never let go again. Soldiers poured from the Judge's old house (now the conquerors' headquarters), mobilizing soldiers to help in the search. Sirens whined and searchlights spurted to life. It became a game of cat and mouse, as Anna and Nehemiah ducked through doorways and under bridges, working their way out of town and toward the woods. The mice had the advantage. They had lived here and explored this town all their lives. It wasn't that hard to make it into the woods. Once under the tall pines and enormous tillandsias, they knew every rock and tree and remembered all the old paths they had discovered and cleared while cracking poor puns and laughing over nothings. Nehemiah paused for an instant, leaning shakily against the rough bark of a tall hardwood tree, as a cough wracked him.

"How can...you tell a dogwood...tree?" he gasped, a tiny smile managing to twist his face.

"By its bark!" Anna finished the ancient joke with a little choked laugh, feeling it mix with a sob as she watched the immense effort it took her brother to force himself up the path. The twins ran deeper into the woods, toward the high mountains on the border of their kingdom. The paths grew steeper and they were forced to walk. For a little while they still made good time. Then Nehemiah began to stumble and his breath, already coming in ragged gasps, began to get more frantic as if he was incapable of drawing in oxygen. Anna remembered the stories she had heard of the Christians who tried to get out, and knew it was no good continuing on anyway. The dogs would be well on their trail by now, and Nehemiah would never make it to the river before they were overtaken. She laid a hand gently on his arm and pulled him to a stop. Nehemiah sank to the ground without a struggle. Anna suddenly realized she was hardly able to stand herself, and her breath came in painful spurts. Anna dropped beside her twin, put an arm around his shoulders, and drew him close. His head sank onto her shoulder and she could feel the effort wracking him with each breath. She smoothed his matted hair as their mother used to do.

"Shh, Nehemiah, Jesus is with us and we'll be fine," Anna murmured.

"Keep the vision–" he started to rasp, but couldn't go on.

"–always burning before your eyes. Our goal is still real, and waiting for us," Anna said, holding him tighter. They sat still under the moon, the woods where they had spent so many happy hours covering them. But running under the cool breeze came the chilling knowledge they were only minutes away from recapture. *Lord,* Anna prayed, as she held her brother and felt the wind on her face, *we need Your help as we've never needed it before. Oh please help, Jesus!*

"Hello," a voice croaked.

Anna jumped, her throat constricting as her head jerked toward the sound. A large black raven stood a foot away from her, its head flicking from side to side and its bright eyes watching her.

"Hello?" she said, her voice trembling. The raven gave a loud, harsh cry, spreading its black wings. A rush of air, feathers rustling, and it rose into the sky and out of sight. Anna stared after it, dully wondering where it had learned to speak.

She wished she had wings like that so she could give them to Nehemiah and let him fly to safety. How very worn she was, worn, worn, worn, in heart and body. Anna let her head slump onto Nehemiah's. They sat still in the gentle breeze, silent except for their ragged breathing.

Bwow! Bwow!

The hound's bay was deep, and guttural, still far away. But before it died on the air it had already come closer. The twins lifted their heads and stared at each other. They lurched up and moved on through the trees, steadily higher. The baying grew nearer. Nehemiah stumbled, clumsy with exhaustion. Anna caught him, but he dragged at her and she just didn't have the strength. The twins tumbled to the ground in a heap, a breathless little cry sliding from Nehemiah. A harsh caw rang over their heads and Anna looked up. A raven circled them. Nehemiah was trying to make her race for the river without him, but she didn't pay attention. She watched the raven, still circling and crying. Nehemiah realized he couldn't make his sister leave him, and forced himself up on shaking legs. Abid had taught his slave how to keep going on. Nehemiah had ordered himself they would keep moving until they were caught, and that self-given order hung in his exhausted mind and forced him on; unspeakable things happened when you didn't follow orders, even his subconscious knew it, and drove him on.

A large figure stepped out of the trees and onto the path in front of them, a huge black silhouette, framed by the dark pines. Nehemiah recoiled, stumbling back with a stifled shriek.

"Shh! Quiet," the figure said quickly, in a deep voice that had an odd quality to it. Nehemiah knew it as the traveling musician with the flappy ears and the blunt nose, but he was too drained to do more than recognize it. The man caught him around his waist, sweeping him off his feet, till he lay crooked in the arm of this great hairy stranger, like a weary child carried by its father. Nehemiah struggled, weakly pushing against the bulging muscles and hair. He couldn't see Anna anymore.

A hand took his. She was there, held on the man's other side. Nehemiah dropped back, too threadbare to do anything else. He didn't have the energy to wonder at the man's strength, but Anna did. The stranger ran, dashing through a dark wood carrying two nearly grown people. He wasn't even breathing hard. She should have been frightened of being snatched by a stranger, but she found she wasn't. Maybe it was how gentle his hold felt. Maybe it was only that all the fear she had was focused on the baying dogs behind her. She didn't know. But Anna felt almost safe as she rested in this stranger's arms.

The pines broke around them and unfiltered starlight poured onto a narrow track, used occasionally for logging. It could hardly be called a road. A wagon hovered over the grass. Painted ravens swirled in mid-flight over the side of the wagon, while an intricately carved railing ran around the top, and she recognized it as the one in the great hall. *What do traveling musicians want with us?* Anna wondered wildly as the man ran up to the wagon.

"We're going to hide you and him, miss," the blunt nosed man growled in his deep voice. Another stranger popped up beside Anna. A boy, guessing from his size perhaps twelve or thirteen, she couldn't tell for sure in this light. A scarred face, a sharp nose jutting from it, and a mop of blond hair spilling over his eyes, were all she caught in a blurred glance. One thin hand held open a small, square door on the side of the wagon, directly underneath the driver's seat. His free hand motioned her into the dark opening through the door. He held a spray can that clacked with the motion.

"Inside," said the deep voice, moving her closer to the opening. A dog's bay filled the forest just behind them, and she could hear the hounds' excited panting growls and the sharp commands of their handlers. Anna made her choice. She did as she was told, scrambling in straight from the man's arms. Her spine bent and her knees pushed against her chin. The big man shoved Nehemiah's limp form in after her, and it was almost too cramped to breathe. The door closed with a click, she

heard something spraying and a sharp smell of anise drifted to her. It would cover their scent. The wagon lurched forward. Pitch blackness surrounded Anna, as she tried to squirm into a position that would let her breathe without her legs pushing against her rib cage. The baying dogs had nearly reached them. Anna could hear Nehemiah's breath getting more and more frantic and felt him begin to tremble violently, his hands pushing on the wooden sides of their hiding place. He wasn't really awake now, and Anna wondered if he could understand where he was.

Bwow! Bwow! A dog bayed right outside their hiding place and Anna started, her heart thundering so hard it hurt. Soldiers shouted, calling the wagon to halt, the sound muffled as it drifted in through the wood enclosing them. Anna finagled her arms around Nehemiah and held him close, praying for God's comfort for him in whatever nightmare he fought, begging he would stay quiet. Her whole being focused on her hearing.

"Two workers fled tonight and came this way," a young, authoritative voice called. "Where are they?"

"Why should we know?" the deep voice of the big man answered, from the wagon seat above her.

"What are you doing out away from home so late?" barked the young voice. The big man chuckled and Anna found herself smiling despite her fear. It was such a joyful and catching sound it permeated even Nehemiah's nightmare. A shuddering sigh slid from him and he grew still in his twin's arms.

"'Out' is our home, soldier," the deep voice answered merrily.

"You can't tell me your home is up here. No one ever comes this high into the woods." The tone was annoyed and suspicious. "Why didn't you stop in a town? And why doesn't your little friend say something?" Anna heard the soldier step forward, his boots hitting the hard packed earth. "Come on, boy, speak up." Scuffling came, the sharp thump of feet kicking and scraping the wood above the twins, as the soldier jerked the blond boy out of the wagon seat. Another thump on the road, the boy slamming into the grass.

"Oh ho! What's this mark on your neck? You're a genetic incomplete! You can't answer my questions." Disgust and triumph laced the soldier's voice. An incomplete. Anna had heard that term before and fished through her mind for the answer. That's what much of the world called those who weren't perfect. The blind, mute, or deaf, or those born without normal intelligence. The soldier's voice cut through her thoughts and she listened in breathless silence. He sounded bantering now, as if he had found a plaything. "Well, that mark may be wrong, you know. Let's find out for ourselves if–"

"Let him go," a voice snarled. It had changed so completely it took Anna a moment to recognize it as the large man. Now it was the most menacing sound she had ever heard. She shuddered in the dark, glad his growl wasn't directed at her.

"I didn't realize you could conceal a rifle that big on your person," the soldier said. He no longer sounded triumphant. "No, lower your weapons," he said, voice muffled as he turned to speak over his shoulder.

"Let him go," the deep voice snarled again, dripping threat. Anna heard the sound of something hitting the ground outside her door, and then someone scampered up the back of the wagon and on to the top.

"Go away," the big man growled.

"I see what you are now," the soldier snorted. His repugnance was almost tangible. "A chimera and an incomplete. You suit each other well." An engine roared, coming up the road in a rush. Anna took two hot breaths in the close dark air, and she could hear a powerful hoverer hissing beside the wagon.

"What's going on here?" a rich, full voice spoke up. Nehemiah started so hard he flailed in the dark, and began to quake, his fingers biting into his sister's arms as a frantic terror took him. Anna winced at his grip and pressed his face gently to her. There was no room to do anything else. "That...creature has a gun on you, soldier."

"What's any of this got to do with you, Simmons?" the young soldier snapped.

"I've had a few dealings with the slave boy who ran, if you insist on knowing what I'm doing here. And Abid just told me his name, finally, so now I'm even more interested. Drop it," the new voice commanded, snapping the order. Something clattered onto the seat of the wagon, the chimera obeying. Chimera... That's right, the people created by a method made by those of the last world, before civilizations collapsed and sent men scrambling for their lives. A mix of animal and human genes. It was said at first they had been trying to create a super-human, the next step on the ladder of science. But instead, the chimeras had come out rather foolish. To the complete disgust of those who mixed and grew them, they had an innate sense of duty and love for their real Creator that could not be trained out of them. Simple faith, some called it. The chimeras had quickly become nothing more than a source for cheap, specific labor.

"You see, I can be useful when I want to be," the rich voice said, bantering. Nehemiah shook uncontrollably, almost writhing, and Anna could feel him murmuring desperate, silent pleas, sobbing them out into the darkness.

"Thank you," the soldier answered, his voice scornful. "Now all this ordinary business must be very dull for you, Simmons, so why don't you get on with your hunt?"

"Not a bad idea," the voice said. His words dripped sarcasm. "You're doing such stellar work, you don't need me, obviously. I'll leave you to it." The hiss of the hoverer began to move, and Anna heard it pass the wagon and shoot off on down the road. Whatever Nehemiah understood of their situation, he understood that. He sagged in his sister's arms, a raspy breath blowing from him. Nehi's weight pressed into her, and Anna could feel his breath coming in slow, shallow steadiness that wasn't from relief. He lay in blank, complete unconsciousness.

"Holding a soldier of The Kingdom of Autonomous Man at

gunpoint is a serious offence, chimera," the soldier spoke up. "You'll come along with me now, and if you object my men will shoot you. You understand? Here it is in your own style. Bad chimera, come now." He sounded positively happy. Anna shuddered and desperately hoped the big man had something up his sleeve. A shrill whistle broke through the night air from the top of the wagon. Of course, the boy. They had all forgotten him.

"Where did you get–?" The soldier's voice was a mix of amazement and fright. He cut his sentence off without finishing it.

"He will throw it," the deep voice growled.

"Don't try to threaten me," the soldier snarled. A moment of tense silence filled the night woods. A clicking started up from the top of the wagon.

"Hurry," the chimera rumbled, interpreting his friend's noise. A frustrated, angry growl broke from the soldier.

"These two beasts aren't worth our time, what are we doing here? Move off, men," the soldier ordered. "Bring those dogs and let's see if we can pick up their scent on the other side of the road." Feet tromped off, moved around them, and then on away to their left. The wagon began to slide down the narrow logging road, rocking back and forth gently as it went. Then it gave a lurch, a cute, rumbling squeak came from the animal in front of the wagon, and the boards under Anna settled into a smooth speed. Her tight muscles relaxed and she breathed again. She hadn't realized she had been holding her breath for that last tense moment. A beaming smile broke over her dirty face. She put her mouth near Nehemiah's ear.

"We're safe, Nehi. Free!" she murmured. He made no sign of recognition. Anna held his limp body, and suddenly noticed the dark again, black so deep it seemed a world of its own. The wagon rose over a bump, and dropped down heavily, jolting her head against the wood. Free from one danger...but had they blundered into another?

Chapter Seven: Joe and Beau

"Defend the poor and fatherless: do justice to the afflicted and needy." Psalm 82:3

The wagon scooted on for what seemed like ages and ages. The cramped space and darkness closed in, until to Anna it felt like a living thing trying to smother her. Nehemiah didn't stir, and Anna envied his oblivion. She leaned her head back against the cool wood for what seemed the hundredth time, wishing it was still a tree trunk.

The wood fell away. She fell with it, air and light flooding over her as the cubbyhole wall landed on a bunk inside the wagon. Anna lay on her back and blinked, gulping in air, stars sparking in her vision. When she could see again, she saw the boy's face above hers. He grinned down at her, his green eyes sparkling merrily. Seeing him up close in the light Anna realized despite his size he must be about Nehi's and her age. Or even a little older. It was difficult to tell. The face was thin, his features sharp, with a host of white scars marring his light skin. One running along the length of his right jaw was particularly ragged and nasty. A part of Anna said she should think it was a disreputable, even a frightening face. But she didn't. She liked it, especially those merry, kind eyes. Her alarm fled away as they met hers.

"Hello," she gasped.

He nodded and held out a cup. Anna tried to sit up to take it. Half of her curled inside the cubbyhole, half of Nehemiah splayed on top of her, and her stiff muscles groaned. She felt two hands slide under her shoulders, lift, and help her swivel around, and she found herself sitting comfortably on the lower bunk of a bunk bed. Nehemiah's head lay on her lap while her back rested against the other side of the wooden panel where she had spent so much time. The cup was suddenly in front of her face. Anna looked from it to the one who held it. The blond boy smiled again and his eyes moved quickly from the glass to her.

"Yes, I am very thirsty. Thank you," she said, not even realizing she was answering a sentence that hadn't been spoken. She took the cup and drank the cool water in one long, delicious gulp. Then she realized very guiltily that she should have saved some for Nehemiah. She looked up to ask the boy for more and found that he was on the other side of the wagon digging through a crate.

She forgot about the water as she looked around her. There were things everywhere, a chaotic clutter of colors and shapes. Musical instruments that she recognized and ones she had never seen, a pile of wood and metal, a chest of drawers overflowing with clothes and tools, a crate filled with food and dishes. Anna spotted a bare place on the wall and caught her breath in surprise. An elm's smooth tree trunk stood there, bathed in moonlight. Anna looked around again and realized all the walls were covered in tree trunks. She followed one of the trunks up with her eyes and let her mouth drop open. The branches of the trees swept the wagon top, interlaced with the ones from the other side, but in the midst of this terrestrial sight sparkled the extra-terrestrial. Stars blazed out in just their proper places. They were so real and so beautiful Anna couldn't decide for a moment if she was looking at the ceiling of the world or the ceiling of the wagon. The wagon rose suddenly over a bump in the road, Nehemiah almost rolled off the bed onto the floor, and she was convinced of where she was. She steadied her unconscious brother and smoothed his long, matted hair. There were several patches missing, pulled out. Their mother used to take such pride in keeping those black curls neat and trim... Oh, Nehemiah.

Anna looked up for the boy again, instinctively knowing he was the only one who could help them right now. He knelt across the room, digging into the crate for something and dropping what he didn't want onto the littered floor. A rubber ball bounced across to her as he tossed it away. A fork clattered to the ground. A matchbook fell. A pencil, dagger, laser goggles, another rubber ball, a mass of unmatched socks, leather gloves, another fork, all came rattling out of the crate onto the floor before the boy found what he was looking for. He spun around and Anna saw he held bandages, a large box of some sort of salve, and two brown medicine bottles. He saw her looking at him and motioned to Nehemiah. His sharp face and green eyes showed sympathy and concern now. Anna wondered if she ever conveyed thoughts as well as he did.

"I'm worried about him too," she answered. "He's been still so long." The boy knelt beside Nehemiah and looked at his face. He pursed his lips, and gently moved the ripped sleeve covering Nehemiah's right arm, in search of something. A look of disgust twisted his face and he jerked his hand away as if what he found burnt him. He took Anna's hand and laid it on Nehemiah's bruised cheek, then took her other hand and en-circled her brother's shoulders, moving him a little more se-curely into her lap. After a quick encouraging wink at Anna, he uncorked a little bottle underneath Nehemiah's nose and slipped to the side out of his sight. Nehemiah spluttered and coughed.

"Ann?" he croaked.

"I'm right here, Nehemiah," she said quickly. "We're in the musicians' wagon, and look at the ceiling. It's your stars, all staring down at you to say hello."

"I haven't seen them in so long," Nehemiah murmured. It took a heavy effort, but he reached up and gripped Anna's hand, his arm shaking. She could see his throat constricting in his terror. "Is he...are they coming back for us?"

"No, Nehi. It's all right, we're safe now," Anna answered, finding the words difficult to get out. Anna began to talk, drawing Nehemiah's mind onto sweet tracks of memory, reas-suring him they were safe. The boy moved silently from his corner after watching for a moment. He ducked around what Anna had taken to be the back wall, but from the clinking and noise she could tell was a dividing wall into another room. He walked back before thirty seconds had slid past, with two

large clay mugs. Steam curled from the top, and they smelled of broth and pepper. He handed them both to Anna and deftly got Nehemiah in a sitting position. In a second he was pressing one of the cups into Nehemiah's hands and motioning them both to drink.

"Chicken soup," breathed Anna as she took his advice. "I haven't had hot soup in ages, it was always cold as ice by the time my work was done. Did you make it?" she asked the boy. He was behind the partition again, but he poked his head out and nodded at her question; he could hear then and wasn't just reading lips. Anna would have liked to say the soup was delicious at that point, but decided it was best not to lie, especially on a first acquaintance. She drank it gratefully despite the horrible flavor, much too hungry to complain. Nehemiah seemed to like it well enough. He drained his cup so there wasn't a drop left. Anna was relieved to see some of his natural color come back as he lowered the mug. He looked at Anna and she beamed back.

"We're free, Nehemiah, free and together!" she said, throwing her arms open wide in her exuberance. Nehemiah cried out as her mug hit his swollen eye and the few contents left splatted over him and onto the rug. The boy poked his head around the corner at the sound of Anna's swift apologies and Nehemiah's quiet responses. He laughed a jolly silent laugh, sent a threadbare towel hurtling from behind the screen at Anna's head, then ducked back. A moment later he poked his head around again and motioned for Anna to come. She stood up from where she had been using the towel to clean the soup stains on the ground (not bothering with the ones on Nehi's rags) but hesitated beside her brother. The boy reached onto a shelf, felt around for a moment, and brought out a pad of paper. He stuck a hand in his thick mop of blond hair and pulled out a pencil. It only took three seconds for him to scrawl what he wanted across the paper. Anna found the note pressed into her hands, as he ducked around the partition again.

There's a bath and warmer clothes waiting for you over

here. Tea after that if you want it. It's all right, I'll look after him.

She looked from the note to Nehemiah, leaning feebly against the wall. The boy stepped back in, carrying a large bowl of steaming water and a cake of soap. Another thread-bare towel draped over one arm, and over the other trailed a pair of pants and a dark green shirt for Nehi. He plopped the bowls down, looked at Anna, pointed to the clothes, shook his head, and motioned her behind the partition.

"You're sure he'll be all right if I go?" she asked. He motioned to Nehemiah, one eyebrow rising, his expressive face saying, *Ask him, not me.* She did. Nehemiah stirred and looked at her.

"We're free. I'll be fine," he said, and even gave a smile with the words. He sounded enough like he meant it that Anna let herself be led around the partition. She was shocked at how much room she found. The boy quickly pointed out a bathtub filled with steaming water, a towel (not quite as threadbare as the others she had seen), a cake of soap, an old but still ser-viceable hairbrush, and a dark blue dress folded neatly on a minuscule stove. She turned to thank him and found he was gone. Anna peaked around the corner and saw him sitting on the bed with her twin. Nehemiah hunched into himself, his arms wrapped around his stomach, crouched against the wall. The boy held out his hand and grinned invitingly. Nehemiah looked at the hand, then at its owner. His shoulders relaxed a fraction, and he took the hand. Anna breathed again. She turned back around the screen and looked around her.

The paintings changed here. The sun shone from a clear blue sky on a mountain meadow surrounded by aspen trees. Their leaves were golden and so realistic Anna expected them to rustle. There was a large oak tree in the midst of the mead-ow, and two ravens sat perched in it. One had green eyes. She leaned forward to get a closer look. The other bird's beak seemed a little blunted, and it was much larger than the

green-eyed raven. His wings spread out so they overshadowed the smaller one protectively and his gaze turned up to the heavens beyond the tree. The smaller raven was frontal, its green eyes bright and very intelligent. She had the idea it was analyzing everything that went on in the room. It was a beautiful and rather strange picture, and Anna stood staring at it, entranced. Then the wagon jolted again and it made the water splash. A hot bath! Elation swept over her and she lost no more time staring at the walls.

Anna was too tired to think much, but she enjoyed her bath. As she slid into the new dress and it fell to swirl around her ankles, she smiled. It was so good to be clean and comfortable. But as she leaned down to sweep up the old worn leather dress a deep sorrow expanded inside her. Mom had bought her that dress. Her mother had been so insistent they go on a shopping date as mother and daughter, even though neither of them much cared for shopping. That had been a good day. Anna dashed the tears away, wondering how long she was going to find herself crying over the little things, and went quickly into the night room.

Dim light closed around her and it took her a moment to adjust. Nehemiah lay on the lower bunk, asleep, several blankets pulled over him. His face still looked emaciated, pale, and hurt. But the dirt and blood no longer clung to it, and something about the set to his mouth seemed a little more normal. The boy sat on the floor beside her brother, hugging his knees and tracing patterns on the ground with one thin finger, his sharp face blank of any thoughts. He looked up as Anna came in. He motioned her to be quiet, pointing to Nehemiah and smiling. Anna nodded and smiled back, agreeing with him that it was a very good thing to see him sleeping. Though he looked more unconscious than asleep. The boy hopped up and collected the wad of bandages (almost gone, Anna noted with a grimace). He grabbed the bowl of water (thick with dirt and scum, and scented of iron), and a few other odds and ends, and quickly moved into the day room. Anna crossed to the bunk and dropped to her knees beside Nehi. She could hear his breath wheezing out of him. But it was the calm, slow breathing of sleep. She reached out and gently tucked a curl behind his ear. He was here.

"Jesus' peace be with you, Nehi," Anna murmured into her brother's ear. She climbed to her feet, joints creaking and muscles complaining, and followed the boy into the other half of the wagon, blinking at the light. The mute knelt by the tub, working the stopper out, his black turtleneck sleeve pushed up to keep it dry. Anna noticed several long scars running down his arm and curiosity sparked in her.

"Thank you," she said simply. He looked up at her in surprise. "Thank you for everything. For rescuing us, and for dinner, and the bath, and your kindness, and the clothes. This dress is even a perfect fit–" Anna broke off and looked at him in surprise. "How did you have clothes for us?" The boy's face went blank and his eyes dimmed, no longer showing any thoughts. He shrugged in a very non-communicative way. The stopper came out with a pop, and he fell over, upsetting a lap harp leaning against the wall. The water began to drain out quickly onto the road and Anna leaned forward to see how the ingenious tub was set up. A beautiful strain of harp music filled the room. Anna looked up quickly. The lithe, strong fingers of the mute darted across the harp's strings, his small form dwarfed by the instrument as the notes danced. One hand splayed over the strings, stopping the sound as suddenly as he began, satisfied he hadn't damaged his instrument. Anna wished he would go on.

The wagon gave a sudden lurch, the incessant soft hiss of steam began to slow, a rocking motion took over, and then even that stopped, as the wagon settled onto the ground. Anna looked at the boy. He stood on tiptoes, calmly putting a stack of dishes in a recess in an elm tree. Anna blinked and reminded herself it was just the wall. She was too tired for paintings this realistic. Two arched aspen trees, their tops interlaced, sunk away into a pointed door. The immense figure of the

chimera squeezed through. The boy put the last plate in the elm tree and made several swift hand motions at the man.

"Yes, it's a good spot," the chimera said in his deep bass. "Dry, level, grassy, safe." He let a small folded table down from the wall, pulled a chair out of a corner, and sat down. With the addition of the table and his large form the room suddenly seemed very small. Anna found herself pushed into a corner and wasn't quite sure what to do about it. The boy grinned and kicked a small stool. It skidded across the ground and clattered into the corner exactly under Anna. The chimera's eyes followed the stool, then rose to Anna as she sank onto the seat. The big man leapt up, blinking and staring as the wagon rocked under his movement. Anna didn't like to see him embarrassed in his own home, and quickly broke the ice.

"Thank you very much for your rescue tonight, sir," she said, vaguely thinking she should come up with something less formal. The embarrassment melted on his big, hairy face, replaced by a look of shocked delight. The chimera turned to his friend as the boy stood at the stove tipping a pot over a large clay bowl. A stream of soup poured from the pot, steam billowing in wispy tendrils around the mute's face.

"She called me 'sir'," the chimera boomed. He chuckled and shook his big head. "She called me 'sir'!" The boy laughed silently, plunked the bowl on the table, pressed a spoon into the man's hand, and shoved him back into his chair. "Sir," beamed the chimera. The boy made several more swift, strange motions with his hands. The chimera paused, his spoon halfway to his mouth.

"I forgot," he said. He stood up and gave Anna a theatrical bow. "We have not been introduced I find, miss. We are Joe and Co. He is Joe," he said motioning to the boy who smiled a smile that said hello, "and I am Cobeau." The two suddenly did a pretty leap to the side and made a sweeping bow to her. It was so perfectly coordinated and unexpected, Anna laughed and applauded. "We welcome you to our little house, and you are welcome to whatever you may find that you wish." Cobeau turned to Joe hopefully. "Is that right, is that what you told me to say, Master?" Joe threw up his hands, rolled his eyes, and glared at Cobeau.

"Sorry," the chimera said, a bashful smile breaking over him. "I mean is that what I was supposed to say, *Joe*." The boy's hands flashed in the light as he moved them in elegant sweeps and dives, and Anna realized that was how Joe spoke. She also realized she was pitifully weak-minded to have just figured that out. Anna couldn't understand much of it, but she gathered from Cobeau's occasional replies that Joe was trying very hard to break him of the habit of calling him "Master." Anna let her tired eyes drift off of Joe's fluid, rapid signs and found they rested on the two ravens sitting on the oak tree again. The feathers were perfect. How were they done? She pulled her leather notebook from the pocket of her old dress, flipped it open, took out her pencil (now only a stub), and began trying to copy the feathers. A shadow fell over her paper and Anna looked up to see Joe peering at her notepaper pressed on the hard white board. He saw her looking at him and pulled back.

"Did you do all these paintings?" Anna asked. He nodded. Joe pointed at her little leather notebook, then held out his hand, his expression questioning. Anna hesitated for just a moment. This notebook was the one thing remaining from her old life; this and her faded dress. Her mother had given it to her. It was her one tangible piece of comfort since losing her parents. But now she had Nehemiah back. And besides, she didn't fear anything from Joe.

"Of course you can see it, but I warn you none of my pictures are very good. Nothing like yours," she said, holding it out. Joe took her book and sank down on the ground underneath an aspen stand. He began flipping through it, pausing every now and then to study a picture. Cobeau slurped his soup as Anna watched and wondered how anyone could eat that much of such a poorly cooked dish. Joe smiled, held up the book, and pointed at a picture. It was a pen and ink drawing of Nehemiah, done sometime last year; he lounged on his back looking up at the sky with that peculiar expression people get when they're creating castles in the air for someone's amusement. Anna remembered that day. They had been in the meadow behind their house and had wandered into a discussion of clouds. Nehemiah had decided that people must live up there and purposely make the clouds look like things on earth. As she sketched him, he had been describing the people to make her laugh. She smiled back at Joe, but her heart wasn't in it. Those days seemed very far away from the young man who lay senseless in the next room. Joe put the book down and gave a short little whistle to get Cobeau's attention. He began to sign something to her. The big chimera rumbled in a sort of monotone, translating for Joe.

"Your brother will be able to daydream and joke like that again," Joe said through Cobeau's sing-song growl. "Don't judge him by tonight. He's too worn down to do anything but exist right now. Love him and help him, like you did earlier, and he will be back to normal soon." Joe smiled again, a gentle look, and handed Anna back her notebook.

"Thank you for that hope," Anna sniffled. "But I don't know how much I can do, he's so hurt and tattered and scared... You seem to know much more about it than me, will you help me with him, Joe? Please?" She suddenly found she was crying and brushed away her tears, mad at this ridiculous tiredness. She didn't like to cry, especially in front of strangers, and especially when asking for help. It might too easily be taken for a woman's ploy instead of real sorrow. But she felt only real sorrow. Cobeau handed her a handkerchief, his face crinkled with sympathy. He looked as if he were about to burst into tears with her. Joe studied her, his face registering nothing of what he thought. Anna's fingers toyed with the handkerchief, winding it in senseless patterns, praying quietly to the heavenly Father she knew would help her sort life out, as it changed again. A quiet moment passed in the little room. Joe stood up smoothly. He gave one quick nod to Anna, opened another recess in a tree where linens peeked out, and motioned to the night room where Nehi slept as he searched for something. He was very quick.

"I'll help him heal," he took a moment to sign and Cobeau rumbled for Anna. Joe tossed two blankets at Cobeau, clicking about something, and the men began to move busily about the little room, allowing Anna to sit in quiet for a moment. Her head nodded and she jerked up. Joe was suddenly in front of her again. He grinned cheerfully and pointed to a kettle sitting on a single burner built into the wall, raising an eyebrow in question.

"No thank you," Anna murmured. "I'm much too tired, I don't think I could stay awake for a cup of tea." The boy nodded from where he knelt collapsing the bathtub and stuffing the pieces into a corner. Joe leapt to his feet, motioned Anna around the partition to the night room, and pointed to the top bunk. He pulled two blankets off a shelf and handed them to her. Anna's hand brushed over them as she took the blankets and he gently pushed her around the partition into the dim room. They were so soft. And smelled of lavender. She blinked herself awake and realized Joe was pointing to the bed again. He gave a half serious, half comic salute, and moved off.

"But where will you and Cobeau sleep if we take your beds?" Anna asked. He poked his head around the partition again. Joe circled a finger around the ceiling, mouthed the words, "under stars," pointed firmly at the bunk, and ducked back out of sight. Anna climbed obediently into her place. It seemed they had fallen in with kind people, whatever else they were. Anna found the energy to lean over and check on Nehemiah as she finished throwing the two blankets over her bunk. He was so deeply out she doubted he would wake up even if they crashed. Anna lay back and pulled the blankets up deliciously close to her chin. Her one thin blanket in the cellars had been too short and had smelled stale and foul. These were lovely. The light from the day room went out, and a door opened and closed from that direction. In the sudden darkness she saw that the stars on the ceiling glowed with a faint white light. Anna closed her eyes to thank God for a night like this, in peace, with her brother there. Sleep closed down her mind before the words had a chance to form.

Outside the wagon, Joe and Cobeau lay underneath the stars. Sleep hadn't touched them. They lay beside the wagon, wrapped in their blankets, and in silence. Cobeau's face held a large troubled frown while Joe's was remarkably blank.

"Are you sure that's it?" Cobeau finally rumbled. Joe's hands moved out from behind his head and he signed something to his friend.

"But she called me 'sir'!" the chimera almost wailed. The hands moved again, elegantly and beautifully in the moonlight. They dropped down a moment later and let the silence stay. Cobeau broke it once more.

"So we're still doing it?" asked Cobeau, his deep voice as quiet as it ever could be. The hands moved reluctantly now, with only a few motions, then dropped back down. The big chimera nodded, his brow creased.

"You're right. What else can we do?"

Chapter Eight: Notes and Resolutions

"As free, and not using your liberty for a cloke of maliciousness, but as the servants of God." 1 Peter 2:16

Warmth enfolded Nehi, seeping into his bones. Soft blankets draped around him and lay tucked against his skin. A hint of lavender danced in his senses, speaking of freshness and good things. It smelled like what his mother used to sprinkle on his bed. He lay still, his consciousness slowly dragging itself up from the blackness. The pain still clung to him. But it felt a little better. He drew in another breath, relishing in the scent, the warmth; the comfort. It made him feel like a man again instead of a slave, to wake up in a bed, in ease and peace. Dread crawled into his heart and up his throat, muscles tightening. It must be a trick of his master, or Simmons. If he opened his eyes they were sure to be there, leering at him, with some new devilry in their hands. Very slowly, Nehemiah cracked his un-swollen eye open.

Silver stars twinkled down at him. His other eye opened and he stared at interlacing tree branches with the beautiful stars shining down, giving him hope and joy in what lay beyond them. Nehemiah lay still and stared. He blinked, holding his eyes closed for a moment before looking again. Daylight shone around him too. He ran a hand over his eyes. No, the stars were still there. How could there be both? He moved to sit up. The pain lashed through him, every fiber of his being complaining at his movement. His mind reeled and the nausea was so bad only *his* strict training kept it down. He sat up anyway, his face tight, eyes slits. Nehemiah lifted his head and rolled his shoulders. It still felt better this morning than it had in ages. But it shouldn't feel better, not after his master having tossed him to Simmons and being locked in that man's room... Nehemiah glanced around again, groggily knowing he was missing something.

Anna, their flight, that horrible baying, the musicians' wagon! He staggered to his feet, his gaze darting everywhere, searching for his sister. His eyes fell on the top bunk by his shoulder. Anna's tousled black hair poked out of a pile of blankets, a pile that breathed rhythmically.

It was true. She was alive, and here! Nehemiah stood and blinked, swaying on his feet. The pain was still with him, so he wasn't in heaven, which meant he was really out.

He was free.

They both were. They were free. A smile curved over his face. His head dropped to his chest and he gripped the bunk to keep himself on his feet as the room spun around him. Free! After a moment he could think again. That was why he felt a bit better this morning, that little fellow with the hot soup and the soothing salve. He must have fallen asleep right after the salve had lessened the pain. Nehemiah didn't remember much else from last night, but he remembered that.

A shaft of sunlight spilled around the corner and onto Anna's black hair, making it shine. That was all he could see of her with the blankets pulled up. Nehemiah moved them down so she didn't suffocate, and smiled again as she swatted his hand and pulled them back up. Still feisty. Maybe life...maybe it would be all right now. Nehemiah gripped his stomach with one hand and kept his other on the bunk for support. Boy, he wanted food. His eyes swept the room nervously. The memory of the little fellow's sympathetic face came to Nehemiah and he risked walking away from his bunk. It took a lot of courage to step around the partition by his own free will. But the young man was desperate; and he knew he would have to use a great deal of courage in the coming days to be able to leave *him*– Abid. He was master no more, and no longer held Nehi's every moment in his hands. Nehemiah would think of him like a man now. Give the horror back his name. And so take his own back too, and leave behind "slave."

When Anna had turned the corner she saw space and art. When Nehemiah turned it he saw space and efficiency. Each item was engineered to fit in the little room, or had a place in the room designed to fit it. The light streamed in from a hole in the ceiling, painted to look like a sun. It was very clever, and very nice. Nehemiah decided he liked it as his eye swept the room. He caught sight of the ravens sitting in the oak tree. The green eyes stared into his. Those intelligent eyes were the ones he had seen in the hall yesterday, but they were somehow different than the ones that had looked into his on the bed several hours later. Or maybe he had just been too exhausted to register them properly. A note hung from the raven's mouth, and Nehemiah leaned forward to read it.

Food is in the oak, choose what you want. We're on top, climb up after breakfast.

On top? On top of what?

"On top of what?" Anna yawned behind him. Nehemiah jumped and spun around. But the alarm left his face as he saw Anna. He smiled and handed her the brush sitting on the cool burner. "That bad, is it?" she said and began to brush the tangles out of her hair. "It's good to see you smile. Seeing you last night I wasn't sure if you would ever manage it again. But Joe said you would."

"Joe?" Nehemiah asked, feeling the oak and trying to figure out how it opened. Anna set the brush down and began to tell Nehemiah about last night. As she unfolded two chairs and let down the table, he got the oak to swing open, revealing an ingenious combination of ice and shelves. Nehi's hand shook as he snatched a block of cheddar. Anna studied the contents of the chest, carefully ignoring the way Nehemiah scarfed down the cheese. A very strange mix of food lay in the chest. There was also a pair of wadded up shorts. Anna couldn't help grin-

ning at these musicians' very masculine housekeeping skills.

"Nothing is made up yet, it looks like," Anna said, deciding to ignore the shorts.

"I choose scrambled eggs and bacon," Nehemiah said around cheese, a bit more decisively than the situation demanded. "What do you say to those two?"

"Nothing, I only eat them. But I do that with great joy and anticipation," answered Anna. Nehemiah grinned, real happiness stealing in as he handed the ingredients to Anna and the cheese settled in his belly. Suddenly being free, helping Anna cook breakfast... It was so like the half-formed dreams he had created in the darkness, Nehemiah was afraid this was all a blessed, wonderful dream, a moment of relief given him by God, and he would wake up in that nightmare of a life again. He bumped his shoulder against the wall as the wagon jerked. Fire pulsated through him, and he grunted, swaying and eyes slitted again. It was real. Nehemiah sighed, thanked God in fervent silence, and picked up the conversation, interrupting Anna's rambling monologue as she tried to find the cooking implements and turn on the stove.

"You should have heard Joe's music. It was amazing!" Nehemiah said, and his words flew on to describe his first sight of the Ravens. Anna interrupted, telling Nehemiah of her conversation with Samuel, and he interrupted to tell her how brave she had been. Then she interrupted to tell him what a triumph their escape was and how clever he had been to try it. Nehemiah burst in to say it wouldn't have worked if Joe and Cobeau hadn't come to their rescue, and of course that brought them back to where they had started. The conversation was so like their old ones (moving so fast it made little sense to anyone but themselves), they both felt better. Life might be able to return to some sort of normal. Anna began to sing a hymn as she stirred the eggs and bacon. Nehemiah hesitated, his gaze darting around the room, and then joined in quietly as he pulled out the plates from the elm tree.

"Oh world of grace and wonder,
I must sing these words aloud,
For by God's might is sundered
All sin's bonds that held me cowed!"

A shadow filled the skylight with a flutter of wings, and a harsh voice cawed. Nehemiah started back, the plates clattering to the ground as he shrank against the wall, gnawing his lip, his eyes glued on his feet and chest heaving. Anna laid a hand on his arm.

"It's all right, it's just the raven from last night," she said cheerfully. "Unless I'm a 'raven' lunatic and mistaken."

"Bird puns always fly over my head," Nehemiah murmured, a tiny smile creeping over his strained face. His hand still shook as he leaned down to pick up the plates. He might be better this morning, but... Weariness pulled at Anna's limbs and she sent a silent request for strength to be all he needed flitting to heaven's throne. A memory popped into Anna's head in that moment. Afternoon sunlight playing over the crocheted lace tablecloth, her mother's beautiful, calm voice talking with the ladies as steam curled from their teacups and Anna scarfed cookies and toast. She could remember every word of that conversation and knew what her course should be. The best way to help a man be a man was for a good woman to treat him like he already was a man. To let him be the leader and protector. For just a moment her will rebelled. This was her twin! But letting him take charge was right, and the best thing she could do for him. In an instant she made a resolution; Nehemiah would take the place her father's absence left. A deep breath, letting go again.

She chucked her brother under the chin teasingly to get his lowered head to lift and asked for another plate from the elm,

since she couldn't reach. Nehemiah obeyed, his tenseness beginning to relax. He looked up as he turned around. A large black bird perched on a twig that jutted out from one of the aspens. The raven cocked its head to the side and surveyed the twins.

"Hello," it croaked. The light was blocked and cleared again as Joe landed lightly on the ground beside them. He held up his hand and clucked to the raven. The big bird fluttered down and landed on his shoulder, pecking at his head in a friendly way.

"It's your bird then?" Anna asked as Nehemiah sank into one of the unfolded chairs. "Does it have a name?" Joe shook his head then nodded it almost in the same motion. He slid a pencil out of his shaggy blond hair, flipped his note about breakfast over and wrote.

Her name's Jewel. I call her one of mine, but it was Beau that brought down and trained her, and she's really too free to be anybody's.

Joe tossed the paper to Anna, replaced the pencil in his hair, and ran his hand down the bird's black feathers. Nehemiah saw his hand pause for a moment when it reached her leg. For just a second he thought he caught a glimpse of that bright gleam he had seen in the hall in Joe's eyes.

"She's the one that found us and told Cobeau where we were, isn't she?" Anna asked. Joe nodded. Now the eyes were simply the friendly, merry ones Nehemiah had seen last night. He couldn't quite understand this. But the friendly quality was enough, and he should get in the conversation.

"I hear you're Joe," Nehemiah said, holding out his hand. "I know we've met, but I can actually respond this morning, thanks to you. Hello, and thank you." Joe grinned and pumped his hand up and down enthusiastically. Then he sniffed and looked at the eggs Anna had cooking on the burner.

"I hope you really meant to pick anything for breakfast. I made extra," she said. Out came the pencil again and he scribbled on what little clear place was left on the paper.

Breakfast I've had, of a sort, quite a bunch/ But I very much hope that you will make lunch.

He grinned at her as she laughed and nodded, shooing his bird out the skylight in the same second. Joe leapt and caught the edge of the skylight with his fingers, swung out feet first, and was gone.

"I guess that's the 'up top' we were wondering about," Nehemiah commented. "Are the eggs done yet? They sure are taking a while. And I want to go talk to these people. I wonder why they picked us up?"

"And how they knew our clothing sizes."

"And boots even," Nehemiah said, lifting his foot to show a gently used pair of boots that were very comfortable and fit him well. And would help keep the bandages clean as he healed. "How did they find us?"

"And where are we now–"

"And where are we going?"

The eggs finished cooking, and breakfast interrupted any conversation. Anna realized she was going to have to re-think her ideas on extra with Nehemiah around. After Nehemiah was done using his fork and fingers as a kind of desperate shovel, the twins tried to do the washing up, but couldn't put the sink together, and left the dishes piled on the table. They had to use the table anyway to reach the skylight. After a few tries, they scrambled out onto the roof. Anna and Nehemiah had expected to come out on a shaking, sloping roof with not much to hold on to and had braced themselves for it. Instead they found hand and toe grips sticking up in two paths beside the short railings on the side of the wagon, and comfortable

seats carved out of the wood near the front. A hoverer's clear wind shield bubbled the top of the wagon. A half oval of crystal-glass[8] formed to fit over the wagon top, the bubble was all that made traveling at a hoverer's high speeds comfortable. This bubble rose high enough Nehi didn't feel cramped as he scooted forward, and it was a pleasant surprise. The landscape was a green and brown blur as they sped along the grassy road.

The twins found Joe and Cobeau settled on the bench set a little ways down the front of the wagon, and looked past them, just outside the bubble. Nehemiah blinked in surprise and Anna burst out laughing. A leather harness lay over the cylindrical animal's back, trailing up to a sort of leather flying helmet draped over her face, and twisting down to attach to four wheeled boots clamped on her feet. Two small steam engines were strapped on the sides of the harness and rotated the wheels through a gear and belt system; a simple stick design attached to it and allowed the driver to shift the big animal anywhere they needed to steer. The great, round creature seemed to be enjoying its speed. It kept lifting up its nose as far as its thick neck would permit and sniffing the air. She snuffled again, and let out a piercing series of squeaks that rose and fell in a cadence Anna thought she recognized.

"Smart," Cobeau rumbled. The Hillsons looked over to see him smiling at them and nodding at the harness contraption. "Joe made it. He thought Prissy would like it."

"Prissy?" Nehemiah asked, a chuckle escaping at the ridiculous name for the big creature.

"Is Prissy somehow related to a guinea pig? She reminds me of a pet I once had," Anna asked, studying the animal.

---

[8] Due to the high speeds of hoverers, tempered glass shatters at any small impact, and plexiglass scratches too quickly. Crushed precious stones are melted and mixed with the usual concoctions to create a stronger, crystal clear glass shield.

Cobeau looked blankly at Joe. The mute signed something at the chimera but didn't look up from the bagpipe lying in his lap.

"Yes, we think she is something like that," translated Cobeau.

"But she's bigger than you," Nehemiah said incredulously. Cobeau looked at Joe again. The mute sat and scowled at the bagpipe as if he couldn't quite grasp something it tried to tell him. He signed something back, but continued staring.

"He says you'll find all sorts of strange things like that as you travel. Leftovers from the past world." Cobeau looked thoughtful for a moment. "Like me, I guess." His simple face clouded over and crinkled in concentration, as if some half-remembered horror was trying to come back. Joe batted his shoulder. He pointed to Prissy and pulled back, then waved one hand in a sweeping gesture at the woods and stuck the other over his eye as if he were looking for something.

"Yes, I'll watch," Cobeau nodded. He switched the engines to low as Joe pumped the wand for the bubble. The crystal-glass broke in two down the center and sank into its slots, disappearing from sight. Fresh, clear, cool air rushed over the twins, bringing birdsong, a gentle breeze, and the scent of leaves and good dirt. Joe and Beau hopped off the wagon, unconcerned it was eight feet to the ground. Cobeau just landed normally on his feet and walked toward the pig. Joe landed on his toes and fingers, as a cat might, and moved to the opposite side of the pig, helping shrug the shoes and their trappings off. Joe stowed the shoe contraption in a cubby under the seat, and the two musicians snapped wheels to the wagon and shut off the steam. Prissy shuffled off down the road, the wagon rumbling and vibrating as it moved tied to the ground by its wheels. It felt strange to the twins, so different from the smooth, warm ride of a hoverer; but it was a pleasant strange. Cobeau strode off and disappeared into the woods.

"Where's he going?" asked Anna. Joe reached for his pencil and pulled a pad of papers from his pocket as he climbed back on top the wagon.

"Why did you two rescue us?" asked Nehemiah.

"Where are we going?" asked Anna.

"Why are we going? I mean, why are you letting us travel with you?" Nehemiah took up. Joe's eyebrows rose and he held up a hand to interrupt the next question. He pulled off the page, handed it to Anna, handed the next note to Nehemiah and his pencil scratched again.

He's scouting, out watching for danger.

Your father found us once, when we were in trouble. He got us out of it and was so kind. Really kind to us. We hoped to repay him.

Anna looked away from the note in her brother's hand as a new note pushed into her palm.

Came too late to help him. But at least we get to help his children. Taking you out of the country, by the least watched border, takes about two weeks to get there if we don't run into trouble.

"What sort of trouble?" Nehemiah asked quickly. "And what danger is Cobeau scouting for?"

Not sure, but he will know it if he sees it.

"What's that supposed to mean?" Nehemiah asked, his face worried as he scanned the trees. Joe shrugged and pushed one last sheet into his hands.

I'm out of paper.

Joe slid away, dropping back in the wagon seat below them, tweaking Prissy's stick as the pig threatened to veer off the road toward a succulent patch of grass. Then he went back to glaring at his bagpipe, ignoring the brother and sister. The twins sat back on the carved wagon seats, staring absently at the papers in front of them, thinking about it. From the way the note stressed their father's kindness, Anna had the feeling kindness wasn't something the Ravens were used to. Nehemiah stared at the little one stating the Ravens were taking them out of the country. *Then what?* revolved in his mind, pounding at his brain till a headache started to throb. They would get out of the country. Then he and Anna would be on their own, and...they would figure it out. Together. The wheels rotated, Prissy shuffled on, and the siblings sat on top the wagon, watching the woods along the side of the path slide slowly by.

"Nehemiah?" Anna broke the silence in a quiet voice. "I...they are really gone."

Nehemiah dropped an arm around her shoulders and pulled her close.

"Cry on, Ann. It's all right to miss them," he murmured, his voice flat. "We could never have had better parents. God gives and takes away, and we will praise Him at all times, for He is always good." His lips pursed and he looked away, a hardness coming over his face. He sucked in a breath and spoke again, conviction back in his tone. "We'll see them again."

"Yes. What a gift they were, Nehemiah!" Anna turned her face to his thin shoulder and wept. He was strong enough to hold her when she needed it. They could be strong for each other, and life would be all right. The two began to talk. They spoke of their parents, of Daniel, telling each other about the past four months, and bringing comfort and a soothing love. Two hours meandered gently by in the sunshine on the top of the little wagon. Gradually the past was dealt with, and their words moved on to the interesting present. When their new situation arrived in the twins' conversation, a sharp rap sounded behind them. They spun in their seats and saw Joe's arm poking out of the skylight from the wagon, his black leather sleeve an interesting contrast to his white hand. Anna blinked in surprise, automatically looking back toward the front of the wagon where she thought the mute was still perched, absorbed in scribbling something and occasionally tweaking the giant pig's steering stick. The white, freckled hand motioned for someone to come near. Anna slid forward and peeked down. Joe stood on the table, a tray balanced on one arm. He grinned at her and pushed it out of the skylight. Anna heaved it out and carted it toward Nehemiah, noting a pot of tea, two cold bottles of water, a large slab of cheese with a good supply of crackers, a bowl of fruit, and a big cup of steaming broth that looked as if it had come from a can. Nehemiah's face lit up and his hand shot out, snatching the broth. Joe scooted toward the front of the wagon and swept up his paper and pencil again.

"Thanks," Nehemiah murmured over the mug. The mute looked up in acknowledgement, giving him a happy grin that said he was glad to oblige. When the blond head lifted Nehemiah could see the paper he was working on. Their host was expertly transcribing a song. Joe went back to it, wholly engrossed in the effort. Nehemiah set the empty mug back on the tray and smiled at Anna as he reached for the cheese. She grinned and nodded. Their situation now was a good one with these odd, quiet people. They let the subject lie. They had enough to bother about without worrying a good situation wasn't safe. But they couldn't live day by day forever.

"What do we do now?" Anna asked as she poked her fork into the fruit to bring out a strawberry. "I mean, first we get out of the country safely; after that, what do we do?"

"We need to find our book," Nehemiah answered through more cheese, smiling at Anna. It was nice to have someone asking him for advice. "Without it we're crippled and dying. Say, happy birthday by the way, Anna," Nehemiah interrupted himself. "We're sixteen now after last month. How was yours?"

"Good heavens, I forgot all about it," Anna blinked. "I was so busy I didn't even notice it had come up. I hope yours was absolutely splendid?"

"Well, we won't go into that," Nehemiah said, his eyes darting away. A muscle twitched on his jaw. A moment of silence fell, but Nehemiah broke it again. "Mom sure hosted some good ones for us, didn't she? Remember our tenth birthday party, with the goat circus?"

"My favorite, fat, curly-haired one escaped from the merry-go-round and butted Dad into the duck pond while he was holding the cake," Anna giggled.

"'Don't let the goats loose!'" Nehemiah mimicked Titus Hillson's inane spluttering. The siblings laughed, their eyes damp. Nehemiah picked up the conversation again. "We have to get that book back, Anna. Dad spent his life keeping our country safe, and he was right. Sojourner's Way needs to live. Samuel said Daniel's trying to get it?"

"Yes. He's still trying, I suppose, since we haven't heard from him. At least I pray so. It's very unnerving to have heard nothing from him. Though I suppose we were both buried pretty deep, he might have been trying and been unable to find us. Do you think we can find him?"

"Yes, that's what I think we ought to do. Find Daniel, find our book, and restore the kingdom. That doesn't sound like too much for the two of us to do this year, do you think?" The breeze seemed cold as it stirred the young man's hair, cutting through his skin to dig deep into his bones. Anna gave a warm chuckle and poured him a cup of tea. It was strong peppermint, with a hint of vanilla. Just the smell infused vigor and cheeriness around the top of the wagon.

"That may be a little above the powers of even our duo, considering we've never been out of this country. But not of our trio, you know. Nothing's impossible with God, especially if His workers let themselves be led by Him."

"Right," Nehemiah said, not meeting Anna's eyes. His voice was flat again as he went on. "And neither height nor depth can change that."

"You never know where help might come from. Remember that red-haired man at the very beginning of this horrid disintegration? I think you would have been killed right then if he hadn't spoken up."

"You mean the fat one with the annoying smile?" Nehemiah said, and Anna grinned at how well the description fit. "I guess it's true. Did you know his name is Freddy, of all funny things? God does bring help from strange sources sometimes. I just can't believe no one made a copy of our Bible!"

"I know, it doesn't make any sense, does it?" Anna agreed. Nehemiah shook his head, and as he did, his gaze wandered idly, lighting on Joe in the wagon's seat. The mute stared up at them and his face held the sharp, calculating look Nehi had first seen on the little fellow. In an instant, he sat glaring at his bagpipe instead. The look had been so quick and the mute's face seemed so bland and friendly now, Nehemiah wondered if he had only imagined it. He was still awfully tired. Although "tired" didn't really describe it. Joe suddenly snatched his bagpipe and began a beautiful tune, his eye on the page of music. His tune rode the wind, haunting and strange, but exciting and inviting. He played for about five minutes, then set the bagpipe down. He nodded in satisfaction, hopped up, and whistled shrilly.

"What are you doing?" Nehemiah asked. Joe grinned at him, motioned to the stack of used up papers, and shrugged.

"We ask a lot of questions, you know," Anna said, holding a cup of tea toward the young man. Surprise flew into his expressive face. His eyes flitted to the cup the twins shared, so

A crystal whip tail
Pg. 162

he could have this one, and his expression melted into a thankful smile as he took it.

"Yes, and we like to talk a lot," Nehemiah spoke up, offering a hunk of cheese to go with the tea.

"So do you think you could teach us your language?" Anna finished.

"Unless you want us to use up your whole stock of paper," Nehemiah added. Joe looked at them in disbelief as he flipped a piece of cheese five feet in the air and caught it absently in his mouth. He kicked the pile of papers and found one that wasn't entirely used up as he switched to the tea. Joe scribbled in the margins, squatting on his heels in front of them.

You really want to learn?

They nodded. He scribbled again, looking honestly puzzled.

Why?

"So we can understand you, of course," Anna said with a laugh.

"Is it such a surprise that we would want to learn your language?" asked Nehemiah, studying the young man. Joe shrugged and smiled speculatively at them. He pointed at Nehemiah and jotted, *bath.* "Anna agreed quickly, and asked for a pair of scissors for a haircut, shooing her brother into the wagon and turning to gather the things back on the tray.

Nehemiah cupped his fingers around the skylight and swung through. His joints screamed in protest and he landed heavily, staggering and biting his lip so hard he nearly bit through it. A thin arm slid around him, supporting him with expert skill and surprising gentleness. But mostly what Nehi noticed in that instant as he blinked and tried to focus on the mute's face, was the strength behind the maneuver. Every muscle in that wiry arm was like a metal cord, taut and incredibly strong. Joe eased the bigger boy onto one of the chairs, and Nehemiah focused again with an effort, forcing the roaring in his head away as he watched Anna's feet swing in front of him. Her toes sought out the table, and in a moment she moved through the wagon, being efficient.

Nehemiah found himself doctored, barbered, fed again, and put to bed before another hour had climbed into reality. Anna meant to get the breakfast dishes sorted out and make lunch for their hosts as her brother slept. But as the night room quieted, she stayed still, listening as Nehemiah's breath came and went, rattling through bruised ribs. Her stomach churned. She had seen his fresh scars and festering wounds more clearly today. Anna sank onto the bunk beside him, unwilling to leave him alone. Her fingers slid between his and she drew his right hand into her lap. A tear dropped onto the raised scar tissue crisscrossing his olive skin. Anna brushed a hand over her eyes and stayed sitting beside her twin. The calm drowsiness of the night room seeped into her. Fifteen hours later, Anna woke up to morning sunlight streaming into her face.

That morning Joe and Cobeau kept the wagon in the meadow where they had settled for the night, joining the twins at breakfast. It was a merry meal, but different than anything Anna and Nehemiah had experienced. Cobeau shot single word questions at the twins about different plant and animal life in the area, with Joe interposing ridiculous rhyming couplets through his big friend's rumble, usually in praise of Anna's cooking. It could hardly be called conversation, but was definitely entertaining. Anna had the idea Joe's comments were mainly to get Nehemiah to laugh. It worked most of the time. As soon as the dishes were cleared, Joe plopped in front of the twins at the table, closed his fist with his thumb sticking up on the side and circled an 'A' on one of his notes. So began their first lesson in signing. It was much more difficult than it looked.

The fire popped and Nehemiah jerked awake. He blinked around him, his vision fuzzy with weariness. Anna was gone, already inside the wagon asleep. He rubbed his eyes, ignoring the slow-healing right eye. He didn't want to go inside. Out here, even in the dark, it was... A breeze stirred his hair and he looked up. A star peeked through the clouds, incalculably far above his head. Free. It was free. He could *feel* the freedom out here. At night inside the wagon the dark closed in like a smothering hand, and he choked on it. During the day it was alright, there was sun and laughter and company, so many things to keep the nightmares at bay. But at night... Nehi leaned against the log, ignoring the lines of fire that complained down his back, blinking at the dying campfire, and putting off that moment when he had to go inside.

Something soft and gray hit him in the face. Nehemiah started, pulling a blanket away with a little gasp. Joe grinned at him and tossed a travel pillow onto the gray blanket. Nehemiah caught it and glanced up again. Joe settled on his own blanket on the other side of the fire, gave a prodigious yawn, and flopped back on his pillow. The mute didn't even glance at Nehemiah. A smile crept over Nehi. He kicked the folds from the blanket, tossed the pillow on the grass and stretched out on his side, one arm sliding under his head. The clouds parted, and four stars peeked through the blackness and twinkled down at him. Another smile touched his lips, and he slept.

He kept the thick gray blanket and the little pillow and slept outside the next night.

The third night he was outside Nehemiah started up from one of his nightmares, a shriek strangled in his throat, shaking in every joint and gulping in air. His clawed fingers dug deep

into the grass and stuck there. An instant, and at least his mind registered he was free. His racing, pounding heart still needed to catch up to the situation. But he forced his hands to be natural, his shoulders to ease. He stared at the grass around him and didn't lie back down. Weariness and pain clung to him, and Nehi longed to drift off into the oblivion of sleep. But he didn't dare try. He sat trembling in the moonlight, hugging his knees and staring at his feet, unable to dredge up the courage to lift his eyes.

Soft fabric landed on his back and a blanket swung around to wrap him in comfort. He heard a soft thump as someone sat beside him, close enough to feel their warmth. Nehemiah looked toward the comforting heat; blond hair, sharp nose, pale face almost gleaming in the moonlight. Joe smiled at him. *It will be all right,* the mute's gentle smile said. The seconds ticked into minutes, and the two just sat under the stars. Nehemiah's breathing lost its panicked gasps. His tense muscles gradually relaxed. Joe pointed up and looked at Nehemiah, his face questioning. Nehemiah just shook his head, not in the mood for guessing games. Joe began to slowly sign letters. Nehemiah found himself paying attention, watching through half raised eyes.

"'Name.' What's its name?" he finally deciphered, his voice husky. Joe nodded and pointed at the constellation again. Nehemiah steadied himself and looked up. "That's the harp." Joe raised his eyebrow and waited. "It's said it represents David's instrument that he used to praise God and write his psalms." Joe's head tipped, asking for more. "You know, the Psalms." A blond eyebrow rose. Nehemiah drew in another breath and he quoted softly. "'Why art thou cast down, O my soul? and why art thou disquieted within me? hope thou in God: for I shall yet praise him, who is the health of my countenance, and my

God[9].' Words like that. It helps. But there's still..." He drifted off and Joe let him drop into silence. After another few minutes the mute's arm rose, pointing at a different constellation. Nehemiah looked up from his toes again. They went on pointing out constellations and naming them for what seemed like a long, dreamy time. Nehemiah suddenly found he was falling asleep.

[9] Psalm 42:11

Chapter Nine: Stars in the Dark

"Seek Him that maketh the seven stars and Orion, and turneth the shadow of death into the morning...The LORD is his name:" Amos 5:8

A cottony pillow rammed into his head. Nehemiah's eyes jerked open and morning sunlight flew through them and felt like it kept going all the way out the back of his pounding head. Then white pillow filled his vision. Nehi groaned and swiped at the soft club. Anna gave a laugh, danced away, then switched targets to his side. She used to wake him up like this a lot in the old days. This morning Nehemiah really wished he had a more somber sister. Joe sat up beside him, rubbing bleary eyes, his shaggy hair tousled. A shiver ran through the mute and Nehemiah realized he had both their blankets. He handed Joe's back a little shyly.

"Thanks," Nehemiah murmured. Joe smiled gently at him. Then he leapt to his feet and flung the blanket at Anna, as she tiptoed toward the snoring Cobeau, pillow ready. Anna yelled, and flung her pillow at Joe. A moment later Nehemiah found himself in the midst of an all-out war. He got his feet under him and headed for the wagon, arms up to protect his face as the pillows and blankets flew. A strong, thin arm shot around him and swung him around as a shield, and Nehemiah suddenly found himself taking the brunt of Anna's pillow wielding, Joe shaking with silent laughter behind him.

"No fair! Nehi, don't let him use you like that!" Anna yelled. Nehemiah reached behind him, grabbed Joe, and hefted him over his shoulder. The shadows of last night were still heavy on him, though nothing like they would have been without Joe's intervention. He didn't feel like playing. Nehemiah had meant to put him down by Anna and tell them both to stop being so silly. Joe twisted out of his arms and snatched Anna's pillow as he flipped to the ground. Anna shouted and swept up pinecones from the forest floor. The pillow came up again, and before Nehemiah could even shift his stance, he found the mute batting Anna's missiles into his face. Nehemiah grunted, and his hands shot up. His fingers curled around a pinecone and he hurled it back at the two combatants. Anna shrieked and laughed, and Nehi found himself snatching more of the flying missiles out of the air and whipping them off. Pinecones, pillows, blankets, and pine needles spewed through the air, as the three young people darted in and out of the forest, and laughter and happy yells broke the stillness of the morning. Half an hour later, they trundled back to the wagon, sticky with sap and ravenously hungry. Cobeau still snored, curled under a blanket on the ground. Anna ducked inside to make oatmeal and sausage. After her first meal she had become the official cook of the group by unanimous consent.

Joe jerked, surprise flying over his face, hopping awkwardly for balance and shaking his foot and left hand wildly. Leaves he had pulled from his sticky, bare foot stuck to his hand. He pointed at the host of leaves stuck on his hand and looked at Nehemiah, bewilderment and alarm playing over his expressive face.

"Haven't you ever gotten sap on you?" Nehi chuckled. Joe shook his head. "You're telling me you've never had a pinecone war before?" Joe scrawled in a patch of mud with his toe.

No games.

The mute stared at his hand and foot, wrinkles curving over his brow as he frowned. He shook them again and a look of near panic came into his face. "O-f-f?" he fingerspelled and stared pleadingly at Nehemiah. Nehemiah looked back at him and blinked.

"Well, uh, you... I have no idea how to get it off," he said.

Joe stared at him, then back at the leaves covering his hand. For just a moment he looked as if he might scream or burst into tears, and with the look Nehemiah's brain fished deeper into his memory. "Peanut butter." Joe shot him a doubtful look, the panic beginning to subside on his scarred face. "Peanut butter," Nehemiah said confidently. "That gets the sap off. Only we don't have any." Joe looked back at his hand, shaking it furiously, and his panic began to come back. "Boy, I didn't realize you loved them so much, you seem to be really stuck on those," Nehemiah commented with a smile. In an instant the mute's mood changed, the twinkle coming back into his eyes. He scrawled in the muddy patch with his toe as he shook his hand harder.

Trying to shake the habit.

Joe began to chuckle, and Nehemiah joined in, trying to wipe the sap off on his pants. Anna stepped out of the wagon and waved a large, black bucket in the air.

"Get me water, minions!" she ordered, and Nehemiah stepped forward to answer the call. She was more like herself this morning than he had seen her since the disintegration. Nehemiah gave her a dutiful salute as he took the bucket and she rewarded him with a commanding point toward the woods. Her delightful laugh spread around the meadow as she moved back inside.

"Hey, maybe water will do something with the sap," Nehemiah said, grinning at Joe as the mute picked the leaves off one hand, only to get them stuck on the other. "Where do I go for it here?" Joe looked up at him, his face a strange mix of humor and horror as he tried to shake the last leaf off. He pointed into the woods a little to their left. Nehemiah trotted in that direction, the bucket swinging from his hand, whistling. Brilliant blue colored the sky, the trees rustled around him, filled with the song of birds. A squirrel chattered at him and Nehemiah grinned at it. His eyes wandered up to the sky and he wondered what position the stars were in now, behind that blue haze of daylight. And then the ground disappeared into water, and Nehemiah tumbled headfirst into it. He spluttered to his feet, and found he was up to his chest in a cool meandering river. He laughed as he pulled himself onto the bank, reminding himself he needed to look ahead when he was walking, not up at stars that weren't there. Nehemiah filled the bucket and squelched back toward the wagon, thinking of nothing at all.

A harsh caw drifted to him as he neared their camp and Nehi looked up. Joe's ravens, all three of them, flapped clumsily into the sky. Nehemiah paused and looked through the fringes of the trees into the clearing. Joe stood on top of the wagon, watching his ravens circling steadily upward. They gave another cry and soared away in three different directions. *That was strange,* Nehemiah thought, and stayed watching.

Joe hopped off the wagon and walked over to Cobeau. His soft-booted foot shot out and began to rhythmically tap the big man's side, as a happy whistled tune slid from the mute. The chimera shot up, every hair on his shaggy person raised in alarm, and a frightened snarl cutting across his features. Joe put a hand on his shoulder and handed him a hairbrush, pointing to his head and laughing. Cobeau relaxed, smiled and moved toward the wagon, brushing his hair as he walked. As soon as Cobeau went inside, the humor disappeared from Joe. Weariness and a little sorrow settled in the lines on his pale face. It occurred to Nehi that the pinecone war had been started by Joe to remove every trace of last night from Nehemiah's mind, and to keep that teasing happiness alive in Anna. It had worked. And Joe had laughed at Cobeau to chase away whatever worry the chimera had woken up with. That had worked too. In fact, he had to have been carrying that hairbrush because he knew it would be needed. Nehemiah looked back at Joe, yawning and rubbing a hand down his face as he gathered up the blankets. He wondered if anyone ever gave that much thought to Joe's needs. Well, water was needed now. Nehemiah hefted the bucket and squelched out into the clearing. Joe's face lit up with mischievous amusement as he caught sight of Nehemiah's wet clothes. He raised an eyebrow.

"Yes, I walked into the river, not just to it," Nehemiah said with a wry grin. Joe simply nodded, his eyes dancing.

"S-a-p?" he fingerspelled.

"It's still there," Nehi answered with a grin. Joe snapped his fingers in annoyance, chuckling silently. He sniffed, grinned, and pointed to the wagon, his right fingers pressed against his thumb and tapping his mouth, Joe's sign for food. The smell of Anna's breakfast wafted out, and the boys ducked quickly into the wagon with the others.

Evil laughter rang through his screams as he writhed, trying desperately to get out. Simmons' laugh laced the fear-riddled, stinking air–

Nehemiah jerked into a sitting position, his eyes starting open, teeth clamped on a shriek, cold sweat soaking him. He sat rigid, gasping and trembling uncontrollably, trying to will the panic away. A cold breeze ruffled his hair and teased through his clothes, getting into his wounds, and Nehi gasped, each small pain drawing a rending agony into sharp relief in his memory.

A familiar blanket swirled around him and a small, strong hand landed on his shoulder as Joe dropped to sit by his side. Nehemiah's breathing began to even out. Two minutes ticked slowly by. Cobeau's snores filled the quiet night. Joe pointed up. Nehemiah's head felt impossibly heavy as he tilted it to

look.

"That's the lion," he rasped. Joe raised a brow encouragingly and Nehemiah went on. "Some say it's the lion Samson found with the beehive inside of it. Others declare it's the lion that goes prowling looking for the unwary to eat. My favorite has always been the Lion of Judah, constantly watching over us. Or at least... Another view is one of the lions from Darius' den where Daniel was thrown. God sent an angel to stop those lions' mouths, just so they wouldn't hurt His servant. Sometimes He steps in like that. But sometimes for reasons we can't understand He lets His own be hurt. But He never leaves them alone in it and He's always good. At least that's what my dad..." Nehemiah's voice strangled in his throat and his arms tightened around his knees. Insects droned in the grass around them. A bullfrog began its croaking tune as Cobeau snored. A thin finger prodded Nehemiah's ribs, telling him to go on.

"Knock it off!" Nehi growled, jerking aside. He started to rock, his eyes glistening in the moonlight. "I'm sorry. I just...sometimes I... I've doubted Him, even when I fight to keep it off. How can God be good, how can He be both sovereign and really good after all He let happen? He's not answering, Joe, He still isn't! No answer comes, though I've begged and begged..."

Nehemiah's hissed words were swallowed by the night. A long, weary sigh blew from him. There was a strange relief in admitting it. His head dropped, too worn down to look up anymore, and fell on his bent knees. A soft breeze stirred the boys' hair as they sat under the stars. A whippoorwill trilled in a tree to their left. Joe's lower lip slid between his teeth as he studied Nehemiah. One hand went to the mute's pocket as the other reached into his mop of messy blond hair, and he began to scribble on his pad of papers, his letters tiny as he tried to fit the words onto the little sheet. After a moment the scratching pencil stopped. His white hand rested on Nehemiah's arm. The other boy didn't stir. Joe prodded him impatiently, ignoring the way Nehi grunted and started up with a wince. A white paper stuck into his hand and Nehemiah's natural politeness kicked in. He sniffled, squinted at the tiny writing, and read.

> *You know that verse about everything being good? How God will only give His children good things? I hated that verse. It sat in my stomach and boiled because I knew better. But a preacher once made it make sense.*

Another paper slid over the one in Nehemiah's hand, and he read on.

> *Doesn't mean God gives us sunshine and rainbows, things that feel good through life. It means He gives us things that make us good. Things that bring about good. Things that grow us into people He can delight in and can take delight in Him, that grow His kingdom and ultimately bring light.*

"I guess that makes some sense," Nehemiah murmured. Atif's changed face flashed across Nehi's mind. He sniffed and nodded slowly, his dark eyes thoughtful. Joe let him sit for a moment. But he could see the hardness stealing over Nehemiah's face. He slid another note on top of the others.

> *It wasn't God, it was man.*

"That's quibbling, and you know it, if God is really sovereign," Nehi almost spat. Joe shook his head, a sharp movement, his lips pursed as he snatched the note back and scribbled on the other side.

> *It's a really big difference between allowing something to happen, and making it happen. You know that.*

A sniffle came from Nehemiah and he nodded, slowly.

"I do know that. I just, sometimes it doesn't seem like...enough."

Why did you hold on?

Nehemiah blinked, his brow wrinkling as he concentrated. He had to dig into himself to answer. And he dug, for Joe's sake; the mute deserved that much courtesy. His voice, when it came, was hesitant and husky as he felt his way.

"I couldn't give Him up. Jesus isn't talking to me now. But... He's waiting on the other side. This life doesn't last, and an eternity of joy waits for me. That's what matters. That's... everything. I couldn't give up something that was everything."

Joe nodded, a smile crinkling his green eyes. Nehemiah sat stone still, his face turned on his knees, his eyes glazed. That fact had been hammered into him every moment of every day until it had become a part of him. Nehemiah no longer thought or felt it consciously, he had half forgotten he even believed it. But every time he breathed he knew it to be true. Jesus was his all; he had a clear vision of where he would be in the end, and nothing could change that, and nothing could take it away. Eternity was what lasted forever; it was what mattered.

"Hope of life eternal, of seeing Jesus face to face. That's what I held to," Nehemiah whispered. A note slid into his hand.

No. That's what held you.

Nehemiah's head jerked up as the realization hit him like a slap with a wet rag. Yes. Clung to him like iron bands around his soul, keeping him whole as he broke in pieces, and drawing him through the blackness alive. Jesus... He hadn't answered the desperate prayers. But He had pulled Nehemiah through the nightmare. As the young man sat still his soul rang like a bell with the simple truth. All the anger and fear he had spewed at his Lord was while his Savior had wrapped the promises around his breaking soul and carried him patiently and silently through the darkness to the other side.

Joe poked Nehemiah on the arm and pointed at the stars again. Nehemiah's head tipped back, leaning against the wagon as he looked up to see which one the mute had picked. His trembles had stopped and he could breathe again. And there was a peace in him, deep in him that he hadn't felt in ages. Joe yawned, and blinked hard as he pointed at a constellation.

"The behemoth," Nehemiah answered. "It's a mighty beast and sounds enormous. But God is mightier." Joe yawned again as he nodded. Four constellations later the mute lay curled on his side, fast asleep. Nehemiah shrugged Joe's blanket off and dropped it over the mute, drew his own around himself, and slumped against the wagon. His eyes stayed on the stars. He needed to talk to their Maker.

For the first time he realized a truth he had missed.

Whether he *felt* an answer or not didn't matter. Jesus never left.

The morning sun poured over the wagon as the wheeled shoes whirred, drawing them toward the border. Anna and Nehemiah were deep in another signing lesson on top the wagon. Today Joe decided they needed names, his names.

"You're easy," Joe signed, pointing to Nehemiah. He pointed to his knee then held his first two fingers on his right hand flat and moved them upward from his chest to his head, his eyes twinkling merrily.

"Oh no, not that!" Nehemiah groaned. Anna laughed and slapped him playfully on the arm.

"I guess you're stuck with it officially now, Nehi," she said. "Before you get to me, what's your sign, Joe? Or do you have one?" Joe poked Cobeau for translation.

"All signers have one," he said through his big friend. "It's just a name, only in another language. Usually a physical feature or something that defines a person. Typically sign names are given for a reason, by someone who knows you, often there's a story with them, but sometimes they just happen. Now for you–"

"Wait, no dodging like you tend to do," Nehemiah said with a grin. "What's your sign?"

"Sharp Hope," Cobeau said, and a grimace cut across Joe's expressive face.

"Interesting. How'd he get that one?" Nehemiah asked. Joe started to sign something, but Cobeau didn't notice or deliberately ignored him.

"A wise old man met him when he was young. Said his wits were as sharp as his nose and his hope stronger than the sun. Dubbed him that." Joe looked decidedly embarrassed and firmly brought them back to the lesson. He pointed at Anna and fanned fingers in a delicate circle around his face, drawing them back together under his chin.

"What's that mean?" Anna asked.

"B-e-a-u-t-y," Joe fingerspelled. Anna looked away, her eyes turned down in embarrassment, perfect lips turned into a small frown, proving the name an understatement.

"I have a question for you, Joe, and while we're learning your language you can't run away on us like you usually do when we ask you questions," Anna said, rather obviously to change the subject. "Why do you call yourselves the Ravens? Do you just like the birds?" Joe gave a little whistle and signed something, his hands almost blurred with his speed.

"You'll have to learn your numbers before I can answer that question," Cobeau said in the sing-song growl he used when translating Joe. The twins spent the next half hour learning. Then Joe started signing again.

"L-u-k-e 12:24," he signed. The twins blinked at him.

"Of course!" Anna blurted. "'Consider the ravens: for they neither sow nor reap; which neither have storehouse nor barn–'"

"'–and God feedeth them: how much more are ye better than the fowls?'" Nehemiah interrupted, finishing the passage. "It's a good verse. Especially for travelers that have no storehouse or barn, and whose house is a moving one."

"Joe?" Cobeau interrupted. The word growled, laced with worry. They all spun toward the road, searching for what he had noticed. A dust cloud rose ahead of them, spewing behind someone coming their way. Joe stood up, shielding his eyes against the noon sun. All the easy humor left his face as he watched the oncoming vehicle. He tapped Cobeau on his shoulder and the big chimera checked on the short rifle he kept hidden in his belt.

"What is it?" Nehemiah asked.

"Inspection car, for the border," answered Cobeau.

"Shouldn't we get out of sight?" Anna asked.

"That's the trouble," Nehemiah muttered. "They've already seen us."

Chapter Ten: The Wild Lands

"And God said, Let the earth bring forth the living creature after his kind, cattle, and creeping thing, and beast of the earth after his kind: and it was so." Genesis 1:24

"How many?" Joe signed at Cobeau. A tense smile curved over Nehemiah's face as he understood him.

"Six," the chimera said. Anna squinted, but could barely see the vehicle. Joe disappeared again, as he had a disturbing habit of doing. He popped up out of the skylight behind the twins, carrying a black soft-leather bag, and something that glinted in the sunlight. Joe reached into the bag and came out with four rounded laser goggles. He tossed one to each of his companions. Nehi caught his just in time to see a glinting weapon sailing toward him, and grabbed it. The cold stock jerked his hand down with its weight. His grip tightened automatically, his eyes going to the heavy thing. Every muscle tightened and he stared. Nehemiah sat still on the wagon top, forgetting their danger, the sunshine, and everything around him in his awestruck delight.

He held a Compton laser pistol. The wooden stock, reinforced by the shiny copper metal, fitted perfectly in his hand. His gaze ran up the gun hungrily, taking in the two copper-coated balls resting next to each other in the center of the laser, the Z shielding holding the dark matter and dark energy. When a pin-prick hole opened between the two, the reaction caused enough energy to fire instantly, and go on firing and firing. His gaze flew on to study the crystal lens at the end of the copper muzzle and a grin stretched over his face. Perfect aim, each gamma ray invisible to the human eye.

"Don't just sit there, Nehi," Anna's voice cut through his awe, "get your goggles on, quick, before the shooting starts." Nehemiah obeyed, the grin still plastered over his face. The goggle's metal was cold, and the world took on lackluster dimness as the two circles settled over his eyes. But as he

drew the black strap tight against the back of his head, the thought of being able to play with a Compton made it more than worth it. Then his eyes lifted and noted the cumbersome vehicle coming closer quickly. He felt a cold trickle of fear. It wasn't going to be play today.

Joe stood beside Cobeau in the wagon's seat again, studying the oncoming car as it banged over the road toward them. He stooped and flipped the switch to slow Prissy. The water flow to the steam boilers strapped to the side of her harness turned to a trickle, her wheeled shoes rotated slower over the grassy road as the power moving the belt system sputtered. The giant pig squeaked in disapproval, but no one noticed her. They stayed focused on the oncoming car. They could see it clearly now, and the people in it. An open topped vehicle, the wheels bumping and jolting awkwardly along the ground; there were six hefty soldiers in it, and a hoverer that could carry that much weight cost too much for ordinary soldiers to use. The twin's throats tightened as they saw five soldiers train their bulky red laser rifles on the wagon. Nehi looked over at the Ravens. No humor showed in Joe now, every line in his sharp face hardened, calculating. A snarl rippled over Cobeau's face as he fingered his Brunhiem.

"Joe, Cobeau," Nehemiah murmured, "if it doesn't work, just let us go. There are too many well-armed men there for two musicians to handle. Don't get yourselves killed for no reason."

"You and Miss Beauty are good reasons," Cobeau growled. Joe laid a hand on the chimera's shoulder and nodded, flicking the engines to the lowest setting. The wagon slowed more, the pig shuffled forward, and Joe pumped the wind bubble down, letting in the fresh breeze and the smell of exhaust and rubber and dirt from the car. The twins sat rigid, waiting. The vehicle jounced to a stop in front of them and five soldiers leveled lasers at the wagon top.

"Stop!" the driver commanded. Cobeau obediently pulled Prissy to a standstill. Joe was gone. Anna blinked, but he was

still gone and she had no idea where he went.

"Your passengers are wanted," the driver told Cobeau, "as suspected Sojourners attempting to escape over the border."

"You can't have them," Cobeau snarled. His voice dripped menace, every ounce of the big man bent on protecting his friends. A sense of thankfulness welled up in Anna at hearing his tone. She slid the safety off the old-style projectile pistol she held and waited.

"You are only one," the driver said. "We have you under our sights. What do you think you can do to stop us from taking them?" A sharp whistle sounded from behind the soldiers. The driver spun, his gaze fixing on a small blond headed figure, pointing a Brunhiem laser at his head. Behind the goggles, Joe's green eyes shone, icy and dangerous. The driver's face paled.

"Four," Cobeau growled. Anna and Nehemiah swiveled their weapons and leveled them with steady hands. "Drop your weapons, or you might get hurt."

"All right, so we're even," the driver said. His voice was strained, but he forced it steady as he turned back to Cobeau. "You have the drop on us, and we have it on you. If a battle starts, I can promise you won't survive." A titanium dirk shone in Joe's hand. For an instant, it glittered in the sun, whistling down to the tire. The rubber and steel of the tire severed, swallowing the glittering blade. A bang, sharp hissing air, the car jumped, and Joe moved.

An explosion seemed to burst in the midst of the soldiers in the back seat as the mute rammed into them.

Anna couldn't see Joe, but she saw soldiers doubled over and tumbling out of the car. The twins just registered the sight when Cobeau vaulted off the wagon. One roaring bound, and the chimera launched into the enemy. Lasers flew, gray uniformed arms shot over heads, bodies collapsed. Anna watched in awe as the giant chimera broke one of the red lasers in half. A low whistle cut through the cracks and shouts and laser whines and Cobeau vaulted back into the driver's seat, flicking the engines to high. The engines on the harness sputtered to life, the wheels dug into the grass, and the pig shot off with a delighted squeal. Anna grabbed her carved seat as the G-force bent her backwards. Trees and grass blurred, the air whipping around them as Anna gasped out frightened questions about Joe.

Nehemiah tuned his sister out and lay on the back of the wagon protecting their rear. The Compton made no sound as he fired it, but he could see the beam through the specially tinted goggles. It was perfect. The balance was exceptional, and he could feel the energy leaping back and forth between the dark matter and the dark energy in the two balls. And the accuracy! The red dye lasers were good, but this! This was perfect. Two seconds and four quick blasts from Nehemiah, and every tire on the car was nothing but a pile of ash. One more, and the engine burst into a red flame. Nehi watched in satisfaction as the soldiers piled out, racing away from their burning vehicle and pointedly leaving their weapons with the wreckage; they had no desire to be picked out as a threat by the shooter on top of that weird wooden wagon.

A white hand flailed up from the back of the wagon and gripped Nehemiah's wrist.

A surprised shout came from Nehi, and Anna spun to see him leaning over the back of the wagon, reaching for something. Joe clambered over her twin, one hand catching Nehemiah's jacket front and pulling him along. The mute looked like he always did, calm and happy, his shaggy hair blowing in the swift breeze. He ignored Anna's questions and Nehemiah's surprise and scampered over to Cobeau, dropping onto the front bench. He shoved his palm against the pump for the wind bubble. Nothing happened. Joe frowned and pumped it harder. Nothing happened. He kicked it with a frustrated grimace and slammed his hand down on a slab of wood by his elbow. The click of a cubbyhole swinging open drifted to the twins. Nehi leaned over, staring past the little mute to see an unknown cubby filled with large, rolled papers. Joe dug

140

through the papers, drew one out, glanced at it, then handed it up to the twins. Nehi grabbed it, and so did the wind. It whipped the big paper into his face, driving it and sucking at it, trying to pull it away. Another roll shoved up, and Anna took it. Another, and another, till their arms filled and their vision blocked with flapping white papers.

Joe pulled one out and stopped. He laid it on his lap and unrolled it, fighting the wind to keep it open. It was a map, Anna thought, though she couldn't see much with her hair and papers blowing in her eyes. Prissy's speed still increased, and Anna swallowed, a niggle of worry eating into her. The large pines flashed by inches from the wooden wagon, and anytime the giant pig shifted on her wheeled shoes, it shifted the hovering wagon dangerously close to the enormous hunks of wood. Joe reached over and flicked the engines to low, then pointed to their right at what looked like a hiking trail. Cobeau spun the stick. The twins grabbed wildly for a handhold as the wagon flew up and down over the potholes and rocks, one minute rising to its right side, sparks flaring from the left as the coils hit the track, the next jouncing up onto its nose and back down with a bang. Nehi bit his lip, visions of steamed, mutilated bodies filling his mind; you didn't take a hoverer on a rough track like this, you just didn't! The track wound up a steep hill, the wagon jolting and jumping and grinding as it raced. The pig jolted and jumped with the wagon, her squeaks vibrating hilariously as her wheeled shoes pulled her over the rough trail.

A dark hole appeared in front of them. A cave carved into the mountain side. Anna caught her breath as pitch blackness swallowed them, devouring the sunlight and fresh pine scent. Close, cold air swirled around her, and a fist-sized fly slammed into her face as they sped through the opening. She spluttered and flung the clumsy, flapping insect off. Her lips tightened as she squinted and blinked, trying to see. Darkness swallowed the light from the opening and blackness claimed this world. She could hear Nehemiah's breathing speeding up, rising in pitch, getting nearly frantic in the dark beside her. Anna clung to the wooden seat, hoping she hadn't dropped any of Joe's papers in this wild ride, and wondering how he knew where he was going. They darted on and on, over the rough cave floor, Prissy's squeals echoing eerily through the rushing air. Sparks cut through the blackness as the coils hit a rock, and Nehi gasped. The darkness wrapped around them in a whistling fury of biting wind.

After what seemed hours a faint gleam of light came from ahead. It grew into a definite opening, with soft green light showing more clearly every moment. It grew very quickly. The wagon shot out, green light flooding everything. A canopy of trees overspread the sky, and a wild forest stood sentinel over the hill, flowing down a sharp slope in front of them. There was hardly even a trail. The hoverer rocked and fought, hissing as it shot down the grass, nosing around giant tree trunks, flattening saplings and undergrowth. Prissy squeaked her head off in delight, her rumbling squeals vibrating as her wheels jolted along.

"We're overrunning her!" Nehi yelled through the damp wind, and Anna shoved her flying hair aside in time to see he was right; the hovering wagon pushed against the breeching strap on the pig's harness. She teetered on her skinny legs, any minute and they would overbalance her, run over the broken pig, and keep on going to smash into whatever was at the bottom of this mountainside. Cobeau pulled wildly on the brake, but too many rotted leaves littered the damp ground, the brakes couldn't catch. The huge trees (gigantic oaks and towering magnolias) flashed by faster and faster as they whizzed down the mountain. A razor-leaf tillandsia crashed down just in front of them, shaken loose by their wildly careening ride. One of its eight-foot razor leaves nearly decapitated the giant pig. Joe slammed his hand on the emergency cut-off switch. The water flow to the coils curled underneath them snapped closed. The wagon dropped to the ground, metal screeching, wood shrieking and cracking. Cobeau jerked the

pig desperately around the rolling air plant.

Anna yelped as she lost her hold and felt herself jolting off the edge. Nehemiah caught her collar and jerked her back up, his arm wrapping around her waist, and she heard her gasping thanks mingle with a yell from Nehi. He threw himself on top of her, pressing them both into the wood of the wagon, papers crushed under them. A razor-leaved tillandsia flashed past, suspended precariously between two great oaks. Its sweeping leaves cut through the air two inches over their heads. As they rushed under it with their horrible grinding noise, it trembled, teetered, and fell. The great plant began to roll, slicing gashes in tree trunks and decapitating bushes. Screams and yells mingled with the grinding crunch of the wagon, squealing pig, and the terrible swishing rumble of the rolling plants. Prissy's squeaks turned to a high-pitched keening scream. Anna felt the wagon bang into something and bounce level, and their wild speed suddenly stopped. A vein stood out on the chimera's neck as he pushed against the steering stick, forcing the pig around by pure strength. Her engines gave one last spluttering, steaming effort, and jerked the grounded wagon two more yards down a green road. The razor-leaved tillandsia rolled past them, one of its great leaves scraping the back of the wagon as it tumbled on into the woods. One last hiss of steam shot out of the two engines strapped on Prissy's back, and then quiet fell around them. The air filled with buzzing insects, bird song, and the incessant quiet mutter of stirring leaves.

The soft, quick breaths of Joe's silent laughter drifted into the heavy air. The twins' shocked expressions melted into smiles. Joe's laugh was a catching, merry sound. The mute reached for his papers and began putting them back into the cubbyhole, and the twins turned their attention to what they held. They looked curiously at their loads as they passed them back.

"I can understand having maps of all the roads in the world, it looks like," Anna commented as she fumbled two more of the huge rolled papers down to the mute, "but a map of the interior of the Kingdom of the Wise's treasury?"

"And what about one for the mines of the People's Kingdom?" Nehi asked, studying one of his papers. Joe just shrugged.

"You never know what you'll need," Cobeau rumbled. Joe placed the last map back, shoved the cubby door closed, and hopped off the wagon to inspect the damage. Nehemiah began to climb down and join him, but the mute waved him back up. A sharp bang sounded from the back as Joe kicked something hard, a spluttering shudder ran through the wagon, and then the soft hiss of steam invaded the rustling leaves. The twins felt it rise smoothly to its three inches above the ground. But it shook and sputtered, and Nehi could tell some of the jets were plugged, jammed or bent from that wild ride. Joe sighed, pulled the wheels out of their slots above the axels, snapped them on, and shut the steam off. A sharp hiss sounded from in front, and Nehi looked over to see Cobeau closing the lid of the water tank on Prissy's engines and tossing an empty pail toward Joe. An instant later the two Ravens were back on their perch, and the wheeled pig rolled off, dragging the wagon at an easy pace. The green road snaked into the distance till the huge trees swallowed it, and it was a deep, deep green. No clean sunlight fell anywhere, it came filtered through a tangle of dense tree branches and leaves. Tillandsias (mostly the beautiful, unnerving razor-leafs) hung down every few yards along this road, thriving in the dense chaos of the forest.

"What is this place?" Nehemiah asked softly. "We're nearly out of the Sojourner's, aren't we? I thought the nearest country this direction was something called Kallipolis, but this looks like..."

"Nothing?" suggested Anna. Joe looked at them in surprise.

"You've never been out of your kingdom?" he asked through Cobeau. The twins shook their head and he paused, digesting the information with a blank face. He began to sign again. "You're in the wild lands. Most of this world consists of wild lands, places in between kingdoms. As far as I know there are no kingdoms built right up against each other, they all have spaces between. Some bigger, some smaller."

"The wild lands?" Nehemiah asked, looking around him with interest and wishing he had actually paid attention to his mother's geography lessons. He saw neglect and disorder everywhere. Chaos ruled. Rotting tree carcasses littered the ground, the trees that still survived stretched out everywhere, fighting for a chance at light and air. Nehi smiled and pointed at a particularly knobby hardwood tree glowering over the road.

"Hey Ann, why did the oak tree get into trouble?" he asked.

"Because it was being knotty?" Anna suggested. Joe grinned at them as the sounds of the birds and the occasional creak and groan of shifting trees took over.

"It's a very sad forest, isn't it?" Anna murmured quietly.

"No one's ever tended the ground in this place, or cared for it at all," Nehemiah nodded. Joe looked at them, his green eyes deliberating and bright. Nehemiah had the feeling he was following on the heels of their ideas. After a moment, he nodded and went back to looking down the road. His sharp face seemed a little sharper than usual and his green eyes stayed bright instead of dimming to their usual friendly look. It put Nehemiah on his guard, and he found himself watching the woods. They rode on in silence, and nothing seemed to change. The air stank of decay. The minutes ticked on, crawling into an hour, and Prissy's shoes started to squeak. Anna's curls plastered over her forehead, and when she reached up to brush the hair aside, her fingers brushed water. She looked up and blinked as a rain drop splattered on her nose. It turned to a drizzle, slow, soft, steady.

"How long does this go on?" Anna asked finally.

"The wild lands or the forest?" Cobeau rumbled.

"Both, but especially this unhappy forest," she said. Joe whistled for Cobeau and spoke through him.

"The wild lands go on for miles and miles, but we're almost

out of the forest. Look, it's starting to clear ahead." He looked relieved as he signed it, and Cobeau smiled as they rode through a patch of brighter sun and heavier drizzle. The chimera's face suddenly rippled into a snarl and he sniffed loudly. Joe sat up, every muscle taut, staring at his big friend.

"Trouble coming," the chimera growled.

"What trouble?" Nehemiah asked, and fingered the safety button on the Compton laser. He let his hand run over it again. A beautiful weapon, like the one he had been going to buy on his sixteenth birthday. His sixteenth birthday definitely had not turned out like he hoped.

A bellow ripped from Cobeau, shaking the air, as his arm shot out to point behind them. The twins twisted, hearts racing. Anna screamed. A huge tongue swept toward them; deep purple, forked, thick, slimy, and hideous. Anna and Nehi jerked out their daggers and stabbed down hard, burying the weapons to the hilts in the fleshy, purple tongue. It pulled back, zipping into the mouth it belonged in, and Anna gasped. A gigantic lizard stood on the road behind them, blunt nosed and wide mouthed. Bumpy black skin, crisscrossed with orange, covered its huge back and ran down its thick, stumpy tail. Its body nearly touched the ground, but its legs stuck up higher than its body and were as tall as some of the younger pine trees along the road. The beast raised its flat head and opened its mouth to hiss at the little thing that had stung it. Slimy, gray flesh oozed in the tooth-filled mouth.

"What is that thing?" Anna gasped, as Nehemiah aimed his laser and tried to decide which of the hundreds of black bumps on the creature were eyes. Two shiny, black beads focused on him, and before anyone had time to answer Anna's question Nehi fired twice. He steadied his hand to send a third beam and Joe grabbed Nehemiah's arm, his blond head shaking in a warning. But it came too late. The beast gave a screeching, rattling roar and reared, forelegs clawing the air. Its thick body slammed down into the road, jolting the wagon. Its claws dug into the soft green grass and it dashed toward them, tongue lolling in fury.

"They didn't go through," Nehemiah murmured, eyes wide. The rushing wind whipped his black curls into his face as he spun to the mute. "I know I hit those black eyes, but the laser's rays didn't go through. What do you do against something that only gets mad when you shoot it in the eye at close range?"

"It's getting closer! What now?" Anna asked, her face tight. Joe motioned the twins into the driver's seat. They scrambled to obey. Cobeau shoved the steering stick at Nehemiah, gripped the carved seats above them, and the two Ravens leapt onto the wagon top. Joe handed something to Cobeau, and with a running leap launched into the air. He sailed out like a black arrow with a blond tip, twisting gently. He landed on the end of the huge creature's nose, one hand digging into the bumpy flesh as the toes of his soft boots clung to the monster. He raised his hand and pounded on the lizard's snout. With an annoyed snort the beast opened its mouth to send its purple, slime-coated tongue shooting toward Joe. Cobeau's arm whipped forward as he launched two little balls straight down the creature's huge throat. The mouth clamped shut. The beast stopped short, gave a mighty shake of its head, and sneezed; Joe was flung off, like an insect on a bull. He hurtled through the air toward the wall of trees on the right of the wagon. Nehi's hands shook as he flicked Prissy's engines off and pulled the wagon to a stop, sick to his stomach at the expectation of the thump he was about to hear when Joe slammed into a tree and dropped to the ground in a broken heap.

Joe back-flipped in midair, his boots hitting the tree instead of his head. His white hand caught a branch as he began to tumble to the ground. He spun around it twice to give himself momentum, and launched off, arching through the drizzling rain. With a sharp thump, the mute landed in Cobeau's strong arms as the chimera stood solid and ready on the wagon top.

Anna and Nehemiah gaped at the two musicians. Joe

grinned as he slid easily from his friend's arms, motioned for Nehemiah to steer the wagon, and looked back at the lizard. Anna followed his gaze and giggled. The monster stood with his mouth open and his purple tongue hanging out on the road. Acrid smoke trailed out of his throat, snaking slowly through the rain. As they watched he groaned, sneezed again, and sank to the ground, his four legs splayed around him.

"What did you throw inside him?" Anna asked Cobeau.

"Smoke bombs," the big man answered. "Doesn't agree with their stomach."

"How did you know to do that, are there a lot of those creatures around?" Nehemiah asked quickly.

"Practice, and not around here. I don't think," Joe answered through Cobeau as he scrambled down into the driver's seat beside Nehemiah, and Anna hopped up to her usual seat on top the wagon.

"You don't think? That's not too encouraging," Nehemiah murmured, eyeing the trees uneasily. He handed Cobeau back the stick and moved to sit beside Anna.

"You never know what you'll find in the wild lands, Knee-High," Joe answered through Cobeau. He paused to move the wet, blond hair out of his eyes. The drizzle grew stronger as the trees thinned and when Joe's messy bush of hair got wet, his bangs hung down past his nose, and the rest of it dangled past his shoulders. "Usually those types of beasts are only in the deserts, like out by the Battle Kingdom. I don't know what this one was doing here. I was expecting a two foot or a green back, so that was a pleasant surprise."

"Pleasant surprise?!" Anna gaped. Nehemiah's Adam's apple bobbed as he swallowed hard, his eyes darting to the trees.

"The stumpy tails," Joe signed and Cobeau rumbled over the noise of the growing rainstorm, "are usually slow and uninterested hunters. Not like a lot of the other creatures out here." Anna and Nehemiah decided they'd rather not know about the other creatures and the conversation abruptly stopped.

Anna looked behind them again and froze. She pointed back as she saw what the stumpy tail's attack had kept her from noticing before. Nehi spun to look. A sign stood by the road. The pole had been scored by laser fire till it listed to the side, and deep gouges in the wood marred the words. But it still stood, proclaiming its truth for a few more days.

Sojourner's Way

"For the Kingdom is the Lord's; and, He is the governor among the Nations."
Psalm 22:28

A songbird landed on the sign, ruffling her feathers as she trilled to the wet world. The pole broke and cracked. The sign tipped slowly and hit the road.

"That's behind us. We're out. Nehi, we're really free," murmured Anna. She smiled, her eyes bright with too many thoughts to put into words, and slipped her arm through his. Nehemiah's lips twitched in a smile back at her. But he heard her through a buzzing in his head, and his eyes stayed on the broken sign leading into his broken kingdom. The verse seared through his mind; there was no kingdom now for the Lord to govern. Why?! Why had all this been allowed by God, if He really did rule? Nehi shut the thought out with a firm hand and turned toward the road through the forest, his back straight. They were out of the country, free and facing... what? *What do we do now?*

The wagon moved on, as the rain fell and the company watched the road. The trees thinned quickly, and the roar of the tumbling drops began to surround them as the forest's cover left. The pouring rain looked to Anna like a wall of liquid sunlight framed by trees, bringing a delicious wild tune of God's washing day. Two more yards and they were out in it. Warm, thick drops pounded on their skin, soaking them in seconds. The raindrops were almost an inch in diameter, tingling with the force of their fall, smelling vaguely of flower petals. It would have been enchanting if it wasn't so hard to find oxygen in the water-doused air. Anna did find a bit of enchantment in the thick rainfall, covering everything with its liquid shimmer. Prissy made very unhappy noises as she rolled down the road, looking like a disheveled dishrag needing to be rung out.

About five minutes of wet travel, and Cobeau turned off the road into what Nehemiah could just make out was a flat, yellow plain. But that was all he could see in this sheet of thick rain. The wagon shuddered to a stop, and all four tumbled off and grabbed Prissy's tent. They had it set up over the giant pig in two minutes, then they made a dash for the wagon and barreled into the day room. The bedraggled group stood dripping and gasping, glad of the clear air inside.

Chapter Eleven: Vision Keepers

"Then we which are alive and remain shall be caught up together with them in the clouds, to meet the Lord in the air: and so shall we ever be with the Lord. Wherefore comfort one another with these words." 2 Thessalonians 4:17-18

Joe turned on the kitchen burner for heat and reached into the cubbyhole they used as a linen closet. He tossed everyone towels and the company quickly dried off their weapons. Nehemiah handed his host his dagger and the wonderful laser as soon as they were dry, but he couldn't help feeling a little reluctant. It was such a nice laser. Joe hefted the Compton for a moment, staring at it. His eyes flew up to Nehemiah, he smiled, and handed the laser back.

"It's yours if you want it," the mute signed and Cobeau rumbled. Nehemiah stared at Joe, delight beginning to light up his face.

"Are you sure?" he asked hesitantly, his thumb running over the smooth wooden stock. "I mean, this is a Compton..." Nehemiah knew what it cost. Joe grinned, pulled a black leather holster out of the weapons cabinet, and tossed it to Nehemiah.

"I like the idea of having a good shot prepared," he signed.

"Thank you," Nehemiah said simply, his eyes shining as he strapped the holster to his thigh and slipped the laser into it. The weight dragged on his leg, but his grin only spread.

"A Compton, Nehi?" Anna murmured, her lips pressed tight. "You realize those things can create black holes?"

"That's only theorized," Nehemiah said quickly. "Besides, the connection between the dark matter and dark energy is only a pinprick, and that's been proved not to be enough to cause a black hole."

"And if you drop it and it breaks?" Anna snorted. "Then what happens when a whole ball of dark energy jumps into a whole ball of dark matter? Bam, we're all pulled apart by gravity and sucked into nothingness."

"It's only theorized that might happen," Nehemiah shrugged, then rushed on, his words fast and excited. "It shoots gamma rays, Anna, when the safety's flipped off, they start bouncing between the crystal insides of the two balls, creating a Compton scattering! And the rest of the balls are a carefully constructed graded-z shielding that's awfully thick and been proven not to leak the rays out. Here, feel how heavy it is, you can tell the shielding is–"

"I'm not touching that thing!" Anna grinned, throwing her hands up and backing away. The huffing breaths of Joe's silent laughter cut into the scene.

"Even if it did break," Joe said through his friend, "and even if the dark energy and dark matter mixing really did cause a black hole, it might not do as much damage as you think, Beauty. Science doesn't know too much about the effects of black holes and all that yet. But ever since those lasers came out ten years ago, I've been around people who use them, and I've never seen one break. Even when one got crushed by a two-ton weight falling on it, the laser was still fine after they dug it out."

"Really?" Nehemiah asked in delight. "Thanks again, Joe, I...thanks. And thank you for saving our lives back there. I'm sorry I made that thing mad, I've never heard of anything that couldn't be taken down by a direct shot in the eye."

"If it has scales, you can't hurt it with lasers. Or bullets," Cobeau said, smiling at his success at following this conversation.

"Well, if you're going to keep the Compton, it ought to have a name," Anna said. "What are you going to call your new dangerous weapon, Nehi?" Nehemiah paused for a moment, his mind on the days before the disintegration when he was first planning on getting one of these, and the days after when every expectation he ever had was lost to him, and the days now with his own Compton suddenly strapped to his leg and no idea what might come next...

"Hope," Nehemiah answered. Anna and Joe smiled, and silence fell in the room. The rain pounded on the wagon top, mottling the light drifting through the skylight. As he listened to its steady drumming, it flashed across Nehemiah's mind that he and Anna were out of the kingdom. His stomach tightened. But they had already taken so much from these kind Ravens. Nehemiah shifted his weight and cleared his throat.

"I suppose this is where we part then," he said. The other three looked at him in surprise. "You two have been wonderfully good to us, Joe and Cobeau, and I know God will bless you for helping the needy and fatherless."

"You mean...you're leaving?" Cobeau said, his voice trembling.

"Well, you did mean to take us out of Sojourner's Way, and here we are," Anna said a little reluctantly.

"And you've already almost died because of us. Three times just today," Nehemiah added. "You've given us our lives, and then supplied us with everything we needed, and I know its cost you a lot. We can't ask you to do more. Except maybe advice; I could sure use that."

"Nehi's right," Anna said quietly. "You two have been wonderful, but we've taken up enough time, and food, and belongings, and trouble for you. It's time we leave." Cobeau slumped down in a chair and started wailing. The sound was so sudden, immense, and sorrowful the twins stared at him. Joe gestured at the big man sobbing at the table and signed something. Nehemiah and Anna didn't understand it and just stared helplessly back. Joe sighed, squared his shoulders, and started moving.

The mute stepped up to the wailing chimera and his hand clenched as if he were holding something as he stretched it out to Cobeau's chest. He stabbed down, the thing becoming an imaginary knife in his hands. Joe's pantomimes were very real, and Anna gasped as the mute began to saw a hole where Cobeau's heart lay. He set the imaginary knife down, wiped his hands together to clean them, and put his knee on Cobeau's stomach. The chimera's tears calmed down as he watched, but Joe ignored him. The mute reached into the hole he had just made, and pulled. He fell back, staggering, as if the heart had come out with a snap. He looked at his hand holding the imaginary heart and made such a disgusted face the twins chuckled and even Cobeau smiled through his tears. Joe reached into a chest of drawers, drew out a hammer, sat the heart down on the table, and swung. The action and reaction of the hammer springing back up were so real Nehemiah expected to hear a bang. Joe squinted and wiped something from his eye. He picked up the heart again, surveyed it with a face screwed up in disgust, and tossed it into the garbage pail. Then he pointed to the twins and back to the still sniffing Cobeau.

"Well, I certainly wouldn't want to do *that* to poor Cobeau," Nehemiah said, grinning. Cobeau remembered why the pantomime had started and his face contorted. His enormous wail filled the wagon again. Anna ran over and hugged him, brushing away the tears as they fell and telling him not to cry. He only wailed harder. Joe watched for a moment, his expression blank. He reached up to his shelf, pulled out a pad of papers, and began scribbling. As he wrote he handed them to Nehemiah.

> *Look, when you've been defended by Beau and he sobs for you like this, you're a part of the troupe. He honestly would be broken if you left.*
>
> *And I wouldn't be too happy myself. Consider this: we can be pretty useful, Beau and me. Stick around and we'll go book hunting together. Your way is our way now.*

Nehemiah looked up sharply. Joe stood in front of him, holding out his hand, an inviting smile on his sharp face. There was something else there too, a...hesitation, a sort of shy worry. As if something in the mute pulled back, afraid to hear Nehi's answer.

"You want to help? Wait, you know about our wanting to hunt for our kingdom's book?" he said in surprise. Amusement flitted over Joe's face. He started to scribble again, handing Nehemiah notes as he finished them.

You and Anna aren't exactly secretive. You have a lot to learn if you were trying to be. And in case you hadn't picked it up yet, we Ravens are Christian brothers.

I've seen more of this world than you yet, we need that Bible and your country more than you can guess. I'm going to look for it anyway, whether with you or not.

Why don't we do it together? Another point, you two obviously have no idea how to survive in this world, and we can't just leave you in the wild lands.

That would be like murdering our friends and we Ravens don't generally do that.

Nehemiah glanced up, caught the twinkle in Joe's eyes, and accepted the tease with a grin that was more cheerful than called for by the note itself. After that giant lizard episode he really wasn't sure they could survive on their own out here, and was relieved Joe knew it. Another note tapped his hand and Nehemiah took it.

If you're willing to join up with a genetic incomplete and chimera, we're willing to take on a crack-shot and cook. What do you say?

Nehemiah looked at the sobbing chimera and his sister trying so hard to comfort him, and back at Joe. The expression on the sharp, scarred face was hopeful and hesitant at the same moment; the mute was half-afraid Nehi would say no, and "no" was the last answer Joe wanted to hear. He really did want them to stay. Nehemiah broke into a smile and took Joe's hand. Thank heavens they wouldn't have to face this world alone yet! Joe grinned at him, took a firmer grip, and stuck both hands under Cobeau's nose. The chimera stopped sobbing and stared from one to the other.

"Thank you for the violent invitation, Cobeau," Nehemiah said, "we'll stay on. But–" he continued, raising his voice as Cobeau leapt from his chair, grabbed Anna, and capered about the little room, as she kicked and laughed and yelled at him to let go. "But we'll only stay if you can make use of us. We don't want to be a constant drain." An acoustic guitar shoved into Nehemiah's hands, stuck there by a smiling Joe. He gave his little translation whistle and answered through Cobeau.

"I've wanted someone to work with for a while now. We'll make use of you, believe me." The green eyes twinkled as he signed it. But he had a twist to his lip, and a squint to his eye that sent a niggle of uncertainty into Nehi. As if there were something deeper in the words. He chose to dismiss the thought.

"So, if we're going book hunting together, as you put it, where do we start?" he said, handing his sister the notes he had just gotten. Joe nodded to show it was a good question. He grabbed his hammer again, shoved Cobeau playfully in a chair at the table, Nehemiah in another, and motioned Anna to join them. Then he hit the table with the hammer and took on a dramatic, serious air.

"Order, everyone, order!" Nehemiah called.

"All rise for Judge Joe!" Anna said. She and Nehemiah popped up and sat back down again to Beau's bewilderment and Joe's amusement. He nodded in mock seriousness, then suddenly dropped the playacting and into his chair. He whistled for translation and started to sign.

"I don't know for sure who has the Bible. It's going to take some probing and lots of patience and trouble to find it. I think the best, and nearly only, method is to start traveling and keep our eyes and ears open."

"You mean just go from place to place looking for any

A razor-leaf tillandsia
Pg. 142

news?" Nehemiah said doubtfully. "You really think we can learn anything useful that way?"

"You would be surprised what you can learn out there," Joe signed with a mischievous smile. "You just have to know where to listen and what to watch for."

"I would love to find Daniel," Anna interposed. "That needs to be one of the things we listen for."

"Yes," Nehemiah said. "According to Samuel, Daniel was the one to get the messages from the group who stole our book. He might be our only lead. And I really, really miss him."

"Okay, find out about your Daniel as we go," Joe signed and Beau rumbled. "Can anyone think of anything else we need to cover in this meeting of..."

"Book Lookers Anonymous?" Anna offered and Joe laughed.

"Good, Beauty," he signed. "Anything else we need to cover in the first meeting of the BLA?"

"Wait a minute, that spells 'blah,'" Nehemiah said with a chuckle. "I think we need to cover a name with a better acronym. How about Bible Hunters Across the World?"

"'Bhaw?'" Anna said doubtfully. "That's not much better."

"What about just two letters, Vision Keepers?" Joe offered, and then suddenly colored and started signing so fast his hands blurred. "Yes, I've heard your conversations about keeping the vision. But it couldn't really be called eavesdropping, because you two never try to keep it private–"

"You approve of it then?" Anna interrupted, smiling at his embarrassment. "What is it you like about it?" A bashful smile crept over the mute and he looked away as he signed.

"Because Jesus is waiting to gather us home, everything here will be all right. That hope never leaves. But we can forget about it sometimes if we're not careful, and that's when life gets really tough. Yes, I approve." Joe's hands started to twiddle the hammer as he studied the ravens painted on the wall, and Anna and Nehemiah glanced at each other, amused at how ill-at-ease Joe was with a normal conversation. Their companions were odd sorts.

"Well, I like it," Nehemiah put in. "It can be the name of our Bible hunting fellowship–"

"And also a reminder to the four of us to keep the vision burning," Anna interrupted. "VK it is!" Joe hit the table with his hammer again to close the meeting and stood up.

"Rain stopped," he signed, and darted out of the wagon whistling a merry tune. Cobeau ambled cheerfully after him. The door slammed behind the bulky chimera, and Nehemiah leaned back in his chair, his cheeks puffing as he blew out a relieved sigh, staring at the sunny sky painted above him.

"Me too," Anna answered his mood, her eyes running over Joe's notes again. "I really didn't know what we were going to do when we had to leave the Ravens."

"I know," Nehemiah grimaced. "Gosh, I really wish Dad took us on some of his trips out of the kingdom! I don't know what to expect out here! And I'm not sure what to expect from these Ravens either, this whole day has suddenly brought them out in a new light."

"Yes," Anna said slowly. "That meeting of the VK was extremely abrupt, in the way it began and ended. I had no idea the Ravens were interested in our book at all, much less actively hunting for it. They were so proficient at dealing with that patrol!"

"Did you notice all the strange maps they had? And how expensive and expansive their weaponry is? Ann, I don't think Joe and Beau are just musicians, or even mainly musicians. What do they really do? What do you think they really want us for?"

"I don't know. But I like them. And Nehi, I don't think Joe is going to tell us more than he wants us to know," Anna said, a warning in her tone and a twinkle in her eye. She recognized the mood overtaking her brother. This was a mystery, and he was going to dig and prod until he understood what it meant. He loved understanding things. "I think we should thank God we landed with fellow Christians, but keep our eyes and ears open even in this lovely wagon. And not be rude by forcing out facts they don't want to give. Nehemiah?"

"All right, I'll be subdued in my fact hunting," Nehi sighed. "But I'm going to hunt, and I think you should too. Don't you want to know who these people are?"

"They are Joe and Cobeau, fellow Christians who have been remarkably kind to us, and whose help we need, and who don't seem to like people barging into their lives opening doors they want shut," Anna smiled, watching Nehi squirm at her summation. She could see his old inquisitive, pushy self coming back and Anna could have yelled in joy. But then his eyes snapped to hers, new lines cut into his face, and he aged again.

"Anna, what's God been doing these past months?"

"Moving us closer to Him," Anna answered. A little smile quirked over Nehemiah's face. She hadn't even had to think about it, she just trusted He had a purpose. That was Anna, always so solid, so sure of her footing. Nehemiah nodded, staring at the floor. A whistle sounded from the door and they looked over to see Joe leaning into the wagon. He grinned, crooked his finger for the twins to join him, then ducked out again. Anna and Nehemiah hopped up and slid out of the wagon. The twins found themselves in a damp, pretty country with yellow grass waving around their knees. A wall of forbidding trees stood a short distance from them. In every other direction they saw flat ground with more yellow grass. Lakes and pools were scattered everywhere, connected by hundreds of little streams, and the insect drone was almost maddening. Joe pointed to their right and Nehemiah and Anna blinked and stared. The yellow over there wasn't just grass, it was smooth-haired animals.

"Why, it's little yellow cows!" Anna said in delight.

"But they only have one horn. And it's stuck on their forehead," Nehemiah said in surprise. He laughed as one of the little grazing cows accidentally walked into a tree and got his two-foot horn stuck in the thick trunk. "What do you call

them?"

"One horns," Joe signed slowly and the twins understood it and grinned; they were making progress. The little creature bellowed in annoyance, twisting and pawing as it tried to pull his horn loose. Nehemiah trotted over, gripped the horn, set his boot to the tree, and pulled. He grunted as his back muscles tightened around the healing whip cuts. But a vitality ran through him which made it easy to ignore the pain and he jerked back harder. A scraping pop, and the horn came away from the tree. Nehi staggered back, watching sap ooze out of the hole as he wiped his hands absently on his pants. The little beast shook its head, snorted, and its brown eyes rolled up to stare at Nehi. Its head stood only a little over Nehemiah's knee, but its horn reached up to his middle. In fact, it hovered around his stomach and suddenly looked very sharp.

"I suppose they're friendly?" Nehi asked Joe. The little mute laughed.

"Now you ask?" he signed and fingerspelled slow enough for Nehi to follow. He nodded and walked into the middle of the herd of grazing cows. Anna ducked into the wagon and came out with a bag of carrots. She pulled one out and waved it under a slobbering, velvety nose. The animal's eyes lit up and white teeth crunched into it. Ears pricked throughout the herd, heads lifted, and drool started dripping. In half a minute Anna was surrounded by a milling herd of little mooing animals, tossing their heads and begging for carrots. Nehemiah shoved his way through to her and joined in the fun. A loud bellow pealed from their right. They looked over to see a large one horn jogging through the yellow grass with Joe perched on its back, whistling merrily as he did a shuffling dance step. Beau vaulted out of a pond and shook his head at Joe.

"He doesn't like it," the big man called, and paused, shaking off water like a dog. Joe grinned, gave his friend a salute, and backflipped off the one horn into a series of cartwheels. The one horn moved up to the chimera, mooing at the big man. Cobeau nodded sympathetically and laid a hand on its head.

"Don't worry, he's off," he rumbled. The one horn snorted and nuzzled Beau's leg. "You're welcome," the chimera answered.

"Does Cobeau really understand it?" Anna asked Joe as he leaned against their tree. He shrugged and reached for a carrot. "Don't eat them all please, I want some for stew tonight. Which reminds me, say Nehi! What do you call a poor cow without any legs?" Anna asked.

"Ground beef?" her brother grinned, swallowing his carrot and reaching for another one. "With a joke that corny, Ann, it's best you're seen and not 'herd.'"

"You had better come up with 'an-udder' theory on that or it might put me in a grumpy moo-d," Anna grinned and left the boys with the animals as she hopped back into the wagon to start water boiling. She had the sink assembled in a moment and pulled open the cabinet under the oven to get out the stockpot. Anna started back in surprise. A little animal skittered on the cabinet floor sniffing the crumbs that had fallen from the small oven. The creature was clear. Anna could see through it to the back of the cabinet, except for its pink eyes. And a little white splotch in its middle that moved and seemed to be attached to its mouth by a slender thread of the same filmy white. It looked a little...a very little, like a glass mouse about the size of her palm. She moved closer, trying to get a better look. The creature found a particularly good smelling crumb, and swallowed it. Anna sat back on her heels feeling a little queer in her stomach as she watched the crumb moving down the filmy white thread into the filmy white splotch in the middle of the creature.

"Well, I suppose you had an empty stomach, didn't you?" Anna told it. The mousey creature whipped around to face her. Its mouth opened in a vicious snarl, and a high-pitched whistle rang from it. Anna scooted across the floor away from the cabinet. The creature began to stalk toward her, still snarling, glassy-clear rows of needle sharp teeth dripping with a foamy white saliva.

"Nice...thing," Anna muttered. Her hand flailed on the counter for the paring knife she had gotten out to cut the carrots. The 'thing' crossed into the patch of sunlight from the open door and Anna's mouth dropped open. When its body caught the sunlight, its clear turned red, green, yellow, blue, and purple, all shimmering and shifting from the tip of its whiskered nose down to its foot-long tail. Anna blinked and looked again. The colors reflected on both sides of the floor as the creature stalked toward her, shifting and dazzling in prisms. The tail slashed toward her and caught Anna on the toe of her boot. A thin white scrape dug deep into the leather toe. Anna tightened her grip around the paring knife and turned to call for Joe.

The creature hissed and leapt toward Anna's face. She squeaked, slashing out with her little knife. Anna caught it squarely in the nose, and the knife clinked, as if it hit something hard. The little creature fell back, gathering itself, its tail twisting and curling around its body. The high whistle sounded, the tail trembling and writhing. *Time to move!* Anna decided and she spun around, her boots pushing into the wooden floor. Anna scrambled into the night room yelling to the others outside that there was something inside. The creature raced after her, bounding and snarling. A flap sprung up behind its head, a circle of skin six inches tall, making the animal seem twice as large. Anna's fingers fumbled on the wooden wall for the painted knot on the aspen. Her thumb brushed it, and shoved down hard. The slab to the cubby clicked down, dropping onto the bottom bunk, and Anna rolled into the little compartment under the driver's seat, jerking the wood back up behind her. The catch clicked home, and a sharp thump banged from the other side; the thing's whip tail at work again. Sunlight flooded over her as the outside door clicked open. Anna slid out, her boots hitting the muddy ground in the middle of her three friends.

"There's a thing in there that looks like a clear mouse and changes colors like a prism when it gets in the light, whistles, whips things with its tail, and a knife only chips it," she blurted out breathlessly.

"This I've got to see!" Nehemiah said, and started to run toward the door into the day room. A hand clamped onto his shoulder, and he jerked to a stop, his feet flailing for an instant, his breath catching in his throat. Cobeau's simple face stared down at him. The grip was gentle enough. But Nehemiah fought the urge to cringe at the inexorable strength of that hand; the chimera held him as firmly as an iron clamp.

"Don't get near a scared crystal whip tail," Cobeau rumbled.

"A crystal whip tail?" Nehi asked, forcing his voice to stay steady. *Only memories, only a fear of being helpless,* he told himself over and over.

"They get scared easily," Cobeau nodded. He let go and strode for the door, and Nehi swallowed his gasp, keeping his face even with an effort; he didn't want Anna and Joe to see how raw one hand on his shoulder could make him.

"Well if I scared it, it certainly scared me," Anna called after Beau. Joe nodded sympathetically and handed her a carrot. "You don't like them?" she asked. Joe picked up a stick and scribbled in the mud next to the little pond.

I've been whipped by them too many times, they scare me.

He pointed to deep, white scars on his hand and shivered melodramatically. Then he grinned and motioned to the chimera disappearing into the wagon. He rubbed out his sentence to write another.

Beau loves them. They're his favorite creatures out here.

I think his hide is too tough to feel their tails.

Anna nodded and leaned against the wagon, munching on her carrot. But her eyes darted around the wetland, a frown on her face, and Nehemiah guessed what was bothering her.

"It's a little disturbing how much we don't know about this world, isn't it?" he sighed, slumping against the wagon next to his sister.

"I can't even make stew out here without something trying to eat me!" Anna burst out. "And what a something; a prism mouse that whips things with its hard tail."

It's venomous too.

"Oh, thanks, I think I'd rather not have known that," Anna drawled. Joe grinned and took a better hold on his stick.

Not very venomous. There's a lot of danger here, but as you learn to overcome it, you'll lose your fear of these lands.

"Joe, how come you and Beau know these lands so well?" Nehemiah asked. "I mean, why do you come out in them at all since they're so dangerous?" Joe shrugged and scribbled again.

We're traveling musicians. You have to cross wild lands when you travel.

"But why did you pick traveling musicians as a trade if traveling is this dangerous? We've already had a giant lizard and venomous prism mouse–"

"Whip tail," Anna corrected.

"–try to eat us and we've only been out here one afternoon."

"That's a good point, is it always this bad?" Anna asked, and Joe scribbled again.

This is good. Bad days in the wild lands are very bad.

Anna and Nehemiah grimaced at each other.

There's a lot of beauty in these lands, you might start to like them.

"The crystal whip tail was very pretty, I'll give it that," Anna said grudgingly. "There certainly were a lot of colors when it got in the light."

"I like the cows. I mean one horns," Nehemiah put in. "Are there a lot of them?" Joe nodded and motioned that they were everywhere. "They'd be awfully easy to catch, I wonder if they taste good?"

"Don't be a beast! Poor little things," Anna said, slapping her brother's arm. Joe's green eyes twinkled as he scribbled again.

They do taste good, Nehi, but don't worry Anna, Beau won't let us go hunting unless we need to.

"He's gone," Cobeau rumbled from the door of the wagon, and Joe trotted toward him, signing as he went. The chimera roared out his great laugh at whatever Joe had said, and the twins grinned as they followed the Ravens into the wagon. It was impossible not to smile when Cobeau laughed. They had sandwiches that night instead of stew, and Anna collapsed in her bunk a little after dinner was finished. She pulled her blanket over her head and tried not to worry about crystal whip tails creeping up on her in the night.

Chapter Twelve: Hunted

"...Lord, how oft shall my brother sin against me, and I forgive him?...Until seventy times seven." Matthew 18:21-22

"We've been walking out here for ten whole minutes, and nothing's tried to eat us!" Nehemiah said. Joe grinned but his eyes kept roving, scanning the tall-grass prairie. A flower towered over the mute, and Nehi stared up at it as he skirted around the huge plant, each pink petal longer than his arm. "I don't suppose any of these flowers are carnivorous?" Joe rolled his eyes and scrambled up a hill to get a better look. "It's not like I want them to be," Nehi explained as he followed, "but we've been out in these wild lands for two weeks now, and every day you and Beau seem to save us from something. We haven't needed saving yet today. Why do you go out in these wild lands so often? What do you really do?"

Joe crouched on the hill's summit and ignored Nehemiah. For a moment Nehi wondered why he wasn't standing to see more. Then he realized this hill was taller than anything he had seen in days. If they stood on the top they would be silhouetted against the sky for miles. He hunched next to the mute and waited. Joe just kept looking, surveying the beautiful grasslands. He was very good at ignoring Nehi. And today, being ignored rankled the young man. "Come on, Joe, what do you really do? I know you're more than a musician, your skills are impressive." No response. Except that Joe's jaw tightened and his face grew blanker. He didn't even glance at Nehi, even when his eyes turned to scan the land around him.

Joe slid off the hill, slipping through the grass as if it were a slide, and Nehemiah followed him, still talking. Still asking the same questions. *Surely, like the widow and the just judge, a little perseverance will yield up something,* he thought. So he pushed, and he prodded, and he demanded as the two boys kept walking through the grassy prairie, looking for a spot with a deep enough pond to refill their tanks. Joe led the way up another hill, ignoring Nehi as if he weren't there. For two hours Nehemiah watched him as he wheedled, poked, and even insulted to try and draw out an answer, and saw his face hardening, his muscles tightening. He was getting to the mute. Which meant perhaps, just perhaps, he would get an answer out of him soon. Nehi kept pushing. They crept to the top of a hill and looked down on a perfect, shimmering lake. A herd of one-horns crushed the grass around it, thousands of the little animals milling and mooing. Which meant large predators must not be a problem here, or the one horns wouldn't have stayed.

"Perfect for a camp," Nehi said. By now, frustration at getting nowhere mixed and boiled with his curiosity. Joe's gaze roved over him with the same interest he showed in the muddy log resting on the mute's other side. Nehemiah's kindness, politeness, all his finer feelings suddenly snapped, swallowed by the burning ball of frustrated curiosity. He rolled on his side, one hand propping up his head, and looked at the mute. "But why do we need a camp, why be out here at all? You haven't told us the truth yet, Joe." A muscle twitched along Joe's set jaw. "Are you and Beau maybe wanted criminals, too easily recognized if you get around people? A thief maybe, with your penchant for black? Or even a murderer? (Hey, accidents happen, it might not have been on purpose.) I'm pretty sure you're a liar, with the way you won't tell me anything. Come on, what do you really do?"

Joe spun on him, his green eyes flaming, that muscle still twitching.

"You gave up and begged for death. I give no answer to you."

The words seared Nehemiah's mind, too shocked and burnt to be surprised that he understood them. Joe slid to his feet, easy and graceful, a sneer cutting across his face.

"D-o-u-b-t-e-r," the mute signed, his movements slow and deliberate. The color drained from Nehemiah's face as heat rushed through him, feeling wounds breaking open inside.

Joe's face was distant, cold, his eyes still blazing. "W-h-i-p feeder, no courage, you begged."

"Stop it," Nehi murmured, his voice low and shaking.

"Begged for food. For m-e-r-c-y. Lost courage. Not strong enough. Held helpless. For months, just c-u-r-l-e-d helpless, and took it. Not a man, you're something l-e-s-s. A screamer. A crawler. Worm. S-l-a-v-e."

Nehemiah's fist lashed out, almost without his thinking it, a move of self-defense, to stop the words breaking him open. Joe spun out of the punch with a sneering laugh, elegantly, easily, and fainted a jab at Nehi's kidney. Nehemiah staggered back, clumsy, his feet tripping over each other, feeling the slightest touch of Joe's knuckles; the mute hadn't connected, but it was on purpose. The move was so swift Nehi couldn't have done anything to stop it, proving the mute could dance rings around him in a fight. Joe laughed, a scornful chuckle, and his hands began to move in signs again. Nehi spun on his heel before he could understand the words, stumbling and tripping down the hill. He stormed back toward the wagon, shaking and hot. How could he? How *could* he? *You forced him into it, you wouldn't shut up,* Nehi's brain told him. But to rub salt in those wounds, wounds Nehemiah was more than half afraid would never heal. Wounds Joe knew about only because of Nehi's most vulnerable moments, when just the mute sat awake to help him through... How could he? *You called him a criminal, told him he was a liar.*

Scenes of Abid and Simmons played through Nehi's mind with a vividness he hadn't seen in weeks, and he stopped thinking. His arms snaked around his chest, still shaking as he shoved through the grass. His feet moved into a jog, then a run, as if he could outdistance himself. He ran and ran, till he spun around another hill and staggered to a stop, gasping for breath, his eye on the wagon settled peacefully in the meadow. Meathead, one of Joe's ravens, looked up from the wagon top, eyeing him. Nehi ran his hands over his cheeks, clearing the hot tears, and took a moment to get himself under control.

But only a moment. He wanted Anna. He wanted to be near her, to know she was safe. To hear her tell him he was safe.

Anna heard the door open and glanced over her shoulder as she shook the salt over the stewpot. Nehemiah slunk in, head down, face strained and lined. He slumped into a chair, his eyes on his feet and hair a mess. Anna set the salt back in the spice cabinet and gave the stew a stir before she said anything.

"Did you find water?"

"Yes," he mumbled. She nodded, and reached for the skillet. A plop, a sizzle, and the smell of melting butter filled the room. Two pieces of fresh wheat bread dropped into the sizzling butter. Anna hummed a hymn as they browned, carefully choosing one about joy and their eternal security; one she knew Nehi liked. She turned the toast onto a plate with one hand, poured a cup of tea (that she had been about to settle down and enjoy herself) with the other, and plopped them in front of Nehi with the honey and a smile.

Anna busied herself about the wagon, finishing dinner, singing softly to herself, and pretending she didn't notice her brother's sudden relapse. If he wanted to talk about it, he would. So far, since that first day when they had shared their stories, he hadn't told her anything but the barest overview about...his condition. How he got the scars, inside and out. She wouldn't press him.

The door opened again and Joe slid in. He was smiling and friendly, but...it seemed a blank friendliness, like that first day she had met him. Anna suddenly realized it felt fake. And it was different than the way he had been acting around them these past two weeks of traveling through the wild lands.

Nehemiah jerked up, his chair knocking over behind him, and stormed out of the wagon, skirting around Joe as if the mute burned him. Joe ignored him. He bounced over to the stew and asked her how soon he could eat. Anna answered

mildly, neutrally.

Whatever had happened, she didn't want involved. And she realized she didn't like the fake Joe. She wanted him comfortable enough his real self came back.

Or had she even met his real self?

Nehemiah settled on the bottom bunk in the wagon that night instead of out with the Ravens under the stars. And he spent most of the dark hours wrestling for the strength to forgive the mute, and forcing himself to admit he had pushed Joe into it. The next morning he was tired, but resigned to forgiveness; he *was* sorry and ready to put the whole matter behind him. But when he tried to state it, the mute didn't sign a word to him, or even look his direction. For three straight days Joe ignored him as if Nehemiah was an inconvenient chair in the wagon.

On the fourth morning, Joe suddenly popped up in front of Nehemiah as he squelched over the mud toward the lake to reposition their water hose. Nehi stepped back, a little warily. But Joe shoved a note into his hand and shuffled back a step.

I'm sorry. Really, really sorry, I should never have delved into any of that. I know it hurt. Believe me, I know. It was more than just immature and wrong. It was cruel. I'm sorry.

Nehemiah hesitated for a moment, staring at the words. He looked up at Joe, the mute's messy hair spilling over his face as his head hung, shifting uncomfortably from foot to foot. Nehemiah's shoulders squared and he nodded, handing the note back.

"I pushed you into it," Nehi admitted. "I'm sorry too. Truce?"

"F-o-r-g-i-v-e?" Joe corrected, that shy hesitancy Nehi had seen when he asked the twins to join up peeking through his

blankness as he watched Nehemiah.

"Yeah. Forgive," Nehi nodded, and shook the mute's proffered hand. A sigh blew from Joe and he visibly relaxed. But he stood in front of Nehemiah for a moment, still blocking his path, staring at the mud. He flipped the note around, jerked his pencil out, and scrawled something quickly. He shoved it into Nehemiah's hand and walked away, almost scurrying. Nehemiah looked at the note, unsure what he would find. The words slipped into the cracks broken in his friendship with Joe and patched most of them neatly.

I should never have told you those things, you're better and stronger than anything I signed or anything you've felt in the past. I would never tell anyone else about it, ever. Promise.

By a mutual effort, things returned to their cheerful friendliness as the days climbed into weeks and the Raven wagon spun on in their travels over the wild lands.

For a long time after that, Nehemiah didn't dare press for facts.

Two days away from the Kallipolis border, Cobeau sat up and sniffed the air, and Joe became alert. Anna and Nehemiah didn't bother to break off their conversation about chocolate trees. The Ravens usually found danger that way in these lands and found it often enough to be classified as almost normal. The twins had lost most of their fear of the wild lands, just as Joe had predicted; the Ravens knew how to keep them safe.

"People," Cobeau rumbled. Joe's features hardened, tightening more than when he faced a green back the day before. He pointed to a grove of oaks. Cobeau steered the wagon deep into the trees and cut off the steam. The wagon settled on the leaves with a soft thump. Birdsong and the angry chattering of

a squirrel filled the silence.

"What's so wrong about people being around?" Nehemiah asked curiously as he glanced back, trying to see the road; a ribbon of land, pressed down, grooved, and hewn by the monstrous machines of the metal caravans. Almost everyone went by the caravans if they needed to travel internationally. The wild lands were too dangerous for people to cross alone, the only options were a private army or the caravans. The three story, rectangular, armored machines transported anyone and anything. And never asked questions. Their treads left a massive gash in the land, and people took to calling it a road, and using it for travel. But even with its size, Nehemiah couldn't see it through the oak trees.

"Bad men," Cobeau frowned.

"Don't any decent people cross these lands?" Anna asked, but Joe's hands flashed in signs to Cobeau, not answering her. The big man pulled his Brunhiem out and stood on top the wagon, muscles tense and ready and his gaze sweeping every inch around their hide-away. Joe leapt off of the wagon and began to make his way silently through the oaks, back toward the road. Nehemiah hesitated, one lip tucked under his teeth. He turned a smile to Anna, gripped the side of the wagon, swung off to dangle, then dropped. His boots scrunched into wet leaves, and they slipped beneath him as he followed the mute. Joe looked over his shoulder and eyed him as Nehemiah began to catch up. The mute hesitated, then shrugged.

"Quiet," Joe signed. Nehemiah nodded, and the two slid off again, Joe leading the way. He moved with absolute silence. Nehemiah did his best to do the same, despite the wet, squelching oak leaves littering the ground. They reached the edge of the oak grove, lowered themselves to rest under the swaying trees, and looked out. A metal centipede, three jointed armored cars seamed together, rested on the road. So it was a private army, not the caravans, not something you saw often. A group of militarily-armed people milled beside the vehicle, gesticulating and complaining. They stared up and down the road, and Nehemiah shifted on the ground next to Joe, to see farther and try to guess what they were watching for. The driver's door to the lead van opened and a tall, supple form slid out.

Nehemiah's breath sucked in and froze into a solid lump that choked him.

It was Simmons, standing only a few yards away! The man strolled to the milling people, and they froze, staring at him. Nehemiah's head ducked into his arm and he lay and shook. It took half a minute to get himself under control enough to lift his head and register what was being said. He couldn't hear it all, the wind kept snatching bits away. But he heard enough to know they were looking for someone and had just run out of ideas of where to look next. Intense pity filled him for whatever poor soul was being hunted by Simmons. Another wisp of wind blew away the voices, and then died down. The name "Hillson" drifted clearly to Nehemiah. He felt as if he had been kicked in the stomach by a steel-toed boot. No. No, surely not! This well-armed group couldn't be searching for them! The wind suddenly stopped, the air grew still and close, and Simmons' voice curled around the two boys lying at the edge of the grove.

"If you don't find those Hillson twins, every one of you is going to regret you joined the FFs. And I'll make sure you regret you were even born." His tone was warm, low, enjoying the fear he knew coursed through those around him. It rose as he went on, ending on a shout that shook Nehemiah's guts. "So I suggest you stop saying you can't figure out how they got this far from the kingdom, and especially stop saying you don't know where they could be now, and find them!" The group scattered and scrambled back into the armored centipede. Red headlights flicked on, a soft electric whirr came from the machine, and it snaked up the road carrying Simmons away. The machine shifted over the horizon, out of their sight, and the birdsong and sunshine took over the world again. Joe stood up, prodded Nehemiah, and started back toward the wagon. Nehemiah followed him automatically, his head humming and stomach sick. He felt his knees wobbling under him.

"What was it?" Anna's voice cut into his spinning mind.

"He was after us," Nehemiah murmured.

"What? Who is after us? Nehi, are you all right?" Anna asked, her voice sharp and quick. Nehemiah swallowed his horror and shook himself mentally.

"Yes, I'm fine," he answered steadily. "They left. It was a well-armed group that called themselves the FFs. I only knew one of them, and don't know what he does. Or at least what he makes his living at. But, Ann, they were after us!"

"Why on earth would anyone be looking for us?" Anna asked, turning to Joe. The mute signed something to Beau.

"You should know that better than we do," the chimera translated.

"He's right we should," said Nehemiah, one hand running through his hair as he stared unseeingly at the wagon's side.

"But we don't," responded Anna. "I don't suppose they're good people, a sort of rescue party sent from Samuel or something?"

"No!" Nehi almost yelled and Joe's head shook so hard his hair flew, a tight frown hardening his eyes. Anna raised her eyebrows in surprise and Nehemiah stared at Joe. The mute knew more of the man than he admitted.

"All right, that idea was definitely wrong," Anna said as Nehi climbed up on the wagon again. "Anyone else have any?" They talked it over for the rest of the day. Or rather the twins did, the Ravens didn't seem to have anything to add on the subject. The brother and sister finally put it down to the elusive, mysterious 'treasure' Samuel had mentioned, the something their family was supposed to have. Reluctantly the twins laid the matter aside, knowing they couldn't do anything else with the slim facts they knew.

That night Nehemiah woke up with a stifled scream strangling in his hot throat. Sweat soaked him, dark dreams and memories flooding his being again. He started upright, gasping for breath and staring wide-eyed at the starlit grasses around him. It had been over two weeks since a dream this bad played through him; he had hoped they were gone. Nehemiah held his knees and laid his aching head on them, trying again to make the memories flit away. Would they never leave him alone?

A familiar blanket fell over him, and Joe's hand gripped his trembling shoulder. Nehemiah's breath slowed from its panicked gasps to a more normal speed. The mute dropped down to lean against him, offering a solid comfort, and after a long minute Nehi stopped shaking. His eyes shifted, lifting to look at Joe.

"Thanks," Nehemiah murmured, and the mute gave him a gentle smile. "I was almost as scared as you were when that pot of honey fell on you yesterday." He tried to make a chuckle and Joe took it over with his merry, silent laugh. He began to sign and fingerspell in the half serious, half joking way he had.

"S-t-i-c-k-y equals dangerous, truth."

A small smile crept over Nehemiah's strained features. He loved that mood in Joe. They settled comfortably on their blankets next to Cobeau's bulk and turned their eyes to the sky. The gentle night noises and Cobeau's snores hung around them. But Nehemiah's mind couldn't dwell on the stars tonight. He turned away, a little sigh escaping him. A low whistle came from Joe, asking for attention. Nehemiah looked at him listlessly.

"The d-r-e-a-m-s will grow f-e-w-e-r, Knee-High," the mute signed and fingerspelled, several times, slowly, patiently. After staring a moment, Nehemiah understood the words and looked at him in surprise.

"How did you know that's what I was thinking?" he asked. Joe started to shrug, as he did to get out of answering a question. But he looked at Nehemiah and paused. Nehi got the feeling he was being assessed, that the mute was making a decision about him. A moment later the decision, whatever it was, had been made. Joe absently ran a hand over the jagged, deep scar on his jaw. His easy confidence melted, leaving him small, shy, and a little sad. Nehemiah had the sudden realization that Joe wore a front instead of his real self most of the time; and he had just dropped it for Nehemiah's benefit.

"I have d-r-e-a-m-s too, s-o-m-e-t-i-m-e-s," he communicated with patient slowness. Then his hands moved on, swifter, almost violently, and Nehi thought he caught a disgusted scowl on his sharp face just before the mute spun to the side, hiding his expression. "Some music I hate!" Joe paused, drawing in a breath and letting his face turn back to the tall young man beside him. Nehi knew that last sentence hadn't been meant for him. He was surprised he had understood it. The mute gave his sign for dreams, and went on. "The dreams f-a-d-e with time," Joe signed slowly.

"That's good to know," Nehemiah said softly. "Very good. I know something else, mine are fading faster because of your voluntary sleepless nights. Thank you for that, Joe, for not leaving me alone to..." His voice faltered and Joe smiled and pointed to the stars.

"I like night," he signed. Nehemiah nodded. The two sat in silence again. But it was a very companionable silence.

"Joe... I've thought about what you said, that second night, about that verse. You're right. I still can't see it all, how God has been working through it, but...the doubts don't trouble me so much. And that...it makes it all easier, to not have that gnawing at my soul."

"You never really d-o-u-b-t-e-d," Joe fingerspelled and signed. Nehemiah blinked, wondering if he had seen that right.

"I kind of think I did," Nehemiah admitted, his voice curious. A twinkle sprang into Joe's eyes and a smile twitched at the corner of his lip as he shook his head.

"T-h-e-o-l-o-g-i-c-a-l questions, maybe. Real d-o-u-b-t? No."

Nehi sat still thinking back on it all, the mute beside him staring up at the white stars. There was some truth in that. He had never lost his faith through the questions, not really. Nehemiah's foundation had stayed solid, even when he couldn't feel his Savior near, and he knew where he was going to be in the end. Questions, anger at the silence of God, even bitter resentment, had gone through him. But hope had never really left. Not the hope of heaven and the resurrection by Jesus' blood. Nehi sat and blinked at the grass, his eyes opened to a new world of dark musings.

"I wouldn't have lived without hope," Nehi murmured. He took a deep breath, his shoulders shifting in the moonlight, glancing almost shyly at the mute. "Thanks for making it stronger." Joe shrugged, his eyes still on the stars.

"That's why God gives us brothers."

"Keep me remembering that hope, will you?" Nehi murmured, his voice a little husky. Joe nodded, and let him just sit. The minutes ticked by, Cobeau's snores the loudest noise in the night.

"I just realized you answered my question," Nehemiah broke the quiet.

"I answer s-o-m-e-t-i-m-e-s," Joe got across with a smile.

"Yes, but not usually. Here, how about answering this one finally. Why do you and Beau go out into the wild lands enough to be so comfortable in them? I know you're traveling musicians, but why did you choose to be something that involves such dangerous travel?" Joe sat very still looking at the stars. The seconds slid on, turning into a minute, and kept moving. Nehemiah was just resigning himself to no answer (he wasn't about to press for it), when the mute pulled out one of his pads of paper. He slipped a pencil from his hair and began to write. Nehemiah felt honored, and a little guilty. He knew by now that Joe regarded his papers as precious commodities, and didn't use them lightly.

We aren't wanted in the kingdoms of this world, Nehi. The wild lands are safer and more comfortable for us Ravens. Your kingdom was one of the very few exceptions.

"Not wanted...why?" Nehemiah asked. Joe reached up to

the left side of his neck, pulled his turtleneck collar down with one hand, and moved his shaggy blond hair away with his other. Nehemiah saw a small, black circle tattooed on his neck. A GI stood out stark in the center, a line slicing through the letters, cutting the circle in half.

"What's that mean?" Nehi asked quietly.

"Genetic Incomplete," Joe fingerspelled. He pointed at the snoring Cobeau. "Chimera. It's dangerous to be us." While the grammar was a little confusing, Nehemiah got the gist. Sorrow settled on his chest, and he couldn't think of anything to say. He realized after a moment of sitting in the silence, it made him sad because it made Joe sad. His green eyes turned to the ground, his focus a thousand miles away from the moonlit grasses around them. His usual easy humor, like his confidence, snuffed out. The silence suddenly didn't seem such a cheerful one, and Nehemiah broke it quickly.

"Thanks for answering my question," he said. Joe stirred, stopped staring into space, and smiled at Nehi.

"One, a-n-y-w-a-y," Joe made Nehemiah understand and winked cheerfully at him. They sat on for a while just listening to the wind and snores, then Joe began to sign and fingerspell again.

"There's another r-e-a-s-o-n I like these l-a-n-d-s," he managed to get across to Nehemiah after four tries.

"What's that?" Nehemiah asked. Joe hopped up and rolled Beau over on his side so he stopped snoring. He held up a finger and placed his hand to his ear, his eyes shining. Nehemiah listened. The light breeze rustled the tall grass. A one horn bellowed in an uneasy sleep. You could hear the streams rippling, and the insects in the grass. It melded and danced when you actually listened to the sounds.

"It's beautiful," Nehemiah murmured. "It's the song of God's glory even in the unseen places. When we move on, this land will still be singing the same praise to its Creator." Joe snapped his fingers and nodded, showing Nehemiah had hit it on the head. His smile was a thoughtful one and his hand strayed absently to his neck, rubbing it where the mark lay hidden by the sleeveless turtleneck he wore under his ever-present leather jacket, as he plopped back down next to Nehemiah. Out came the pencil and paper.

I love listening to this land because it reminds me you can sing praises to God even without a voice.

Nehemiah read it in the moonlight, and nodded and smiled at his friend. There was a thoughtful soul underneath that cautious, humorous mask. Cobeau rolled over onto his back and began to snore like a lumberjack trying to cut down a metal tree. Each boy tossed his blanket around himself and dropped to the ground, staring at the stars. A moment later Joe began to scribble in the margins on the notes he had already handed to Nehi.

Tomorrow you start music lessons. If you think you can 'Handel' it.

"Oh clef-er," Nehi grinned.

I am 'sharp.'

"Yeah, well your jokes are falling a little 'flat.'"

I'll stop, before I get in 'treble.'

The mute slipped his pencil back into his hair, then he pointed up at a constellation. Nehemiah followed his slim, pointing finger.

"That's the twins, Jacob and Esau," he answered Joe. For the next hour he told stories and scriptures from the stars. Joe fell asleep during a description of Gideon's horn, and Nehemiah couldn't blame him, he had been going on much too long on that one. Nehemiah lay on his back, his hands comfortably behind his head. But his mind wouldn't be still. He found himself imagining what Joe and Cobeau's lives had been like to make them more at home in these wild lands than amongst their fellow men. Dark possibilities swirled in his mind, and he turned on his side, his face lined and stomach tight. Nehemiah pushed the depressing visions away and switched thoughts. Tomor-

row they would start their music lessons in earnest. That sounded interesting. Hopeful and cheerful musical thoughts ran through Nehemiah's head as he finally fell asleep, with a friend near and the rustling yellow grass waving over his head.

Chapter Thirteen: Taken

"And be not conformed to this world: but be ye transformed by the renewing of your mind, that ye may prove what is that good, and acceptable, and perfect, will of God."

Romans 12:23

The next day Anna and Nehemiah began their induction into the Ravens' musical show. They started with how to play Joe's rhythms, until Joe heard how Anna sounded when she actually concentrated on singing. His eyes widened and he let his jaw drop as Anna launched into her favorite hymn, Nehemiah's bumbling attempts on the rhythm makers setting it off. With the smattering of knowledge the twins had of his language, Joe began to teach her how to sing. Anna thought she already knew. But after the first lesson with Joe, she found Nehemiah and sang for him as Joe had taught her. Nehi's eyebrows rose and he declared he had never heard anything that pretty.

The days started with music, switched to travel for a few hours, and then dove into music again. The mute's perfectionism hadn't shown itself in other things, but in his own musical realm everything had to be exact. Joe was a fanatic. The first two days of trying to teach Nehi on the rhythm makers proved a trial to everyone. The mute's nasty mood hovered under his mask the end of the first day, as he forcibly held back barbed comments. Nehemiah mentally termed the angry mood threatening to break out "the mad fox" and walked with care. The second day Joe went to bed with a migraine. But his foot dug into Nehi's ribs in the morning, tapping the bigger boy awake and sending him back to the rhythm makers. Nehi went obediently, yawning and stretching. As he stepped into the midst of the pile of wood and gravel, he noticed he wasn't even sore. No pain plagued him, and vitality fired his veins, making his stomach growl almost pleasantly. He smiled and glanced up at Joe. The mute stood pale, his face set and lips tight. Nehemiah took a breath, eased his shoulders, and tried with everything he had. Joe deserved at least that from him.

Nehi's movements were slow and clumsy compared to Joe's elegant speed. But as he went through the movements, Joe's green eyes lost their slits. A smile touched his face and he started to nod. Nehemiah's eyes crinkled in concentration as he spun and kicked, twisted and stamped, setting the wild lands alive with a pulsing, beautiful rhythm. The tangy notes of Joe's bagpipe leapt into the air around Nehi and he concentrated harder, shutting out the mute's work and just breathing as he spun and danced. The droning, wild shriek of the bagpipe crescendoed, then dropped into silence. Nehi dragged his boot over the gravel one last time, and stopped, blowing hard.

Anna started clapping, cheering with unladylike volume. Nehemiah looked up to see her in her cotton pajamas, leaning in the open wagon doorway, her hair disheveled, Cobeau plopped by her feet. He glanced over at his teacher. Joe's eyes shone as he lowered his bagpipe. The mute held out a hand, a smile teasing the corner of his mouth. Nehi grinned and slapped his hand into Joe's, exultant to have done it. And a little surprised at the strength of the warm glow in him, fired by the knowledge he had made his little blond friend happy.

"Again," Joe signed. Nehemiah rolled his eyes and Anna giggled, sliding back into the wagon to get ready for another day with the music tyrant.

Nehemiah had a clear melodic baritone, but his main focus stayed with the instruments. He began to accompany Joe, learning to blend and stand out as Joe decided what the music called for. They were only hours away from the border of Kallipolis when Joe decided Nehemiah had gotten good enough at the rhythm makers to try a duet. Nehi wasn't so sure, but he started up the easiest rhythm he knew. Joe jumped in, his feet striking where Nehemiah's had just left off, creating an intricate, strange, and poignant rhythm. And incidentally, looking very neat. The two boys twisted and kicked, stomped and circled, around the little pile of wood, metal, and gravel. Anna was clapping for them and Nehemiah was just beginning to think he could do this, when he forgot to scrape the gravel and kicked the wood instead. Or it should have been wood. Joe staggered away from the rhythm makers holding his stomach. Anna stopped clapping and started laughing as Joe plopped cross-legged on the ground trying to convince his breath it was safe to come back, and Nehi followed him, apologizing.

"That was amazing, for a moment," a voice spoke up from the dusty road. All three looked up to see a five-foot racer lizard, his bright green scales brilliant in the sunshine. A leather saddle draped over his back, and a tall woman in a blue and red military uniform straddled him, holding the animal's reins. A gleaming projectile rifle dangled from her shoulder strap, and a truncheon, taser, and riding crop hung strapped to her belt. Nehemiah noticed a dull blue glow in the lizard's mouth and his expression tightened at the electric bit and harness. The woman smiled again, the expression not moving her eyes. "I hope you're coming to my country to play, I would love to see more of that. Except for the last part, perhaps."

"We will be coming into Kallipolis tomorrow, Ma'am," Cobeau rumbled from where he stood on top of the wagon keeping watch. She nodded and urged her lizard forward, between the rolling green hillocks. The racer shook his head and scuttled over the ground in a snaking motion. A moment, and they were lost to sight among all the little hills.

"That was a very stern, sad-looking woman," Anna commented.

"And a really large lizard," answered Nehemiah. "Though not as big as the birds in the green back flock that tried to eat us last week." Joe stared down the road after the woman, his face blank. The twins knew that expression (or lack of one) meant he was thinking and they waited for his decision. He spun to Nehemiah and motioned him back to the rhythm makers.

"Let's try again," he signed. It was one of the few full sentences the twins knew of his language, because it was Joe's

main method of teaching.

"You're a very brave fellow, Joe," Anna grinned. Joe signed something quickly as he and Nehemiah took their places again.

"It was my fault too, I wasn't paying enough attention to Knee-High," Cobeau translated for Joe. "And my stomach is strong enough to take the fall if I'm wrong." Joe grinned and winked at Nehi, then suddenly stood still, looking down the road again with the same non-expression. He stirred and signed something as if he had made up his mind. Joe began quickly gathering the rhythm makers.

"Time to go," Cobeau said. It was abrupt, but the twins had become used to the Ravens' abruptness by now; and for once Nehi was too excited about coming into their first new kingdom to wonder what had caused the sudden change.

The simple sign disappeared behind the wagon as they whizzed past. Anna and Nehemiah's heads swiveled, drinking in the sight of their first country outside their own. There didn't seem to be much difference from the wild lands. The dusty road snaked on, and the green hills rose and fell around them, covered in six-foot grasses and buzzing with the loud drone of insects. But gradually they began to see signs of people. A small farm spread over the hills, an old square house watching over it. Two more twists of the road, and a mill stood at the top of a hill, the cogs and wheels squeaking as they rotated. Ten minutes later Beau pulled Prissy to a stop as a flock of sheep baaed and bounded over the road. A shepherd boy walked behind the flock, an enormous wooden crook dwarfing him. The boy only glanced at the giant pig and painted wagon, his cheek discolored by a large purple bruise. Anna thought he looked as sad as the woman had...or maybe even sadder.

"Is he all right?" she asked softly as the wagon pushed past. Joe glanced at the boy and then away again quickly.

"One of the Outsiders," he signed and Beau rumbled. "He's better than many of them, at least he gets to be outside by himself with the sheep."

"Outsiders?" Nehi asked as the wagon sped up and the sheep and boy dropped to specks in the distance.

"Children not perfect or not supposed to be here."

"Not supposed to be here, like immigrants?" Nehi asked, his insatiable curiosity sparking as he twisted, trying to catch another glimpse of the boy.

"No, they –" Joe broke off, his face wrinkled in frustration, as if he couldn't decide what to say, and would rather not say anything. "Not supposed to be born, an accidental baby, unsanctioned by the state."

"Unsanctioned by the–" Nehi started, but Joe's face went stonily blank; Nehemiah was starting to recognize that look. It meant a desire not to be talked to, a sharp wish to be left alone. The mute fidgeted, his eyes darting away. Something had Joe on edge here.

"Look, it's a stupid, awkward method the state has here for propagating children, and I'd rather not go into it," the mute

signed quickly. Nehemiah let the subject lapse.

The farms began to grow more frequent. They began to turn into single houses. Small, simple squares of wood, all painted white but most with the white fading and cracking. The single houses started to clump together. And then they were in a town.

Houses leaned and gaped at them, windows boarded up, paint cracked, yards decayed and torn. Squat, single story shopping malls sprawled along the road, signs faded and sagging. If Nehemiah had to choose a single word to describe it, he would have picked "dumpy." Everything seemed dingy, as if no one cared enough to repair their broken porches or repaint their faded fence. Except those in the uniforms of the Kallipolis military, the auxiliary. Soldiers strolled through the town, in twos and threes, each one pristine and proud. Their brass gleamed, their outdated weaponry sparkled. Even to the most casual observer they were men proud of their station, and proud of serving their country. Nehemiah blinked and looked around the streets again.

"I don't see any lady soldiers," he commented. "But the one on the lizard this morning sure was."

"She must use pounds of lipstick," Anna murmured.

"The requirements for being in the auxiliary are pretty high," Joe signed absently, his eyes still darting around them; he hadn't looked at the twins since they rode into town. "Women are born considered 'inferior in most things,' and so have to leap that bar as well as the regular one for being chosen for the military. Not many make it."

People milled around them, in slightly better repair than their buildings, watching the strange wagon and giant pig. Nehi studied them, and found himself staring into sullen faces. Most of them turned envious and angry when they saw the auxiliary stroll by. An ancient gabled house, with patched peaked roofs soaring into the blue sky, rose on their left. He and Anna spun toward it, studying the peeling brown paint and the large iron fence around the bare yard. Children of all ages played inside the fence, ordinary children's games that the twins recognized immediately. It gave them a sense of normality and fun, and seemed nicely out of tune with the depression of the rest of the town.

"What's that?" Nehemiah asked as they passed it.

"Children's home," Cobeau rumbled.

"An orphanage?" Anna asked.

"No, just home," the chimera answered. Joe started to sign and his large friend translated absently as he maneuvered Prissy through the dirty streets.

"The children are raised by the state here, not families. They live in homes like that till they're old enough to be placed where the state puts them."

"Where the state puts them?" Nehemiah asked.

"There are three classes; Auxiliary are the warriors and sheriffs, Guardians or Philosopher-Kings are the ruling class, and Producers are everybody else. The Guardians decide what everyone does, they have people watching the children all through the growing years, and everything's a test."

"The children grow up just like orphans, even if they had families?" Anna gaped, appalled. Joe nodded.

"Families don't really exist here," he signed. "Real marriages aren't encouraged."

"No wonder everyone looks so sad and glassy eyed," Nehemiah grimaced. Anna said nothing and the conversation stopped as the wagon rolled on. She leaned comfortably against Nehemiah and watched the town, but her eyes kept darting to the mute. He had turned remote today, almost as if a part of him were distancing himself from the twins, ever since that woman had stopped by their wagon. Anna wondered if it could be her imagination, or if Joe could be up to something... She didn't mention it to Nehi, not wanting to give him another reason to fret over their friends. But a vague unease played through her.

Their road snaked to an end at a simple square of dirt, cast-off cans and rubbish flitting here and there in the breeze,

and a few trees struggling to survive beside it. A faded sign proclaimed it "The Square." Cobeau maneuvered Prissy to the top of the place, and the Ravens and consorts hopped off and began to set up for a concert. People straggled in after them, and kept coming. In a few minutes, people lined The Square, packed deep, trying to see over each other. The sun shed red beams on the little band of musicians as it dropped toward the horizon, bathing the group in a natural spotlight as they leapt into their places. The twins watched Joe as he tucked his bagpipe under his arm, the stares of the crowd boring into their bodies. But excitement roared through them, and the crowd only inspired their best. They would do what they could to lighten the sad faces around them, and play their best for their King. The droning wail of the bagpipe split the air. Nehi leapt into his rhythm dance, and the concert began.

Anna and Nehemiah found it surprisingly fun to put everything they had learned together, and let other people enjoy it. Cobeau strolled as their announcer, collecting money from anyone who felt like giving it. He came back with an overflowing hat. Anna and Nehemiah also found giving concerts was very difficult work. Setting up the show, doing the show, and then putting it all up again wasn't easy.

Exhaustion hung on their limbs and fuzzed their minds when Cobeau pulled the wagon to a stop just outside of the town, where they rested alone between two hills. Anna gathered dinner sleepily with Nehi's help, grabbing the leftover ham and the mushrooms, and making something new. They plopped at the little table to eat. Joe's chair stared back at them, empty. For a moment the twins sat, waiting. Nehemiah snuck a bite of the soup and his eyebrows rose.

"Hey, this is actually good," he murmured around a hot mushroom.

"Oh thank you for that vote of confidence in my cooking skill," Anna said, covering a yawn with her hand.

"It's just that you got it together so fast, I expected..." Nehemiah let his voice drift away as he saw Anna staring at him, her mouth twisting in amusement. "I'll stop there before I dig the hole deeper. But it's good. What do you call it?" Anna blinked at the soup, watching the bits of cheese at the top swishing gently back and forth.

"Cheddmusham," she said with decision. Nehemiah chuckled and it turned into a yawn. "It would be better with potatoes in it too. 'Cheddmushpoham' is too long though."

"Decidedly."

Joe's chair stayed empty.

Anna and Nehemiah looked at each other. The sound of Cobeau's sloppy manners filled the little wagon as he devoured Anna's cooking. Nehi shrugged and reached for his spoon. Soup and sandwiches disappeared inside the chimera and Nehemiah, but Anna hardly touched hers. She was too tired. And Joe's seat stayed empty. Beau slumped back, his chair creaking dangerously, and swiped a hairy arm over his mouth. "Cobeau, where's Joe?" Anna asked.

"Business in town," Cobeau said, a placid smile on his face as the food settled in his massive belly.

"Should I keep his dinner warm, will he be back soon?" Anna prodded. The chimera shook his head. A peculiar keening hum, tuneless but happy, slid from him as he slumped and smiled. The sound came from the big man when he was content, unworried, and had nothing to do. The twins glanced at each other again. Anna shrugged this time. If Cobeau wasn't worried about his little friend, Joe was fine. She hoped that meant they had nothing to worry about.

It's awfully long business, Nehemiah thought three hours later, as he sat against the wagon wrapped in his blanket. The insects buzzed around him, zipping up to study the young man, or clumsily bumping into him as they went about their night business. He shooed them off irritably and wished they would leave him alone. A six-inch, fat beetle ran into his foot, teetered for a moment, and rolled over on its back, its legs

waving miserably. Nehi smiled at the thing, picked it up, and tossed it away into the grass. Then he leant back and heaved a deep, long sigh. Nehemiah missed his friend. Where was he? He looked over at Cobeau, framed in the dirty yellow light spilling from the town. The chimera sprawled on the grass, fast asleep and snoring. Nehemiah mentally shrugged off his unease, slumped down, grimaced as another beetle scurried out from under him, and dozed off.

White light cut into his face, slicing through his eyelids into his brain. Nehi cracked his eyes open, shifting uncomfortably. A bright beam shone in his face, so bright he could see nothing but white. And that hurt. Nehemiah shielded his face with his hand and blinked, his eyes watering.

"Joe, that's not funny. If–"

"Yes, he's one," a strange voice said from the direction of the light. Nehemiah froze. Two sets of hands darted from the darkness. Strong fingers grabbed his arms, hauled him to his feet, and jerked his hands behind his back. A rope slipped over his wrists and cinched tight. Nehemiah woke up the rest of the way. He bent his arm and rammed an elbow strike back into the man holding the rope. He felt ribs and heard the air go out of the man in a rush. Nehi pivoted on his left foot and brought his knee up fast. He caught a glimpse of soldiers, navy blue and crimson uniforms starched and neat, projectile rifles slung over their shoulders. One directly behind him was doubled over, wheezing. Nehemiah's knee connected with the man's face. The soldier went over backwards, his nose broken and his eyes rolled back in his head. Two more shouted and leapt toward their captive.

Nehi took two quick steps back to gain room. He centered himself on the ball of his left foot and aimed a roundhouse kick at the knee of one of the soldiers rushing him. He was fast and well-trained. A sharp crack sounded as his foot connected and he snapped it back. The soldier's face went pale and stricken with shock. He folded onto the ground as Nehi spun to the second soldier, dimly noticing more moving around him as he focused on the nearest threat. His stance was still solid and he snapped his leg out again, catching the soldier on the inside of his knees. The man fell backward with a pained cry, and Nehi stepped back again, his eyes darting around the circle of white light he stood in, trying to see into the shadowy blackness on the fringes of the light to tell which way to run.

A bullet dug up the ground in front of his foot. Another ricocheted off a rock and whined past his ear. Nehemiah froze.

"Ah, you do have some sense in you," a bored voice drifted from the source of the light. "We would rather bring you in whole, but if you do continue to insist on objecting, it would be very easy to shoot you in the leg and *make* you docile." A pause came as Nehi stayed still, his heartbeat pounding, trying to think of any way out. Alone in the center of a pool of light, he had no chance.

"Well, why are you waiting?" the voice snapped.

Four soldiers stepped into the light, their rifles held ready, eyeing him warily. They moved cautiously as they approached him and it gave Nehi a little satisfaction to see he had worried them. One burly soldier lunged and grabbed his arms, wrenching them back. The old ache in Nehi's shoulder seared into him; he thought that had healed. Iron-shod boots slammed into his shins, driving his legs out from under him. The ground was cold and hard as he hit it. A heavy body leapt on his back, holding him in place. Nehi lay still on his face, breathing hard and forcing himself under control. He knew when not to struggle, and what might happen if he tried. The heavy someone stayed on him as the rope was checked over, and a second biting length added just above the elbows. The someone clambered off, the ropes pulled, he stumbled to his feet, and a hand shoved into his back, pushing him toward the source of the blinding light. A large group of soldiers stood behind the light, all armed with outdated projectile weapons. Outdated, but still deadly. The hand rammed into his back again and Nehemiah stepped into the middle of the soldiers. Two rifle muzzles pressed into his sides, the round tips boring into him.

"What do you want?" Nehemiah growled, forcing his fear deep inside. A tall, commanding man with an officer's stripes on his uniform looked him up and down.

"You're wanted for questioning," he answered, his voice the same bored tone Nehi had heard earlier. The wagon door opened, and two more soldiers hopped out. Nehemiah's throat tightened and his heartbeat paused. Anna's wrists were bound behind her and a burly soldier pulled her out of the wagon. Her messy black curls tumbled over her shoulders and waved around her cotton pajamas. The dullness of a heavy sleep clung to her, but confusion and fear quickly overtook Anna's lovely face.

"Is this the other one?" the commander asked, turning to his left. Nehemiah followed his gaze automatically, and fixed there, wide and staring.

Joe stood beside the soldier.

His sharp face was blank, his eyes lowered, showing nothing. The shaggy blond head nodded. Anna stumbled beside Nehemiah. The biting hands gripped his shoulder again and jerked Nehi away, Anna next to him. The twins were half dragged toward a group of trucks, rifles prodding into their backs. Nehemiah lost sight of Joe's small form in the swirl of soldiers. He shuffled obediently where they pushed him, his dark eyes watching for any way out. But his stomach rolled as he tried to grasp what had just happened.

Cobeau watched the group of soldiers moving off toward their trucks, his face puzzled and anxious. Joe stepped out of the shadows beside him and some of the worried wrinkles vanished from the big man's face.

"Why did you do that, Master?" he asked mildly. Joe slapped him on the arm and shook his finger at him out of habit. He didn't like being called master. The mute looked up at his friend. Beau's trusting eyes melted the stiff blank mask away; Joe sagged, his scarred face lined with depression and exhaustion.

"I had to. You saw Tarin this morning patrolling on her lizard. I found her later and...the FFs are in town and found out the twins are here," he signed. Cobeau looked back toward the trucks, his big face confused.

"But I thought you thought–" he started to rumble, and Joe interrupted irritably.

"If they are with the FFs we can't let them come together, if they aren't we really can't let them together," he signed. Joe's eyes suddenly snapped urgently at the chimera and he began to sign in a blur.

The trucks pulled out into the road, with Nehemiah and Anna sitting frightened and silent in the last of the line. If they had looked back they might have seen a large, dark shadow race up behind them and latch onto the back of their truck. They might have even recognized Cobeau in the hunched form clinging to the handrail as the truck rumbled deeper into the kingdom. But neither twin looked up; they were too scared and preoccupied to notice a shadow.

Chapter Fourteen: The Guardians

"The fear of the LORD is the beginning of knowledge: but fools despise wisdom and instruction." Proverbs 1:7

Nehemiah and Anna sat still, jaws tight, listening to the roar of the engine. The truck bumped and jerked uncomfortably, clumsy and loud on its rubber tires. Anna turned to Nehi, her mouth opening to say something. The guard beside her glared and lifted his rifle. She slumped back, her nose wrinkling. The truck turned sharply, and its movements became slower and jerkier. Nehemiah assumed they had turned off the main road. He tried to get a look at where they were, but three soldiers stood blocking the opening. The truck rattled to a stop, their guards piled out, and a hand shoved into Nehi's shoulder, knocking him out of the van. He stumbled to his feet, as Anna rammed into his side. She looked up at him as she got her feet under her. Nehemiah gave her a smile. No one had hurt them yet, he kept reminding himself, and it was helping him stay calm...a little. A rifle dug into his spine, and his lips pursed. Boy, he wanted to break that thing over its owner's head. But he just started walking.

They marched through the moonlight toward an enormous, ancient building. Its gray stone walls rose three stories into the air, crowned with elegant crenellations, and pitted everywhere with deep-set windows. Ivy covered one side, but it was the brown spider web of ivy deceased. It must have been beautiful in its day. Now with its crumbling walls and faded paint it looked depressing and a little sinister. The brother and sister were pushed up three flights of creaking stairs and into a large, well lit room. It was an elegant place, with carved marble faces watching them from the top of the white walls. The frowning group of old men sitting around the large table seemed austere and prosperous, and they fit the room. The soldiers prodded and pushed Anna and Nehemiah to the center of the room and shoved them into chairs facing the table. Then they stepped back to the wall respectfully. Fear played over the soldiers, and they kept glancing from the old men at the table to the door. For just a moment Anna considered using their distraction, eyeing the windows leading to the spiderweb of ivy outside. But as she leaned forward their gaze shot to her, fingers shifting along their rifle barrels. She sat back obediently. An elderly man in a flowing yellow shirt and white pants stood up and stared at the twins.

"Are you the children of the Sojourner Judge?" he asked. Anna and Nehemiah blinked, wondering how on earth they knew that, and why they were asking. And why they cared. There was no Sojourner's kingdom now.

"Are you the youngest two Hillsons? Answer!" the man demanded. Nehemiah decided they had better obey.

"Yes," he said, and was surprised to find his voice was strong. The group stirred and looked at each other significantly. The man in yellow waved the commander forward. The soldier bound the twins securely into their chairs. But not cruelly, Nehemiah noted.

"You and the other auxiliary may go now," the man said. The soldiers almost rushed the doorway. The door clicked closed, and every old man turned toward the twins. Questions shot out, a bedlam of noise, and they couldn't pick a coherent phrase out of the jumble of voices. The man in yellow raised his hand and stood up again. Silence dropped into the room.

"We are the guardians of Kallipolis, the philosopher-kings," he said, his voice echoing off the walls. "We wish you to tell us who took our book."

"Don't say it like that, Acacius," a slightly younger man said (gray hair clinging to his head in thin strands). "It sounds as if we do not have our book." The whole group reeled in horror, and Acacius quickly spoke again.

"You understand we paid the full amount, and our glorious *Republic* is back in our midst. But it is just we find who has taken our money, for that was taken from us unjustly."

"Why do you think we know anything about it?" Anna

gaped.

"You have lost your book, child of the Way," Acacius said, his eyebrows lowering over his watery eyes as he peered at her. "Besides, we have information from a fairly reliable source that says you may know something."

"He would not dare to tell us a lie," the second man spoke up confidently. "He has too much to lose."

"It is true but hardly to the point, Eusebius," Acacius said crushingly and turned back to the twins. "You must know something of who has it."

"It doesn't follow that since our book was taken we know something about who took it," Nehemiah said. Acacius bridled, trembling as he reared to his full height, glaring at the boy.

"Would you dare to put your reason over ours?" he demanded, anger making his voice shake. "We have grasped the form of goodness, we will not be contradicted by a young follower of the Way who does not even grasp the form of the sensible particulars!"

"We don't know any more about the book being stolen than you do," Anna spoke up, as Nehemiah sat and stared, trying to figure out what the old man was talking about. "We didn't even know it was stolen until long after the act had happened. Actually, you should know more than us. Your book is back." The group at the table sat still for a moment, trying to decide what to respond.

"Do you know, she might be right?" said one, in a voice quivering with age.

"I think she is only trying to appeal to our spirit to try and save herself," spoke up one in a crimson robe at the end of the table. In an instant the room divided between the two schools of thought. Each held their own view tenaciously, and the volume of the debate began to grow. The twins waited, tense and silent, watching to see which side would win. This was a very strange turn of events. Another book stolen, another country blackmailed to get it back! Anna's brow wrinkled as she thought furiously. Could this be the reason they were hunted?

One reason Samuel warned them not to give out their name? If there were more kingdoms like this, people who had been blackmailed out of their book and shook in their boots now… When powerful people grew scared, ordinary people got hurt. And she and Nehi were ordinary people now. No, they were more vulnerable than that. Without a family, without a country, without protection of any kind.

The volume of noise lowered in the room, and Anna started paying attention to the Guardians again. The first theory had won. The Guardians were convinced the two young people had no information to give. Elation swept over Nehemiah as he heard it. But then Acacius rose again.

"If we no longer have need of them, what are we to do with these two?" he said. Nehemiah stopped feeling elated.

"The Way says belief should rule over reason," the man in the crimson robe took up, rising shakily to his feet and studying the twins with dislike. "That a man may have one woman, and only one woman no matter their age. That there is only one good and it is God, and cannot be discovered by pure reason. We have seen how their foolish ideas can spread in the weak minds of the Auxiliary and Producers. I do not believe we can let these two out in our midst."

"It is a just thought, Diodorus," Acacius spoke up. "Also, we have told them of our book's disappearance, and though we have also told them of its return, this knowledge going out into the world might cause friction with our neighbors." A murmur of agreement ran through the room. Cold began to seep into Nehemiah's bones.

"We do not need the boy; I can think of no use the State has for him," Diodorus spoke up. "But the girl is very pretty, and her reason seems adequate. We are always in need of more children, it seems ours do not come out very wise, of late."

"You cannot have my sister," Nehemiah snarled. The vehemence and threat in his voice made everyone look at him in surprise.

"And what do you intend to do, boy? You are helpless, in

case you haven't noticed," Diodorus said. Images of horrors Nehemiah had seen and more he heard talked about at Abid's table filled him and his heart shook in his fear. Nehemiah had never felt terror like he did at that moment. They couldn't have Anna. He looked around him at the cold faces, his lungs constricted.

"You can't have her!" The words were almost gabbled, the desperate pleading choking out of him. "Think of your own sisters, wouldn't you let her go for their sakes?"

"All members of the State are our sisters, child of the Way, or mothers, or grandmothers," one man said, his lip curled in an imperious sneer.

"I will call the auxiliary back," Acacius said, "and tell them of our decision."

"You will not touch these two," a deep growl came from a corner behind the door, black with shadow. Everyone in the room jumped and twisted toward it. Cobeau's huge form towered in the shadows. A whine slid into the silence and a red circle glowed as his short laser rifle primed, pointed at the table. An awkward silence tingled in the air.

An incoherent shout broke it, drifting from the road outside the hall. Voice after voice took it up, yells of challenge, anger, a few rifle shots and high-pitched keening lasers. The noise came toward them. One of the men at the table stood up and looked out the window. His mouth fell open, then he grimaced and sat down heavily.

"Our neighbors from the Kingdom of the Wise are calling," he told the company. Another silence fell, but to Anna it felt much angrier than the last. The noise of a large group of people came closer to them. Shouts, clashes of metal on metal, and pounding feet filled the courtyard outside and poured into the building. It climbed the stairs till it was right outside the ornate room. The doors crashed open, banging against the walls. The room flooded with people, most of them waving red dye lasers, shiny and new, led by a tall man in a long brown coat.

"Good day to you, Guardians!" the man said with what was

almost a yawn. "If it is a good day. We heard you had visitors and have come to ask them to leave this stuffy old building of yours and come with us."

"To use one of your favorite words, Bertrand, why?" Acacius said, his old face wrinkled in abhorrence as he glared at the man.

"I expect for the same reason you have them here, old man," answered Bertrand. He spoke with a flippant tone and looked down his nose instead of over it. "Though of course I don't know that. Of course I don't know anything."

"Some people's reason is so faulty they can know nothing, yes. Especially you skeptics it seems," sneered Acacius.

"Why do you think that?" asked Bertrand, a smile curling his thin lips. "Why reason, why not breakfast instead? We can know as much by breakfast as we can by reason; nothing." Acacius spluttered something about reason, but Diodorus interrupted.

"How did you know we had visitors, Bertrand?" he asked.

"I was told by a source we sometimes use for news, but as for knowing–"

"Yes, I used the wrong word for you, I admit that," Diodorus said quickly. He pointed behind Bertrand. "Is that your source?" Bertrand reached behind him and pulled Joe to the front of the crowd. The mute stood still, eyes fastened on his black boots as the crowd of people stared at him; small, blank, his messy hair spilling over his face.

"Yes, it is," Bertrand answered. "Why?"

"We have also used him as an information source, for some years," Diodorus answered, studying Joe. As someone might stare at an interesting beetle. "This time we thought we had his services to ourselves, due to one of our auxiliaries accidentally stumbling on an old owner of his among our producers. A nasty sort even for that class. If he didn't bring us news of what we wanted, we were sending him back to his old home."

"That's a hold I won't mind having on the beast," Bertrand

commented, looking at the expressionless Joe with the same inhuman scrutiny. "He and his large dog can be very useful if they can be made to be."

"Yes, they can," Diodorus said. "I mention it only as an interesting fact, I did think his fear would keep him loyal. His coming to you shows a side of him I did not know existed. A strange source to use perhaps, and only as one passing through, you understand."

"I understand nothing," said Bertrand, making the philosopher-kings glare at him and Nehemiah's head spin. "But I think you mean that you would rather he didn't stay. I agree. No, we need no incompletes in our Kingdom of the Wise, either. Too uncertain, if you know what I mean."

"Oh, so you do know and mean some things?" Acacius answered, but Diodorus interrupted quickly.

"Yes, I believe we agree on that point at least. The wrong blood might send a whole strand of incompletes into the country, and that would be undesirable for the perfect State. He is much better on his way. Why don't you take him there, Bertrand? And by all means, take these two as well. I hope they are of use to you."

"You wouldn't be offering to let me take your visitors if I hadn't come with enough force to bring them out despite you," Bertrand said with a laugh. Hands gripped Nehemiah's arms, as a blade sheered through the ropes binding him to the chair. But not the ones on his arms. The hands gripping him levered him to his feet and shoved him to the door. Nehi marched between two soldiers, their grip strong, faces chiseled and alert. He watched Anna being propelled by her own guards just in front of him. These men were well trained, and well outfitted, all their trappings new and polished. One soldier jerked his arm forward, the other back, and Nehi twisted between them, half-carried sideways down the stairs. The moon shone on laser dye rifles and trim uniforms as he was pulled onto the gravel of the drive, between two lines of Bertrand's soldiers.

An armored, two car centipede waited, its open back looking ready to swallow them alive. The centipede was a squat dome shape with a tapered nose at the front, made of metal sections jointed together to allow for turns and defensive circles. It couldn't move as fast as a hoverer or the massive caravans, but it was reliable, extremely hard to break through the metal, and capable of getting through almost any terrain. Perfect for traveling through the wild lands, if someone had to make the dangerous trek between countries.

Anna's guards lifted her at the elbows and tossed her to two waiting soldiers. The metal bench clanged as they dropped her onto it. Nehemiah clambered up and took a step toward his sister. The soldier behind him grabbed his arms and jerked him back. Fire flared up Nehemiah's shoulder again, and he slammed onto the metal bench opposite Anna. Soldiers filled the centipede's car, silent and orderly. Bertrand stepped in last, his head high and brown leather jacket flaring in the breeze. Two soldiers jerked the doors home as Bertrand perched on a bench, and artificial bulbs blinked into buzzing white light along the top of the dome. A sharp squeal came as the metal legs began to move, then merged into a constant background clanking as the centipede smoothly picked up speed.

Nehemiah's stomach still churned, and his relief at having gotten out of the hands of the Guardians was almost tangible. But where were they being taken now? He didn't like the look of this Bertrand who spoke so flippantly and acted so rationally. Nehemiah looked over at Anna, sitting stiffly across from him. Her eyes met his and worry gleamed there; but she smiled when she saw him looking. She wasn't as frightened as she should be. Or maybe he was more frightened than he should be.

He had a long ride ahead of him to figure it out.

A one horn
Pg. 160

Joe stood under the swinging strands of a willow tree, watching the gashes in the land that served as a road. Soft black leather wound around his head, tied off behind his right ear so it tapered into an elegant tail lying over his shoulder. It hid his blond hair and pale face, melded with his high-collared black jacket, and left nothing visible in the dark but the glitter of his bright eyes. The chimera towered next to him, a larger shadow in the blackness. A breeze brushed past, stirring the willow's weeping boughs and caressing the Ravens. The two stayed as still as the tree trunk, black statues in the night.

A white beam pierced the dark; a vehicle's headlight topping the hill a mile to their right. Joe swiveled to watch it, calculating as the light moved over the edge and disappeared into the valley. Two smaller red lights pulsed farther down the road behind the bright white headlight. Joe slid his gloves off so the chimera could see his pale hands.

"Centipede," he signed. "They're in the back. Last car, you act when the others get out of sight. Board after it passes us."

He slid the gloves over his hands and disappeared into the night again, as if he belonged to the darkness. The circle of white light appeared over their own hill, closer and larger this time, illuminating the ground in front of it as it came. They could hear the metal legs clanking as they dug into the earth, sending the machine skittering over the land.

The headlight swept past the Ravens. It pierced the forest around them, scattering a cloud of bats who rose in a dark cloud with loud complaints, their leathery wings filling the night with a sharp hum. But the swinging fronds of the willow masked the Ravens from view. The nose of the centipede clunked and clinked past, and Joe could see the faces of the two soldiers in charge of the machine staring out the slit; a grizzled old officer and a fresh-faced youth. The first car moved past them, its plates shifting with loud metallic clunks as the drivers turned away from the deepest portions of a pond pooling over the road. Water splashed in all directions from the skittering legs, wetting the ground. The red light blinking to mark the first car moved on past the Ravens, the legs making soft squishing sounds as it traveled over the muddied road.

Joe shifted, smoothly and with a speed that blurred in the dark. A pair of goggles slid over his eyes. His hand went behind him and pulled his hover board from its sling strapped on his back. He activated it as he dropped it and a soft woosh of steam filled the night as the two hundred jets under the board started. The jets caught, pushing off the soft ground, and Joe's feet found the slots. He shifted his stance, feeling the board under him responding to his movements, and gave a slight nod. Always check a hover board before using it. Even a slight miscalibration or clog could cause an overbalance. And an overbalance when zipping at high speeds with no protection except your clothing is a nasty, nasty thing.

The red light of the last car came level with the Ravens. Cobeau shot forward, his powerful legs pumping as he darted to the skittering machine and leapt. His magnetic gloves and boots latched on with perfect ease and he clung to the side as the wind from the centipede's speed rushed around him.

Joe whizzed past, the steam from his hover board leaving a small white trail in the night. He kept close to the side of the centipede, where the driver at the front of this car would have no chance of sighting him, his balance perfect, the board responding to every movement. He leaned forward and it sped up, rushing through the darkness. He came even with the cab and Joe leaned back enough to slow the board, matching his speed with the centipede's as it skittered on. The wind buffeted his body, cold and humid, but Joe shut it out, studying the machine through his goggle's green night vision mode.

This car was a center, not designed to be the front of the vehicle. A metal wall, split from one end to the other with a three foot wide slit of tempered glass, it wasn't aerodynamic or particularly safe without the rest of the cars. The driver in the cab was merely a formality, a safety feature, a last ditch effort if somehow the car became separated from the nose. Joe glanced through the slit at the driver. The man sat stooped over a hologram projection of a mindless throwing game. The mute turned his attention to the couplings.

Twelve of them ran over the dome and around the edges, hooking it to the next car. Simple clamps, nothing too fancy or ornate. But they might pose a problem. Joe's lips pursed as he studied the ones on the bottom of the car. Then he looked up at the driver again. Even someone engrossed in a game wasn't going to miss a black form clambering all over their field of vision.

His hand slid to his pocket, fighting the wind. When it emerged, brass knuckles glimmered in the moonlight. Joe turned to study the terrain coming up on him. His hand rose to tap his goggles and he zoomed in on the ground near the nose. The centipede's lead legs crunched and smashed over a fallen tree, sending splinters cascading into the air. He focused, and the smashed wood came into view in sharp green lines. That would be his chance.

Joe hunched on his board, his arms held even beside his body, his stance relaxed, everything focused on the coming maneuver. He watched the log come closer, the wind tearing at him. His board hit the edge of the log.

The board rocketed into the air, the steam jets pushing off the wood. Joe's arms came out till he stood perpendicular to the ground, a black cross suspended for an instant between earth and sky.

He kicked out of the foot slots, his toe hitting the power button as he moved. The board shut off, he caught its side and flipped it behind his back to snap into its sleeve. Joe's other hand shot out at the same instant, gripping the last car by a joining clamp. He pulled himself to it, fighting the wind and the force of the moving centipede as it tried to whip him backward. His toe found a lower clamp and he clung to the car. His fist came back, he hesitated a quarter of a second to balance, then rolled forward, striking his fist into the tempered glass of the slot, with all the force of his shoulder and

torso behind him. The glass shattered, breaking into lightning shaped streaks, then stars, then falling in a shower of musical tinkling. Joe's right hand gripped the edge of the slit and pulled as his left pushed off the clamp. He shot through the slit, using his force to headbutt the guard in the chest, driving him into the metal back of the car.

It took him five seconds.

But one second could make him too late.

Joe heard ribs crack as he hit the soldier, and felt the air go from him. But he saw the man's hand moving toward the alarm button. If the alarm went up, if anyone got wind of the Ravens invading the centipede, it would end all chances of rescuing the twins.

Hot fire ran through the mute, his desire to make sure the twins made it out a burning fury. It claimed him, his muscles moving under its volition. His gloves planted on the glass-strewn floor and his leg launched out in a back kick. His heel hit wrist bone and he saw shock pale the soldier. A scream formed on the man's face. Joe bounced up as if propelled by a spring. His fist rammed out in an uppercut, the brass knuckles gleaming as he moved. It connected under the soldier's jaw, and his head snapped back. An ugly, hollow thump reached the mute and the soldier's eyes rolled back. He slumped to his side, blood smearing the back of the car as he fell. Under the elegant black mask, anger melted into fear on Joe's face. The mute dropped to one knee, sliding a glove off and pressing two fingers to the soldier's neck, feeling for a pulse. For six seconds he knelt there, face tight, not breathing, just fumbling to find life. A pulse beat under his fingers. His shoulders sagged, a sharp breath sucking into his lungs. Joe pulled a dart gun from his pocket, fired a quick shot into the soldier's neck to keep him down and mercifully unconscious, and turned him on his stomach. The man's skin was split and bleeding freely from the back of his skull. Joe's hands were a blur as he reset the soldier's jaw, pulled a roll of bandages from one of his capacious pockets, made a few quick turns around the man's head to stop the blood flow, and spun toward the slit.

Humid, cold wind found its way through the broken slit, teasing Joe's mask. He let himself just stand for a moment, gathering his breath. Then he gripped the edge, pulled himself through back into the night, and grabbed the clamps. His fingers dug into the top one, tugging and pulling. It wouldn't budge. He frowned and pushed his goggles to the top of his head to study it better, sending his mind back to the terrain, and calculating angles. Another hill had been in the distance when he had located his log. If he tried to use his electric pulse to shove the clamp apart the flashes of blue light would be seen from the drivers in the nose. No, he needed a dark, silent force.

Joe heaved himself up till his head poked over the top of the dome. The wind hit him with all its cold force, whipping the leather fabric hanging by his ear into a maddened, living thing. Joe gave a short whistle. A large, dark shape swarmed over the side of the car and scurried toward him. Beau came even with him and the chimera's large trusting eyes stared down into the mute's, begging to be useful, the eagerness in his expression visible even behind his mask. Joe waved at the clamps. The chimera reached a huge hand down, wrapped his fingers around the top one, and popped it open. Joe nodded, squirmed to the edge, and reached for his hover board.

The mute held a clamp with one hand and let himself dangle off the car into the wind. He slid his feet into the board's slots, turned it on, moved the power level to high, and watched the jets spurt to life. A thin cloud of white steam was caught by the wind and lifted off. He jabbed a small button on the side and a black dye released into the water pipes. Then he jumped. The steam jets caught him, the board lifted to hover a full foot off the ground, and the dye began to turn the steam from white to black. He shifted left, then right, watching carefully as the board followed his movements, zipping him back and forth.

Joe gave his friend a quick salute. Beau leaned far off the

edge, the toes of his magnetic boots clamped to the metal car, popping the clamps open with ease. He waved at Joe in acknowledgement of the salute and went back to work. Joe leaned forward, hunching close and letting his arms go behind him, offering as little resistance as possible to the wind.

He needed speed now. The drivers in the centipede's nose would notice when the last car came undone. He had possibly a minute till they knew something was wrong and set off the alarm. Joe had to reach them before that.

Black steam poured from the jets and the board continued to pick up speed. The wind tore at Joe, finding ways through his clothes to rip at his skin, roaring in his ears. He ignored it, his whole focus on the nose of the centipede. The board came even with the nose and Joe leaned back, his balance perfect against the wind and the shifting of the board as it raced over the rough terrain. The hover board matched the centipede's speed and Joe looked up at the brain of the machine. A control panel took up most of the interior. The slit started at the top and tapered with the nose, nearly five feet wide and six across. And made of crystal-glass; the nose was too important to risk it breaking from a loose rock or a hunting animal's tooth.

Joe swung in close to the machine, near enough he felt the cold from the metal shell seeping into his bones. Moving carefully to keep himself balanced, he flipped a flap from his right sleeve open, shielding it as best as he could from the wind. A myriad of useful items lay strapped to his arm under that flap; throwing discs, scanners, smoke bombs, darts for his gun, nylon cord, a host of tiny things laid carefully in their places. Joe slid the brass knuckles in their allotted slot and popped three ultrasonic nodes from the interior. He glanced up at the slit again and grimaced. The nodes took three seconds to sync, before they pulsed. The drivers only needed a second to reach the alarm. He couldn't afford to risk the extra two seconds to sync them on the slit. He gritted his teeth and hit the activator as the nodes lay in his palm.

Hot fire ran up his arm as the electricity started, blue lightning bolts shooting from one node to another as the three little circles found each other and synced. Another second, and his heart quivered from the pulsing pain. Joe flung the nodes, rolling them in his fingers to get them the right width apart. A gasp slid from him as they left his body.

Three black round pebbles hit the slit and adhered to it. Blue-white lines of electric power pulsed between them, and with it came a whine that pierced Joe's ears. It's sounded like a giant bat, shrieking in mad fury. For that instant a circle three feet across lit the night and the whine shook the mute's brain.

Crystal-glass shards sprayed inward. The two drivers cried out, staggering back, and trying to shelter their faces from the needle-sharp spray. Humid, cold wind poured in, taking the drivers breaths and teasing the glass shards to stinging life.

A black form shot through the hole. He moved as if the dark wind created him. A blur of action, he landed a knife strike with the flat of his hand on the young soldier. Joe kept it a light strike, but when he connected with the base of the soldier's skull his arm jarred with the impact. The soldier's head snapped and he folded into a pile on the floor, a sharp gasp coming from him. Joe didn't stop to check on him.

The grizzled officer's face rippled in a snarl. His hand shot toward the ruby laser pistol on his belt. A small weapon, the battery and lasing medium could not sustain a long distance powerful shot. But it was perfectly deadly at close quarters. Joe launched toward him, moving unexpectedly into a handspring.

The mute's fighting style couldn't be labeled as any one thing. Someone had once termed it Capoeira on steroids, that ran into a mixed martial arts studio, stumbled into a boxing ring, and ended up on the streets. The only thing consistent about it was his reliance on speed. A blow doesn't gain devastating force from the power behind the strike. It's the quickness and cleanness of it that makes it deadly. The less drag, the less resistance, the more powerful the blow when it lands.

Joe had a speed no one could match.

But the officer had a lifetime of dealing with sudden, unexplained threats.

The laser pistol fired as Joe pushed off into his handspring. The mute felt the heat of the beam as it hit the crystal-glass slit centimeters from his arched back. He landed on his hands in a solid stance, his right foot already flying into a side kick. The flat of his foot connected with the officer's jaw and came down in an ax kick, slamming into the man's wrist as he stumbled back. The laser pistol fell from his nerveless fingers, clattering to the metal ground. The officer slashed out with a snap kick, before Joe thought the man had time to gain a fighting stance. The mute brought his hands up, letting himself fall towards the metal ground, and slammed his palms on the incoming foot. It didn't stop it, but it lessened the force, and got it aimed away from his kidney. His ribs bent as the foot connected, the air left him, and he couldn't breathe.

The young soldier on the other side of the nose lurched to his knees. His eyes were unfocused, his hands shaking. But he headed for the blinking, red alarm button.

Joe wrapped his hands around the officer's ankle. He twisted it to the side, planted his palm on the sole of the man's foot, and pushed. With a cry the officer stumbled back, fumbling to keep his feet. It gave Joe the room he needed. He jerked his dart gun from his pocket. The sound of two small pops were swept away by the wind. The officer sank to the ground in a pile, a tiny wooden dart impaling his neck. The soldier collapsed face down on the metal ground, one hand outstretched toward the blinking button.

Joe rolled to his back and gasped. He tried to bring air into his protesting lungs and wondered idly how many ribs were cracked. With an inward groan he pushed himself to his knees and reached for the control panel. He pulled himself upright, shook himself to get the glass shards off, and studied the buttons and switches.

He had never actually been in a centipede nose. Did it even

have an autopilot? Well, if it didn't it was about to. Joe cracked his knuckles, pulled his instrument case from a cargo pocket, and got to work. Time to send these first cars back to the Kingdom of the Wise. Bertrand Galen, younger son of the House of Galen, rulers of all the west sector in the Kingdom of the Wise, a man who wielded almost unlimited power in his own sphere...not many knew he was terrified of the Wild Lands. Bertrand thought it was his own personal secret. But Joe made it his business to know unusual facts about important people.

They needed Bertrand's car alone in the wild lands.

Chapter Fifteen: New Beginnings

"Behold, how good and how pleasant it is for brethren to dwell together in unity!" Psalm 133:1

A sharp squeal of metal rent through the night as the centipede's legs suddenly slowed. Anna grimaced and wished she had a hand free to rub her ears. The vehicle jerked crazily to a stop, tilting and nearly tumbling to its side. It spun Nehemiah off the bench, grunting as he slammed into the metal floor, his shoulder blades butting up against Anna's toes. Bertrand cursed, unclamped the door into the driver's cab, and slid in.

"Contact the nose and find out why we stopped!" he shouted at the driver. Only there was no driver standing at attention. A still, dark heap lay on the floor of the cab. A humid breeze drifted through the glassless slit. No second car in the lead, no nose giving commands, simply empty, dark wild lands.

The door slammed closed behind him, isolating him from his soldiers.

"Don't move if you want to live," a deep voice growled behind him. Bertrand felt cold metal pressing into the back of his skull. The shrill whine of a laser pierced through his ears and a deadly red light filtered around his head. "Order the prisoners out of the truck," the voice growled. Bertrand obeyed, his voice shaking as he yelled the order. Nothing had ever terrified him more than that empty, open expanse of wild land in front of him. Losing the command nose and most of his soldiers, he lost all his nerve and didn't even consider resistance.

The back plates squealed as someone shoved them open. Then came the soft thud of a boot connecting, a grunt from Nehi, Anna's feet scuffling the metal floor, and then two thumps on the hard packed road.

"Now get in the driver's seat and drive, don't look back."

Bertrand did as he was told and he didn't stop driving till

he was back in his own country, at his own front door.

"Are you all right?" Nehemiah asked, helping Anna up as best he could.

"I'm fine, Nehi. Thank the Lord of all grace, we both are." Her voice shook, and Nehemiah knew she had been hiding her terror. Good, brave Anna. "Why did they just dump us like that?"

"I said so," Cobeau answered. They spun on the dirt, hearts pounding, and found the chimera smiling happily at them, his laser resting easily on his shoulder. Joe stood beside him with his little dagger in his hands and a hover board strapped to his back. His green eyes were lowered, and they stayed that way as he sliced through their ropes. He turned and scrambled over the deep ruts of the road to the edge of the dark woods, standing sentinel on both sides. His white hand almost shone in the moonlight as he motioned them to follow. Joe turned and disappeared into the darkness under the trees. Nehemiah and Anna watched him from the road. The chimera stopped at the edge of the forest and looked back at them, blinking, his big hairy face crinkled as he tried to guess why they weren't following.

Anna looked at Nehemiah. He stood rubbing his shoulder, but his expression was easy for his twin to interpret. The pain there wasn't from any physical wound. It came from the anger of betrayal. If he had been a few years younger, hot tears would have been pouring, Anna knew. Nehi considered Joe enough of a friend that the mute's treachery had him bleeding inside. She turned and followed Joe. They needed an explanation for tonight, before anything else was decided. Nehemiah needed an explanation. Nehi watched her march forward, trim feet slamming into the ground so dust rose in her wrath. He followed without a word.

After about five minutes of walking, the twins found them-

selves following Beau's wide back into the Raven's wagon. As soon as the door closed, Joe signed he needed to start Prissy moving. He quickly disappeared onto the wagon top, and Cobeau followed him. Nehemiah and Anna climbed up into their usual seats, still in the same strained silence. The sharp hiss sounded, the wagon rose, jerked forward, and they moved quickly down the road toward...somewhere. Anna suddenly realized she had no more idea where they were going than she knew where she was right now. They went on in silence. A heavy silence that dragged on and no one broke. The big chimera finally decided it was too heavy.

"Exciting," Cobeau said cheerfully.

"Exciting? Exciting?!" Nehemiah hissed furiously. "Yes, I suppose that's one way to describe tonight, Cobeau. Especially if you don't want to mention the fact that you betrayed us and nearly got us killed. Or worse."

"It wasn't exactly what I would call a friendly thing to do," Anna agreed sharply. "Were you really in trouble with those people? They said something about an old owner." Joe signed nothing, and only stared at the darkness ahead with his curious blankness covering anything he might be thinking.

"Not nice people. They would have turned my Joe over to the bad man," Beau rumbled, sorrow almost dripping from the voice. He shook his shaggy head. "No love there, not for God. Sad men."

"Well," Anna said, her voice a little less sharp, "I certainly don't object to helping you out of a scrape. But why didn't you just ask?"

"We would have helped, Joe!" Nehemiah burst in, each word laced with hot fire. "I object strongly to your turning us over to the dubious mercy of those guardians without a hint of warning."

"And what about that Bertrand?" Anna put in, her sharpness returning.

"He didn't have any hold on you," Nehemiah took up. "Why did you go to him except for what he'd pay you for us? I hope he gave you more than thirty pieces of silver, you Judas." Cobeau stared up at them in surprise, obviously struggling to follow the conversation.

"Were you hurt?" he asked, setting his rifle down and looking at them with serious intensity. "I watched so you weren't, and I thought I did it."

"Cobeau, don't you understand?" Nehemiah yelled. "It wasn't what happened, it was that it happened at all! You turned us over to people meaning us harm, for your own gain!"

"No we didn't," Cobeau said, his face wrinkled in confusion. Joe suddenly woke from his stupor and laid a hand on the chimera's arm. After several swift signs at Cobeau, the big man pulled the wagon into a small round clearing by one of the many ponds, surrounded by enormous willows. The chimera hopped off and disappeared into the darkness on their left to do his usual reconnoitering of a prospective camp sight. Joe turned the steam off, the hiss of the wagon settled, and the droning insects, shifting water, and rustling trees took over the night. He looked up from his perch on the driver's seat, meeting the twin's glares. His face was pale, sharper than usual as he begged them to understand.

"Look, I'm sorry," he signed slowly, trying to pick words the twins knew. "In a tough spot, I used a – spot to–"

"We don't know those signs," Nehemiah growled. Joe reached into the pocket of his cargo pants where he kept his papers and pulled out an empty pad. He showed it apologetically to the twins to say he was out of paper, and started another sentence.

"I know it frightened you. I know I – not have –"

"We don't understand those signs either," Anna said. Joe grimaced and started over again.

"I shouldn't have done it," he signed seriously. "I'm sorry. I promise to never do it again." A little half smile flitted over his face. "Without your say so."

"So...you're asking for forgiveness and trust..." Anna prod-

ded. Joe nodded, biting his lip and watching her.

"Well, I still say it was a nasty thing to do," Anna said, her fingers swiftly braiding and unbraiding her hair. But the tone she used let the others know Joe had won. Nehemiah looked away, exasperated at his sister who always forgave anything at the first sign of contrition. "If you had just told us you were in trouble with these guardians and needed our help to get out, we would have said yes. After all, you've already saved our lives more times than I can count, and I've trusted you with our safety, and both of you have been very trustworthy up till now. Yes, I suppose I will forgive you for tonight, but don't you dare ever let it happen again! Ever!" Joe gave her a grateful look, and then turned reluctantly toward Nehemiah, as if afraid of what he would see there. Nehi sat still, his lips pursed, studying his feet.

"Joe, I honestly thought Anna was going to–" he started, then stopped and looked up at the mute. Nervous pleading cut lines in Joe's face, expressions Nehemiah had never seen there before. Nehi remembered the mute's gentle encouragement to Anna on their first night with the Ravens, and how cold and tired Joe had looked after their first constellation party. He had wondered then if anyone noticed Joe's needs. Well, here was a chance. Joe sat there asking for trust and friendship, and he seemed to need it. Some of the words spoken by Bertrand and Diodorus about Joe resurfaced in Nehi's mind, and he remembered the threat that had been hanging over the mute's head. A chill went through him at the thought of someone threatening to hand him back to Abid, someone with the power to make it happen, and his shoulder pulsed. It must have been a difficult night for Joe.

Nehemiah looked back at the sharp, pleading face and had the sudden knowledge he already trusted the mute, and always had. But...trusted him with what? Joe was more than he said, and there was something about the way these two had scooped up Anna and him that rang false with the simplistic story Joe had fed them that first day. Cobeau wandered out of the trees to their right.

"Green backs nesting, we move," the big man said to Joe, then leaned against the seat. The Ravens stared at Nehemiah, both pleading for a return of the simple good fellowship they had enjoyed. The young man looked away, his chest tight and his head aching.

"You have an interpreter now," Nehi said, forcing his voice neutral with an effort. "Is there anything you want to tell me?"

"I'm sorry?" Joe signed and Beau rumbled. Then his hands moved in a blur. "I didn't go to Bertrand for the money, I used him to get you two out of the guardians' hands and back into the wild lands."

"I know that, I realized it after a minute of thinking, I was just mad earlier," Nehemiah said. "Joe, if you were in trouble with the guardians, why did you come into the country at all? Why not just bypass it?"

"We needed things. Our food stores are very low, even supplementing with our foraging in the wild lands we still needed things. And you've seen the way our bubble sticks, and how almost a quarter of our steam jets are jammed and useless after that careening ride out of Sojourner's Way. I had to get parts to fix it. Hoverer parts we can't restock in the wild lands, it takes peopled places for that." Joe's hands fumbled his words. His lips pressed tight then he rushed on, exasperation mixing with a stress that lined his face. "I thought I could slip in and out, with a harmless concert to cover us (they don't know I'm a musician). But then that lady soldier at the very beginning spotted us, and I knew they were watching. They found me when I was out getting things. I didn't mean for all this to happen." Joe's hands clasped together and fell to his lap, and he sat and stared. Nehi stayed still, considering.

"I don't know." The words burst out of Nehemiah, low and automatic. "I'm going to have to pray and think about it. Anna's already falling asleep, I need to get her to bed," he finished abruptly, shoving his sister in the shoulder. Anna's eyes flew open again, blinking rapidly as she swayed from the

shove.

"I'm awake," she yawned, then slumped toward him, her eyes closing again. Nehi gave a tight smile as he herded her off to the bunks. Anna slumped onto the lower bunk, curled in a ball, and snored gently. Nehi wandered into the day room and dropped heavily into a chair at the table. He wasn't going to get any sleep. He wanted time alone to think, and pray. Joe needed an answer. So did Nehemiah.

The trapdoor clicked closed behind Nehi and the night noises closed in. Joe's hands shot up and moved in frantic signs through the damp air.

"They've got me!"

The little mute ran a hand through his hair in a bewildered, desperate motion, his breath almost sobbing out of him. Cobeau looked at him in surprise.

"What?" the chimera rumbled.

"I said I wouldn't trust them, wouldn't let myself like them, especially when I saw they have it, but they've got me!" Joe signed swiftly at the big man. He buried his face in his hands and pulled them away again almost in the same motion. Joe's frantic mood melted into listlessness, as his head dropped back against the wagon's wood, haunted anguish scoring his sharp features. "Why am I so weak?" he signed. Cobeau laid a big hand on Joe's knee.

"It's not weak to love, Joe," he rumbled. A mirthless, silent laugh split Joe's face, pain, not humor in it.

"Whether it is or not, I've lost them before I even let myself admit it's been awfully nice to have the two of them around, almost like real–" The mute stopped abruptly, his fists balling in mid sign.

"Friends," Beau rumbled, finishing the sentence. Joe winced. His head drooped, blond hair covering his eyes. Cobeau vaulted into the seat beside the mute, swept up the steering stick, and started Prissy on the animal-made paths of the forest.

Prissy, frontal
Pg. 222

Beau picked up the conversation again as soon as they were on their way. "Good friends. Nehi will forgive. You will be happy."

"That's your theory," Joe signed, his lip curled. "He doesn't trust us. Why should he? And you say friends, but what if these two are really–" Joe cut it off, his hands trembling. He heaved a soft sigh and pulled his knees up, huddling into the chimera. Cobeau dropped one big arm over the mute. The two rode in silence as the minutes stretched on.

"Master?" Beau rumbled. Joe jabbed him in the ribs. "Ow. I mean, Joe?"

"What?" Joe signed, staring off into the darkness, his eyes reddened and tired.

"Did you actually let them catch you?"

"I didn't sign they caught me, of course they didn't. I signed they found me. I didn't lie to Knee-High! I just...didn't...tell him all the truth." A huge sigh blew from Joe and his head dropped back against Cobeau's thick side. "I'm so tired of this kind of life! The secrets, the almost-lies, always fighting the battles alone..." The mute glanced up, his hands still forming quick signs. He saw a blank confusion on the chimera, as Beau tried and failed to understand the words. Joe's hands gently closed into fists. He leaned against the chimera's hairy side, staring into the darkness and fighting back the lonely frustration again. It would have been very nice to have someone who understood, just a little.

The minutes stretched into an hour, then two. Cobeau pulled the wagon onto another path and they bumped and shuffled over another mile of ground, till he let the wagon settle gently in a grassy meadow. The steam slowly cut off, the gentle hissing quieting in time with the tired squeaks of the pig. But before full silence fell, it was interrupted by the sound of the trapdoor snapping open and Nehemiah scrambling out. Joe jerked up, suddenly his usual confident self. But he let just a little of his earlier pleading show through the mask as he looked up, eyeing Nehemiah.

"You win. I don't know why, but I trust you. You're forgiven for tonight," Nehi said. Joe's mouth fell open and he looked away, blinking at the darkness with an inscrutable face. He turned back, nodding up a sincere thanks. Nehi nodded back, serious and friendly. "Now listen, both of you. You're asking us for friendship, and that goes both ways. No more of this Judas business, all right? At least not without our permission," he added with a wry smile. Joe nodded and grinned in relief as Cobeau gave one of his jolly chuckles, happy to see his dear Joe happy.

"So, did you find everything?" Nehemiah asked, trying a little too hard to make it cheerful and natural. Joe accepted the offer of a normal conversation, and the talk rushed on to the best way to repair the hoverer. They argued in a friendly way over it as they settled the pig, pulled out their blankets, and dropped on the grass around their wagon. Very soon the two Ravens were fast asleep. Hours passed, and Nehemiah still lay with his hands behind his head, staring up at the overcast sky. Something nagged him about tonight. He was certain Joe hadn't acted just from the fear of being turned over to his old owner, as the mute had allowed it to be understood. And he still didn't understand why he had come into the country at all, if he was really worried about that danger hanging over his head. Kallipolis was the closest country, it was true, but the Kingdom of the Wise wasn't that much farther away. There was something else to it. Nehemiah yawned and his eyes closed involuntarily. He would ask Anna; maybe together they could figure it out. The young man prayed he had made the right decision tonight and finally fell into a restless sleep.

Nehemiah woke to something making loud, harsh noises near him. How had Cobeau suddenly caught a cold that made him cough like that? Nehemiah opened one eye and saw Cobeau sleeping with all the deep innocence of a dog a few feet away. He opened the other eye and saw Joe standing by the wagon with a raven perched on his arm. As it flapped, the raven looked bigger than Joe's head and shoulders put together, and Nehi wondered how he could hold him so effortlessly. Joe clucked quietly to it and the big bird quieted down. It sat still, cocking its head from side to side. Joe ran his fingers down the bird's feathers, still clucking quietly, till he came to its right leg. With a deft movement he removed a little leather sack and cupped it in his hand. He petted the bird a few more times, then sent him to a perch on the top of the wagon. From the way the bird began to move happily and its head ducked up and down, there must have been something very tasty for it there.

Joe ignored the bird and sat down. Nehemiah watched, staying absolutely still, while the mute pulled open the bag and drew out a folded letter. He read it once, then again. He reached behind him on the wagon and pulled open a little drawer. Joe took out two large papers covered in his unique scrawl and folded them swiftly into the bag. With the same swift movements the bag was reattached to the bird, and the raven sent soaring away to the north. Joe watched him go for a minute, his sharp face calculating. Then he lay down, yawned, and rolled over. He sat up sharply with a grimace, clutching at his ribs. Joe rolled to his other side and squirmed under his blanket. Nehemiah watched and could see when his breathing changed to the slow, easy way of sleep. Nehi sighed and sat up. There would be no more sleep for him this morning.

As Nehemiah sat in the quiet morning, his inquisitive mind longing to find the answer to whatever Joe was hiding, and his prayers for wisdom high, he realized something. There was no more slavery left in his heart. He was a man and Abid was only a nasty memory, and Simmons only returned to haunt him in his sleep. Joe, Anna, they both looked to him naturally as the head of the two Hillsons here. And Nehemiah realized he was a leader, however poorly he did it. Servitude was gone. Manful leadership had replaced it. Nehemiah lay back down again, staring at a tree branch shifting over his head. Gratefulness welled from his heart to the throne of heaven, pouring out to the God who healed and helped. And thanking Him for a sister who was a strong enough woman to choose to treat her twin like a man even when he failed to be one. Oh Jesus, give him wisdom in their dealings with these Ravens! And if possible, let him find out what it was all about!

Peter Lovine pounded through the streets of Freedom. The wail of the police hoverers cut through the air around him, mixing with his sharp breathing. This wasn't where he expected to be after Anna helped him gain his life back.

One day. Seventeen hours. That's how long it took him in his newly selected country to get in trouble with the police. Surely that was a record of some sort.

He caught a glimpse of circling siren lights, reflecting off the hundreds of windows glimmering in the night as he raced through the quiet street. Peter gripped a corner and spun around it, the sharp bricks of the office building biting into his palm as he got out of sight again. His pulse pounded in his ears.

Peter had found the Christian underground. Well, he had found a Christian in the underground, a jeweler by the name of Michael Wheaton. He had located the jeweler earlier this afternoon after asking questions around the seedier side of town. But Peter didn't know the Kingdom of Autonomous Man offered a reward for information about any deterrents to humanities advancement. He had gotten about four sentences out when the jeweler's eyes went wide and his loupe slid from his hand and clunked onto the counter. A police siren whooped outside the shop. Two well-armed officers strode in, their hands on their tasers.

"A Christian has been reported in this area," one of them said, staring daggers at Peter and Michael Wheaton. "You are to come with us."

"Wait a minute," Peter broke in, his mind racing as he

caught up to what he had just done. "I just stopped in here to get my watch fixed. How can that be wrong?"

"Are you a Christian?" the man demanded. Peter didn't hesitate. If he didn't know the danger he had put Michael Wheaton in before, he did now.

"Yes," he said, his voice even. Then he karate chopped the two of them and ran. Becoming the object of the police's hunt hopefully got the jeweler out of their sights. It wasn't a bad plan, and wouldn't have been so hard to slip away if there hadn't been a third policeman in the hoverer watching. Now, as he pelted through the streets, Peter found himself heaping maledictions on that third officer.

These dad-blamed windows were his downfall! The town of Freedom seemed made up of reflective windows, always showing the townspeople their own fair faces as they went about life. Every time Peter thought he had lost his pursuers his reflection bounced his position back to the police. His breath spat from him in gasps and he could feel his legs shaking with each step. Four hours he had pounded these pavements. It would have to end soon, Peter reflected as he ran down yet another paved street, houses lining the pretty sidewalk.

A hand shot out of a storm drain and gripped his ankle. A yelp broke from Peter as he felt himself jerked off his feet and falling into a dark hole in the street. He landed on his back on concrete. The breath went out of him in a rush. A hand clamped onto his mouth, and he felt someone kneeling beside him. Peter's hand shot out, aiming for where he guessed this new threat's throat would be. Someone caught his wrist and forced it down as he lay gasping and winded.

"Quiet, young fool," a voice hissed in his ear. "It is Michael Wheaton and a friend. Lie still and let the Advancers pass us by."

Peter slumped back, panting and glad of the excuse to just lay there for a minute. Hissing hoverers, wailing sirens, and shouted commands rang in the street above them. For two tense minutes the three men stayed crouched and still under the street. Then a hand landed on Peter's shoulder and tugged gently. He followed the pull, deeper into the darkness. The moonlight drifting from the storm drain disappeared as they inched forward. Blackness closed in. Musty, close air surrounded him, partnered with dark so deep the only thing he could see was stars dancing in front of his tired eyes. The hand stayed on his shoulder.

"We are deep enough conversation is safe now," Michael Wheaton spoke up in front of Peter. "Why were you inquiring for me?" The voice held curiosity, but no suspicion.

"I didn't realize you would be arrested for being a Christian," Peter said quickly, determined to get that out of the way. "'Young fool,' maybe, but only by ignorance at least. I'm sorry I led them right to you."

"You led them away with just as much alacrity," the jeweler said, a chuckle lacing the words. "I have never seen officers as surprised as those two when you chopped them down and ran. No one gave me any more thought."

"Good," Peter said, his relief evident in his voice. "I'm a Sojourner." Silence fell in the darkness. Peter felt the hand on his shoulder squeeze, a moment of silent sympathy. They understood what that simple phrase meant. "I had heard there was a branch of the Way underground here. I would like to do what I can to help. And I won't be quite such an idiot as I was this afternoon again, if I can help it."

"Learning something of the country you're in now might help you not be an idiot later," a new voice spoke up behind him, amusement playing under the pleasant baritone. "Turn left."

Peter turned left blindly. He took two steps and felt the hand on his shoulder pull him to a stop. Something metal clinked in front of him, a sharp click sounded in the darkness, and a chink of yellow light showed the outline of a doorway. The light grew quickly as Michael pulled the door open and stepped through into the cluttered back room of a jeweler's shop.

"Congratulations," the second voice said, still amused, as Peter stepped through behind the jeweler, blinking in the light, "you successfully ran in a full circle. Not the way I would recommend getting a tour of your new home, but to each his own." Peter turned to face him and found himself looking at a tall, thin, sandy-haired man somewhere in his late thirties. A long scar (still pinkish with new skin) lay under his eye, and Peter automatically identified its origin as the bone having been laid bare from a blow; probably a series of punches. The man smiled at him and held out his hand. "Paul Sireton, nice to meet you. I'm the branch leader here of the 'Way underground,' as you call it."

"Peter Lovine," Peter said, taking the man's offered hand. "No offense, but you're awfully trusting to have just told me all that."

"I like you," Paul grinned. "We have to take people on trust sometimes."

"And we did a background check on the name you gave when you approached my counter," Michael Wheaton said with a smile. His finger tapped the wall mount and a hologram picture of Peter's face congealed in the air, turning in a slow circle, his professional description in a green script under it. "Your profile is still active on the International Site of Warriors. Your credentials are rather impressive, young man. The youngest ever to join the elite Judge's Guards, very impressive indeed."

"Oh." Peter couldn't think of anything else to say. Weariness suddenly washed over him, seeping into his bones. It seemed like a lifetime since that title fit him. There were no more guards. There was no Judge to guard. He sank onto a dusty chair and looked around him. He saw no trace of the door they had entered by. It melded into the striped wallpaper with a perfection that left it invisible. Paul Sireton strolled around the room poking things curiously. Michael Wheaton puttered at his bench, doing something with a pile of metal.

"The police and the Advancers will have your description now," Paul spoke up suddenly. "But if you don't mind my saying so, you look like a lot of other people. I don't think there's much danger in your being recognized if we introduce you in respectable circles. So, Peter, have you decided if you'll stay in KAM?"

"Yes. If you'll have me."

"Good. Then you need a token," Michael smiled and snapped his jeweler's loupe on.

"A what?" Peter asked.

"If you're to be a member of the International Discipleship Program (the actual name of 'the Way underground')," Paul Sireton said, "you'll need to carry the symbol we all do." He slid a chain over his head and held it out to the young man, a pendant dangling from it. Peter took it dutifully and found himself looking at a folk-style metal design, loops and swirls making up a test tube. "I'm an analyst, so a test tube was my choice for a shape. But underneath that innocuous little tube..." Paul's finger jabbed something on the top of the pendant. The metal clinked and shifted, rearranging itself. Peter watched in fascination as a beautiful, simple cross formed on his palm.

"Everyone has their own design," Michael said, "something that means something to them and masks the true shape from the world. It isn't safe to carry the cross openly. What shape would you like?" Peter's eyes flitted to the hologram, still slowly rotating. His past self looked so young, somehow, as he smiled from under his uniform's black beret. He had been so proud when they took that picture. His soft brown eyes focused on the badge on the hat; a broadsword sliced through an open book, the symbol of the Judge.

"I think that will be safe enough," Michael said softly, and turned back to his work. Paul Sireton spun toward the young man as the tinkle of metal and whirr of tools filled the room. His thin hands rubbed together in a show of oddly nervous tension.

"That's settled then," Paul said. He squatted in front of Peter's chair and looked up at him, his eyes bright and intense. "Now, Peter. Tell me about the Judges."

Continue the epic in book two of the Sojourners,

Ravens Rescue

Appendices

The Collapse

When the Christian Confederation came to power, the Africas turned into a powerhouse of design and science, the multicultural ruling power of learning. South Africa became the first to harness the dark matter.

It was only an attempt to use energy efficiently in their experimentation that drove the dark matter lab to use nuclear power.

The other countries followed in a close line. First America, whining and claiming they were really the first. It was America that managed to harness both the dark matter and dark energy. The lab learned how to safely keep the two apart and began toying with how they worked together. Then China, England, Finland, Arabia, Iran, India, all across the globe labs began popping up, experimenting with the revolutionary new material. Each lab patterned itself off the South African Confederate Lab of Dark Experimentation.

The first explosion happened in China. No one knows what caused it. There were no survivors left to explain. But the results changed the face of the earth.

A mushroom cloud billowed into the darkness at 3:34 that fateful morning. Few things are dreaded more than that monster of fireball and fallout. But then the night darkened unnaturally, and the mushroom cloud became swallowed by a ball of swirling, devastating, terrifying blackness. Dark matter and dark energy are drawn to each other. And they sense more.

The ball of dark rushed toward the nearest dark lab still standing, ripping up forests, turning buildings to rubble, trailing nuclear fallout in its wake. The Japanese lab was hit at 3:47 that morning. Another mushroom cloud, another larger ball of whirling, sucking, freezing blackness. The Japanese never knew of its coming until they became obliterated.

Around the world the devastating force rushed, hitting lab after lab, growing so large it ripped up countries, oceans, whole civilizations and continents. By 6:21 that morning, only a handful of life still survived on an earth devastated by glowing nuclear waste and the force of energy and matter.

No one survived near enough to see what happened to the dark energy and matter at the end of the spree, after it devoured all of earth's dark stores. Some held it merely consumed itself, running out of energy and mass in a natural course. Others declared it created a black hole inside the ocean's vastness and stays there somewhere, a tireless void consuming water and spitting it out again, like a monstrous farce on a garden fountain. Most of the survivors wanted to forget it had ever been. The tattered remnants of humanity sought sanctuary where they could in the wild lands, far from the ravages of what had been civilization.

The world became a place of survival, a constant struggle for life to hold on longer than the re-settling continent, the ocean's tsunamis as its borders rearranged, and the deadly hold of the nuclear fallout.

One generation survived, then another, and another. Gradually humanity began to reform. Grass began to regrow. Trees grew strong enough to survive the storms. The roaming monsters created by the fallout were pushed back, and humans took over corners of the earth. But that first generation dropped the torch. The survivors wanted only to forget their grieving, devastated by their losses, expecting every moment to be wiped out. They did not teach their children to remember. Generation followed generation, and the past grew dimmer with each new age. But one thing each generation did bequeath to the next.

The ability to read. The knowledge that thinking placed them apart from the animals.

One man of that first generation defied the general forgetfulness. A professor carried with him a bag filled with fifty-four of his most beloved books. He traveled the world after the collapse, making notes, bringing news of other survivors, and leaving behind him at each stop a precious, precious gift. Some didn't heed his hope or his knowledge that the past could heal the future. Some books were thrown away into the arid wastelands of the Collapse. Some pockets of survivors were wiped out and the books lost with them.

But some survived. As mankind began to rebuild, slowly, ach-

ingly, these relics of larger and greater civilizations became revered as the only source of knowledge, the only hope of surviving in this new world.

As the corners where humanity survived took a stronger hold on their portion of earth, and learned of the other survivors in other pockets, only two things became common ground. Humanity, in all its fallen beauty, and the possession of a book as the central relic of each pocket.

And thus the Book Age formed from the glowing ashes of the great Collapse.

Currency

Currency after the Collapse returned to precious metals. During the Book Base Age no paper currency existed. Each kingdom minted their own coinage. The type and rarity of metal, as well as the weight of the coin, defined its worth. Though sizes, shapes, names, and designs varied from kingdom to kingdom, any coinage was accepted so long as the weight and metals were true to the price to be paid. For example:

The 1 oz Golden Marx from the People's Kingdom is rarely seen in the streets of Freedom and most citizens go their whole life without laying eyes on one. A single such coin could buy a cartload of goods in the People's Kingdom. If that Golden Marx is taken to the Kingdom of Gaia, it will purchase only a barrel load, if you will, because gold is more plentiful and prosperity more general in Gaia. But because 1 oz gold is 1 oz gold no matter where you go, it will be accepted as payment. Though it will likely be sliced into first to ascertain it is pure gold, as most merchants are skeptical of Golden Marxes. Once the merchant in Gaia has enough of the Golden Marxes and other pieces of pure gold to make it worth his copper, he takes them to the Stampers. For a fee the Stampers weigh the precious metal, melt it down, and restamp it into whatever coinage the merchant chooses. A merchant will have it restamped in his kingdom's currency as it is a mark of professionalism and business curtesy to barter in your own country's coinage. A Gaia merchant will likely choose to stamp most of it in the half flower ounce (the "half petal" as it is commonly known), as that is the more common payment form. But he will likely have a few full Gaia flower two ounces (the popular name being the "six petal") made for larger purchases and his own banking ease.

August | 3065 | Issue #42

Science Today

Looking forward to what the future will create.

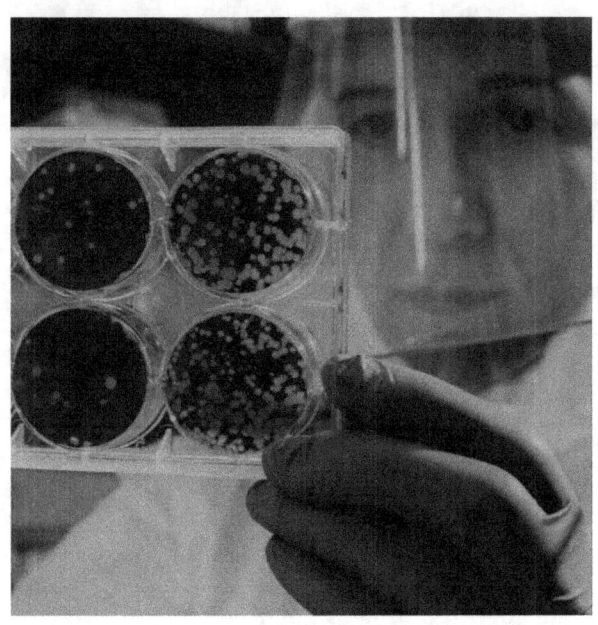

IN THIS ISSUE

News from Hemsha Robotics

The new Mach VII child-care bots are rolling off the lines. What this means for you...

Chimeras today

We once thought chimeras would be evolution's path to higher man. Here's what is happing today...

Design, construct, and maintain

Are you looking for a new design for your lab? See the newest...

News from the Breeders

By Lillian Zupane

A chimera begins life in a petri dish. Animal DNA is carefully manipulated and selected, then inserted into the human embryo. The chimera then begins the growth process, usually in an artificial manner calculated to speed the progression. Some types of chimera are reported able to care for themselves at a younger age than humanity. In some cases (most notably the wilder breeds, such as wolf, zebra, or leopard), an eighteen-month-old chimera has been observed to be completely capable of self care. However, the earlier a chimera is left to itself, the harder it is to train and tame. This, too, might be due to the breed.

At this point in our studies it is clear no higher man will emerge from the animal manipulation. Each chimera grows with limited intelligence and superstitions that cannot be trained out of them. We must keep trusting in Chance to bring our race to higher things. Experiments are changing according to this new understanding of the use of chimeras.

Attempts have been made to create chimeras of bird varieties, but none of the entities had the ability to support their form in flight. The weight and balance of a bird is too delicate to mix with a human embryo and expect Chance to compensate. One study allowed two winged chimeras to procreate to see if evolution would improve the flying ability. The fledging chimeras were weak, the human overshadowing the albatross to such an extent no wings were visible on Fledgling Two. The

fledglings were born sterile, unable to reproduce a second generation for observation, and two fledglings died before able to walk, much less fly. The whole of the experiment was terminated.

The strand of chimeras most useful are those based off Chinese breeder Mai Zhang. Unlike many of her contemporaries, Zhang limits the animal DNA and selects only strands of human embryos noted to be from strong, large races. After the first two breedings she also discarded the wilder DNA animal strands and focused on the domesticated animals. Her Ox-Mountain Breed is especially well noted for its exceptional strength and longevity.

Discussion still goes on in governments about the legal uses of the chimeras, but it is generally believed they are a gift to our underpopulated globe, and will lighten the burden of the manual laborers better than the Hemsha Workers Mach II so widely promoted by the Hemsha Robotics Company.

Reverend Alex

765 N. Mine Rd.
Birmingham, Alabama, United States
Email: crosschurch@hema.com
Hologram: 9745-2361

September, 21, 3065

What are we to do with the chimeras coming out? In our central region, some have been released as "unacceptable for study or practical use" and are roaming wild. "Wild" is unfortunately a very good term from some of the creatures, and we have seen several dozen deaths from people taunting the chimeras, or unwittingly intruding on their "lairs." Most of them however are pitiful, cringing, witless entities that die soon after coming into our midst.

Which brings me to the real question. Are they humans, or are they animals? Do we treat them as dumb creatures in need of food and shelter, or as human souls in need of shepherding and teaching?

Reply soon.

Reverend Alex

Timothy Newman

8954 Cali St.,
Victoria Falls, Zimbabwe
Hologram: 8943-5123
Email: timothynewman@gmail.com

Alex,

I have a parishioner who used to assist Dr. Zhang in her work, before coming to me in tears, hardly able to look at herself in the mirror. She explained to me the chimera begins as a human baby, simply and helplessly an unborn human baby. After the baby's selection, he or she has certain physical moderations, most notably the addition of the animal genes.

These new "creatures" our world is seeing are people. People that have been changed and toyed with, but people nonetheless. Treat them as such, and you will find their souls just as real as yours and mine. Indeed, in my few encounters with the chimeras, I find them innately honest about their Creator, and sharply aware of their conscience. Without any prompting from me, one poor soul (a lurching, part lizard, hardly able to speak through his elongated mouth, with lungs unable to function at full capacity) spoke to me of "the One watching from above" and ran through a list of things he ought not to do because it "made the Maker sad." It was a simplified version of the Ten Commandments. In inquiring further it became clear he did not mean the people working at the lab where he was born and raised. He had not heard of Jesus or the atonement, no one had spoken to him at all on the subject of soul or religion. But he understood as a very young child would, and before his last breath rattled from his underdeveloped lungs, his joy was a beautiful thing to see. If one can be sure of any soul, I am sure I will meet that poor misused lad in heaven when I reach those shining shores; though I don't think I will recognize him, as all horrors will be washed away, and it will be his true, beautiful humanity that I see.

Treat them as the little children they are. For those physically incapable of understanding salvation, I can only trust the same God who takes the baby who cannot tell their right hand from their left will also claim these poor half-creatures.

In Christ,
Timothy

Lasers

The word "laser" started as an acronym, not a word by itself. It stands for Light Amplification by the Stimulated Emission of Radiation. Energy is poured into a lasing medium (a liquid, solid, or gas whose atoms emit light when excited) in order to produce a laser. At its most basic, a laser is a beam of light. But it is light concentrated along narrow, very similar wavelengths. A laser's light has a high concentration of energy. It is able to focus that energy with extreme precision, at the speed of light. (In case you were curious, a phaser is more scientifically accurate than a blaster; the human eye cannot follow the speed of a laser beam, we see it only when it strikes.) If the energy reaches high enough levels, it becomes an effective weapon.

In the early days of research, the main problems with using lasers as a weapon were the source of energy and the heat emitted by the process. It takes so much power to create a weaponized laser, the apparatus used to excite the atoms was too heavy for even a tank to carry, and handheld weapons were out of the question. Also, most of a laser's energy burns off as heat, before the laser light became strong enough to be useful. One more problem with the practicality of lasers was atmospheric interference. A high concentration of dust or water in the air might tamper with a laser's accuracy, bending the beam, or causing it to reflect off the atmospheric conditions.

The first two problems were finally solved by the Pylum battery. A man named Ralph Pylum, in the year 20 of the Book Base Age, discovered a battery powered by heat. It is the perfect solution for a laser weapon energy source. The Pylum battery requires an initial charge, which it uses to start the lasing process in a weapon. The laser passes through its chosen medium and begins to bounce between a complicated series of mirrors, increasing the atoms' excitement and thus the power of the laser. This is called priming. Some take more time than others to reach a weaponized level of energy, it depends on many factors including the size of the battery and the medium chosen. But as it primes, the laser is giving off wave after wave of heat. The Pylum battery absorbs it and uses the energy. This creates a weapon which basically powers itself. If allowed to sit unused for some time the battery loses its charge and needs a "jump start" of external heat to start the lasing process. But if kept in proper order, a Pylum battery laser will provide its own energy indefinitely.

Atmospheric conditions are still an issue with some lasers, throwing off the accuracy. The lens of a laser (what the beam is finally sent through, after the energy has climbed to useful levels) as well as the lasing medium affect the accuracy. It is possible for the beams to be reflected back, or even scattered. This kind of reflection would be too weak to cause much damage, unless they landed in a person's fragile eyes. Because of this danger lasers are never to be fired without safety-dyed goggles.

Brunhiem
The laser of choice for the Judge's Guards, the Brunhiem is a compact liquid fiber laser. The lasing medium is optical fibers, coiled to pack more power into a weapon that is smaller, lighter, and more easily maneuverable than almost all its contemporaries. The Brunhiem employs three separate packets of carefully coiled optical fibers. The packets each have access to the Pylum battery, a relatively small affair for a laser. Because of the smaller size, the Pylum does not consume all the heat created by the lasing process, and so is surrounded by a liquid coolant, running through tubes wrapped around the battery. The separate beams from the three packets combine in the reflective chamber as the weapon primes.
Priming: 3 seconds
Health Length Without Charging: 2 weeks
Weight: 9.27 lbs
Accuracy: Excellent

Revolution
An older model of laser, the Revolution was created by Mark Happley of the People's Kingdom and the rights to manufacture the laser remains in that country's hands. A gas laser, it uses a

ceramic tube filled with the lasing medium. Electricity is pumped through the tube, exciting the gasses and sending the laser into the reflecting chamber where it gains energy till it reaches maximum power and triggers the end priming switch. The battery required is large and heavy, and the carbon stock is thick to protect the ceramic tube. A workable but heavy and ungainly weapon.

Priming: 5 seconds
Health Length Without Charging: 3 days
Weight: 20.6 lbs
Accuracy: Tolerable

Ruby

A mass market weapon, the Ruby is a solid-state laser found in most kingdoms during the Book Base Age. It employs a synthetic ruby rod as a medium and is prized for its small size. Because of the single-handed size, the battery is necessarily smaller, making the power less effective. It creates a lethal laser shot, but only at a range of up to six feet. A popular choice for personal defense, but not optimal as an army weapon.

Priming: 4 seconds
Health Length Without Charging: 5 days
Weight: 6.3 pounds
Accuracy: Average

Krackmens

The Krackmen is a prepossessing weapon with its intricately crafted red carbon stock. It is a dye laser utilizing rhodamine, and the accuracy is legendary, though the priming time is a serious drawback to the weapon.

Priming: 7 seconds
Health Length Without Charging: 1 week
Weight: 15.9 pounds
Accuracy: Exceptional

Compton

A revolutionary weapon, the Compton laser is the first to utilize dark energy and matter as an energy source. Two balls of carefully fashioned Z shielding are bound next to each other in a copper fitting. Inside one is a ball of dark matter, inside the other dark energy; they are small enough as to be almost trace amounts. But when activated, a "window" is cracked between the two. Dark matter and dark energy excite each other when combined, and create what science currently sees as an inexhaustible source of energy. The gun then utilizes Compton scattering between the two balls to harvest gamma rays. The rays are fired through a crystal lens fashioned after the Krackmens' excellent design. Gamma rays are invisible to the human eye, and so most Compton guns are sold with specially dyed goggles to allow the shooter to see where his rays land. Currently thought inexhaustible, nearly unbreakable, and as small as a Ruby laser (though considerably heavier), a Compton is viewed as the best weapons breakthrough since the Pylum battery.

Priming: 0 seconds
Health Length Without Charging: Unknown
Weight: 9.4 pounds
Accuracy: Very Exceptional

Kingdom's Worldviews

Sojourner's Kingdom

Book Base

The Holy Bible: Authorized King James Version. Blue Heron Bookcraft, Family Edition, 3011.

Government Structure

"Now therefore, our God, we thank thee, and praise thy glorious name. But who am I, and what is my people, that we should be able to offer so willingly after this sort? for all things come of thee, and of thine own have we given thee. For we are strangers before thee, and sojourners, as were all our fathers: our days on the earth are as a shadow, and there is none abiding. O LORD our God, all this store that we have prepared to build thee an house for thine holy name cometh of thine hand, and is all thine own." (1 Chronicles 29:13-16)

The citizens of the Sojourner's Kingdom term their government an elected Judgeship under a theocracy. A careful reading of their book base made the Sojourners distrustful of kings, and they had lost the idea of presidents in the past. The name "Judge" is taken from the sections of the Bible wherein God speaks through prophets and judges to His people, exhorting them to stay truthful to Him and so be safe and prosperous. The Judge of the Sojourners never presumes to speak with the very voice of God, but is expected to act according to the words of God given in the Bible.

The Judge is elected by the general citizenry, and he must know his scripture if he expects to be selected. When first organized into a kingdom in the year 2 of the newly declared Book Base Age, a Reverend John Hillson was unanimously elected by the citizens as the first Judge. Any citizen of the country can be elected Judge by law, but it became traditional to have a member of the Hillson family elected. In the history of the kingdom, only one other line has been elected, and they were cousins to the

Hillsons. The Judge is the undisputed ruler over the smaller bodies of state government, such as local court judges, the army, and the penal system. It is the state's duty to deal with the malefactors, outside diplomacy, and protect the kingdom.

It must be noted, the state is seen as only one part of what keeps the kingdom running.

Picture three circles, state, church, and family. Each are their own separate entities, but they join in the center. This is a simplistic explanation of how Sojourner's Way functions. Only one circle is state government. The other two are independent of the state, but it is understood that the kingdom lives and breathes in that small triangular shaped section where all three circles join.

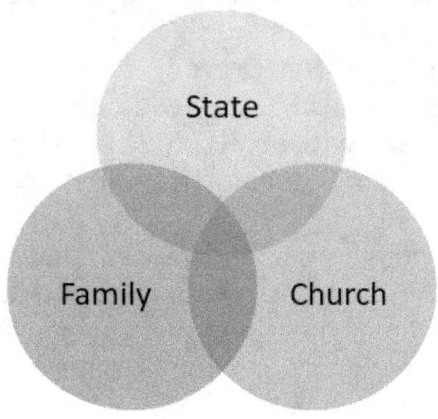

"The church" encompasses all denominations, it speaks of the universal church as represented by the individual congregations scattered throughout the kingdom.

"Let us hold fast the profession of our faith without wavering; (for he is faithful that promised;) and let us consider one another to provoke unto love and to good works: not forsaking the assembling of ourselves together, as the manner of some is; but exhorting one another: and so much the more, as ye see the day approaching." (Hebrews 10:23-25)

This circle inspires a firm sense of local community, as the separate churches serve their cities and neighborhoods. The

churches are in charge of charity, seeing to the needs of the poor, the orphan, the widow, and of course shepherding the kingdom's citizens in religious matters. Involved in that shepherding is the church's opinion on a candidate for state office, especially on if the person in question is truly a Christian. The church has no say as to who is appointed in the state, but they have a traditional role in offering advice to their congregations. They also have a very definite role in the formation of laws.

When a need for a new or amended law is found, a Law Court is formed, consisting of fourteen elected members of the church and fourteen elected members of the local court system, presided over by the Judge. The vote must be unanimous for a law to be passed or amended, and the Judge has the right to refer the law to the general public after the decision has been passed. If over half the citizens vote for a second debate, a Law Court of thirty pastors and thirty local judges will be called, and the process gone through again, with an eighty percent majority needed to pass the new law or amendment. The ruling of the second Law Court is undebatable.

Families are the single small entities that make up the entirety of the kingdom. The point is obvious, but unlike some of the other kingdoms, the Sojourners not only recognize the fact, they encourage it by acknowledging strong Christian families are the backbone of their subsistence.

"Lo, children are an heritage of the LORD: and the fruit of the womb is his reward. As arrows are in the hand of a mighty man; so are children of the youth. Happy is the man that hath his quiver full of them: they shall not be ashamed, but they shall speak with the enemies in the gate." (Psalm 127:3-5)

"And these words, which I command thee this day, shall be in thine heart: and thou shalt teach them diligently unto thy children, and shalt talk of them when thou sittest in thine house, and when thou walkest by the way, and when thou liest down, and when thou risest up." (Deuteronomy 6:6-7)

Families, by working their own individual jobs, are in charge of the economy of the kingdom. By seeing to their own children,

they are in charge of the education of the next generation. And by voting, families choose the leaders in the state.

The state has no right to interfere in either church or family, unless an individual in those entities comes under the heading of malefactor.

Incompletes and Chimeras

"There is neither Jew nor Greek, there is neither bond nor free, there is neither male nor female; for ye are all one in Christ Jesus." (Galatians 3:28)

"Thou shalt not curse the deaf, nor put a stumblingblock before the blind, but shalt fear thy God: I am the LORD." (Leviticus 19:14)

"If a brother or sister be naked, and destitute of daily food, and one of you say unto them, Depart in peace, be ye warmed and filled; notwithstanding ye give them not those things which are needful to the body; what doth it profit? Even so faith, if it hath not works, is dead, being alone." (James 2:15-17)

Most Sojourners would not understand if asked what they thought of incompletes. Inside the Sojourner's Kingdom there are no incompletes, only humans. There are numerous passages in the Bible where we find the blind, halt, deaf, etc. as objects of compassion, specially pulled from the crowd to be healed by Jesus and His followers. Mercy and practical help are also stressed in the Sojourner's book. If someone needs assistance, the Sojourners are one of the most likely places to obtain it.

Chimeras are undeniably different, but still considered fully human amongst the Sojourners. They are generally looked on with indulgence and can easily become objects of charity from the church or individuals as the chimeras attempt to make a living for themselves. Some live on stipends from local churches and do small, menial tasks among the congregation. Sometimes, a job is created in a company especially for a chimera's unique job skill or lack of intellect, solely to ensure the chimera sufficient funds to live on. A chimera is never turned away at the border or discouraged from creating a family and living as normally as possible.

251

Art and Music

"Sing unto him a new song; play skillfully with a loud noise." (Psalm 33:3)

"And thou shalt make holy garments for Aaron thy brother for glory and for beauty." (Exodus 28:2)

Music is a commanded way to praise God, it is prevalent throughout the country. Most music created is sacred, but there are many instances of music used as only as personal expression.

Art in Sojourner's Way notes how the Bible is poetic, paints many word pictures, and begins with a creative God making things of beauty. Art is encouraged, prized, and there is a plethora of styles and mediums employed in its making. The majority of the artistic works are realistic and hopeful; they depict what they see, because God made the seen and the unseen and pronounced them good.

Science and Advancements:

Jesus was a healer when here on earth, Solomon a naturalist.

Within Sojourner's Way the freedom to pursue one's interests combines with little government control and a robust economy. Added to that are the Bible's obvious commands to help our fellow men when we can, Jesus' many acts of healing the sick, and instances of various naturalists recording their observations.

Combine those facts, and you have the perfect position for the sciences to thrive. The study of science, and the uses derived from its advancements, are prevalent throughout the kingdom. The rest of the world is reluctant to acknowledge the Sojourners proficiency at new medical and scientific breakthroughs, but often find themselves using their methods. Ingenuity runs rampant within the kingdom.

Army

"Happy is he that hath the God of Jacob for his help, whose hope is in the LORD his God: Which made heaven, and earth, the sea, and all that therein is: which keepeth truth for ever: Which executeth judgment for the oppressed:

which giveth food to the hungry. The LORD looseth the prisoners: The LORD openeth the eyes of the blind: the LORD raiseth them that are bowed down: the LORD loveth the righteous: The LORD preserveth the strangers; he relieveth the fatherless and widow: but the way of the wicked he turneth upside down." (Psalm 146:5-9)

We see God's people making war throughout the Bible. But it isn't wantonly, there's always a reason behind it. Usually it's defense, sometimes it's a direct command from God in a select circumstance. In the New Testament, Jesus puts forth the command to "turn the other cheek," (Matt. 5:39) and "he who lives by the sword shall die by it." (Matt. 26:52) Sojourners are a strong people, with no love of war but the willingness and ability to defeat anyone coming against them, and a desire to protect those who cannot protect themselves.

A standing army is necessary, both to patrol the borders to keep the wild beasts at bay and to stave off attacks from the rest of the world. In the history of the Sojourners, almost all the kingdoms have attacked at one time or another. The Sojourners are adept at warfare, their soldiers are some of the best trained and best outfitted in the world. Both sexes are taught defense, but only the men make a career of it in the nation's army, as this is the principle laid out in their book.

After the first hundred years of the Book Base Age, Sojourner's Way found itself with peace on its borders and a large number of trained soldiers with nothing to do but patrol. Jeremiah Hillson, the Judge at that period in the kingdom's history, allowed soldiers to place their names in the newly formed International Site of Warriors, making it possible to hire themselves out as mercenaries. The Sojourners were in high demand from small countries without the standing armies to contend with threats. Jeremiah quickly found a few rules had to be put in place (such as, a force of more than twenty men needs the Judge's approval, and a rotation system to ensure enough men on hand for the Sojourner's use). If the cause is a just one, the Sojourners tend to hire themselves at "discount prices" to those who cannot afford their services. It is a politic move, for any kingdom favorably minded toward the Sojourners, and not swallowed by larger enemies, means a little more safety for Sojourner's Way.

Social Structure

"And that ye study to be quiet, and to do your own business, and to work with your own hands, as we commanded you; that ye may walk honestly toward them that are without, and that ye may have lack of nothing." (1 Thessalonians 4:22-12)

"But if any provide not for his own, and specially for those of his own house, he had denied the faith, and is worse than an infidel." (1 Timothy 5:8)

Industry is a national pastime. Private property is a strongly-felt right in the kingdom, as God is the One Who gives and takes away; not other people. The taxes are kept only high enough to keep the kingdom safe (i.e., keep the judicial system, army, and Judgeship in good order). Any interest is allowed to be pursued, so long as it is not directly against the laws of the kingdom (based on commandments laid out in their book). With the freedom to hone any skill, the philosophical and social urge toward hard work, and the safety to enjoy peace, the economy within the Sojourner's Kingdom booms.

"So God created man in his own image, in the image of God created he him; male and female created he them." (Genesis 1:27)

"There is neither Jew nor Greek, there is neither bond nor free, there is neither male nor female: for ye are all one in Christ Jesus." (Galatians 3:28)

"Now therefore ye are no more strangers and foreigners, but fellowcitizens with the saints, and of the household of God..." (Ephesians 2:19)

No man or woman is above another in humanity or purpose. All are all born of the same line, created in God's image. If someone is a Christian, they are even part of the same family and will share the same home for all of eternity. God gives and takes away life, in His own wisdom. Therefore, every life is to be protected and cared for, as the soul is also nurtured.

"Wives, submit yourselves unto your own husbands, as unto the Lord. For the husband is the head of the wife, even as Christ is the head of the church: and he is the saviour of the body. Therefore as the church is subject unto Christ, so let the wives be to their own husbands in every thing. Husbands, love your wives, even as Christ also loved the church, and gave himself for it... So ought men to love their wives as their own bodies. He that loveth his wife loveth himself... Children, obey your parents in the Lord: for this is right... And, ye fathers, provoke not your children to wrath: but bring them up in the nurture and admonition of the Lord."
(Ephesians 5:22-25, 28, 6:1,4)

Women inside the Sojourner Kingdom are not meant to be public leaders. They are to give way in those spheres to their menfolk. You will note, however, that their book says "submit to your <u>own</u> husbands." Women are not called to obey all men, only those God has directly placed in their lives as headship figures. Also note the text immediately after speaks of husbands loving their wives as much as Christ loved the church. A careful reading of their book produces men who respect, protect, and genuinely love the women under their care, which allows a woman to respect, and even enjoy, their man's headship. Recall there is a strong sense of community flowing outward from the church's work. If man in a family is failing in his job as protector and Christ-like leadership (especially if a woman's situation becomes dangerous) there are those around the family who will notice and step in to help. When operating correctly and following the Sojourner's book, a family becomes both a steadfast rock against anything the world can throw at it, and a haven of rest to all those inside it.

"The aged women likewise, that they be in behaviour as becometh holiness, not false accusers, not given to much wine, teachers of good things; that they may teach the young women to be sober, to love their husbands, to love their children, to be discreet, chaste, keepers at home, good, obedient to their own husbands, that the word of God be not blasphemed." (Titus 2:3-5)

Women are generally expected to work in the family sphere. But unlike some other kingdoms in the Book Base Age, they are respected and even in many cases revered. The women hold a high standard for the men, and it is much of what keeps the kingdom stable; deadbeats and jerks aren't likely to catch their sweethearts.

One summation of everything said above can be found in Colossians:

"Lie not one to another, seeing that ye have put off the old man with his deeds; and have put on the new man, which is renewed in knowledge after the image of him that created him: where there is neither Greek nor Jew, circumcision nor uncircumcision, Barbarian, Scythian, bond nor free: but Christ is all, and in all. Put on therefore, as the elect of God, holy and beloved, bowels of mercies, kindness, humbleness of mind, meekness, longsuffering; forbearing one another, and forgiving one another, if any man have a quarrel against any: even as Christ forgave you, so also do ye. And above all these things put on charity, which is the bond of perfectness. And let the peace of God rule in your hearts, to the which also ye are called in one body; and be ye thankful. Let the word of Christ dwell in you richly in all wisdom; teaching and admonishing one another in psalms and hymns and spiritual songs, singing with grace in your hearts to the Lord. And whatsoever ye do in word or deed, do all in the name of the Lord Jesus, giving thanks to God and the Father by him." (Colossians 3:9-17)

All Christians are one in Christ, Who is all in all. And all in Christ are to act like Him, the One who gave His life for the outcasts and sinners. Christians are to be kind to strangers, fierce against evil, watch out for one another, and do their work without causing trouble.

Strangers, those who are not Christians, are welcome within the borders of the kingdom. Their book base has a great deal to say on how a stranger ought to be treated, and it usually comes with the reminder that God's people too were strangers and sojourners in a foreign land (Exodus 22:21, Leviticus 19:34, etc.). Anyone can come into the border professing whatever religion

they espouse. But if the stranger deliberately breaks laws in professing their religion, they will find the full weight of the government on their heads, just as any citizen would. Part of a Judge's job is to know the basic tenants of the other kingdoms of the world. This aids them in foreign policy, but it is also very useful in knowing which strangers entering their border ought to be surreptitiously checked on during their stay, in order to best protect their citizens. To become a citizen with voting rights, however, a person must profess the basic tenants of Christianity and be a member in good standing of a local church within the kingdom.

> "Behold, I send you forth as sheep in the midst of wolves: be ye therefore wise as serpents, and harmless as doves." (Matthew 10:16)

The Sojourners strive to be open and kind, but not stupid.

Kallipolis

Book Base
Plato's *Republic*, edited by J.D. Kaplan, copywrite 1950 by Pocket Books Inc.

Government Structure
There are three classes of people. The ***producers*** are the artisans, farmers, merchants, any kind of worker. The ***auxiliaries*** are the warriors, the standing army in charge of defense and keeping the peace. The ***guardians***, or philosopher kings, are the rulers watching over the health of the State.

The "State" is capitalized in all of their dealings. It is the ultimate end, the good of the State is what each individual is supposed to be focused on.

The producers are basically there because the State cannot do without them. The auxiliaries are honored, especially for bravery and accomplishments, both in the physical and intellectual realm. The guardians have full power over everything. They are to prize justice and truth above all things, though in certain

instances it is allowable for them to lie to their people, for the greater good. How people are selected to be in which class is not specified in the book base itself. When questions about practicalities come up Socrates, the main expounder of the *Republic*, usually states something akin to, "we will leave the details to our guardians." During the Book Age, the guardians devised means to have the children of the kingdom watched closely as they grow and learn. Tests are constantly documented and filed for each child. Every choice and development of a child is recorded, and when they reach an age to be useful, the documents are reviewed by the guardians and the child is delineated to whatever sphere of life they are deemed fit for. The vast majority become producers. This observation and documentation is possible because of the social structure of the kingdom and the importance placed on education:

"Also, I said, the State, started well, moves with accumulating force like a wheel. For good nurture and education implant good constitutions, and these good constitutions taking root in a good education improve more and more, and this improvement affects the breed in man as in other animals."

Children are molded from the earliest age in Kallipolis. Once chosen to a sphere of life, there is no opportunity to change it. You are what you are chosen to be till you pass on to the next life. Being a "just man" is the highest achievement in Kallipolis, and through some mental gymnastics, it becomes that a man focused on his own business is the definition of a just man.

"...justice was doing one's own business and not being a busybody... Then to do one's business in a certain way may be assumed to be justice."

The economic gain gotten from doing business is disposed of thusly:

"Both the community of property the community of families, as I was saying, tend to make them more truly guardians; they will not tear the city in pieces by differing about 'mine' and 'not mine'; each man dragging any acquisition he has made into a separate house of his own where he has a separate wife and children and private pleasures and

pains; but all will be affected as far as may be by the same pleasures and pains because they are all one opinion about what is near and dear to them, and therefore they all tend toward a common end."

Again, there are few practical details laid out as to how this should be accomplished in the kingdom's book base. The guardians chose to allow the producers to keep sixty percent of what they make, to go towards running their businesses, and their needs and pleasures. The other forty percent goes into a pool for the good of the State. It should be noted that the book base prohibits the guardians from owning anything other than basic necessities, or even touching silver or gold. Human nature is such that often in the history of Kallipolis, the guardians have found ways of utilizing the state's funds for their own private enjoyments, but a surprising amount of does go for the good of the State.

"...our aim in founding the State was not the disproportionate happiness of any one class, but the greatest happiness of the whole..."

Everyone in the State is expected to be more concerned for the State than for their own good. This is not always the case in the history of the kingdom, especially among the producers. The producers tend towards a sullen laxity in life, most of them living with the idea of making just enough for their comfort and not caring much about anything else. But the conversations and goals of the auxiliaries and guardians do tend toward the good of the State.

Incompletes and Chimeras

Because of the emphasis on the good of the State, perfecting the breed, and the leeching influence of the rest of the kingdoms, incompletes and chimeras are not encouraged inside Kallipolis.

No official statement has been issued by the guardians about the status of incompletes, except for the general rule of all *"deformed children"* (see Social Structure). In general they are thought of more as humans than as animals, though the influence of the other kingdoms does show itself from time to time. They are easily used and oppressed, and few auxiliaries bother

to step in to help an incomplete.

Chimeras are viewed as useful workers, much more animal than human.

The Arts

"Musical training is a more potent instrument than any other, because rhythm and harmony find their way into the inward places of the soul."

Music and poetry are highly prized in the *Republic*, if they are of a good quality and not merely copies. The book base does not define good quality to its full extent, but a certain kind of literature and music thrives in Kallipolis.

Science and Advancement

The activity of pure intellectual thought is prized higher than any manipulation of creation. Science is not discouraged officially, but neither is it encouraged. As a result, it mostly lies in a state of imports from other kingdoms, and tends to be slow to catch up to the newer advancements.

Army

The auxiliaries are an honored class, though just as firmly under the whims of the guardians as the producers. The standards for gaining the status of auxiliary is very high. The class is small, and a tight-knit community who considers themselves much superior to the "mere producers."

"Are dogs divided into he's and she's, or do they both share equally in hunting and in keeping watch and in the other duties of dogs? Or do we entrust to the males the entire and exclusive care of the flocks, while we leave the females at home, under the idea that the bearing and sucking their puppies is labor enough for them?

No, he said, they share alike; the only difference between them is that the males are stronger and the females weaker.

But can you use different animals for the same purpose, unless they are bred and fed in the same way?

You cannot.

Then, if women are to have the same duties as men, they must have the same nurture in education?

Yes.

The education which was assigned to the man was music and gymnastic.

Yes.

Then women must be taught music and gymnastic and also the art of war, which they must practice like the men?"

Men and women alike fill the ranks of the auxiliaries. But the book base holds up what many would see as a double standard, stating elsewhere that women are as a general rule inferior to men, and it is merely a possibility that one might come along who is fit for higher things than seeing to the stores; women are also termed "possessions" throughout the book. There are fewer women in the auxiliaries than men, for the bar is high to reach that class, and women are already seen as below it.

The auxiliaries are rigorously trained, and often go on sorties into the wild lands against the wild beasts to allow their younger generation to see action. Because of their small size, there is no history of their attacking another kingdom. Their kits are slower to modernize than the rest of the world, once something is deemed adequate for the State it takes a lot to change it.

Social Structure

"Yes you are quite right, he replied, in maintaining the general inferiority of the female sex: although many women are in many things superior to many men, yet on the whole what you say is true...

Men and women alike possess the qualities which make a guardian; they differ only in the comparative strength and weakness.

Obviously.

And those women who have such qualities are to be selected as the companions and colleagues of men who have similar qualities in whom they resemble in capacity and character?...

"The law I said which is the sequel of this and all that has proceeded, is the following affect - 'that the wives of

our guardians are to be common, and their children are to be common, and no parent is to know his own child, nor any child his parents."

Women are allowed to hold office and other places of honor, and historically some have been raised to high ranks in Kallipolis. But the vast majority spend their lives as "inferior" in the ranks of the producers doing the more menial tasks, or as the "companions" to the chosen auxiliaries.

Families, as the rest of the world knows them, do not exist in Kallipolis. Only those few couples selected by the guardians are allowed to come together, and then really just for the usefulness of creating more children. Because of this, most of the producers (who are never among those selected by the guardians for the mating rituals) don't bother to make more than what brings them comfort, instead of creating something of actual quality. Some do, but for most of humanity it takes an idea of leaving something for your own posterity instead of general future generations to inspire making things of excellence, or spending time, effort, and money on things that will last more than your lifetime.

Licentiousness from those under a certain age is strictly outlawed in the state. Instead it is operated like a breeding program, as one would for dogs or falcons to improve the herd. There are sweepstakes, drawings, to choose those allowed for the yearly mating rituals. The guardians actually select carefully, but they use the lie of the sweepstakes to keep the population from rebelling. That way the "inferior" will put it down to their ill-luck that they are never chosen, instead of the more desirable people the guardians select to allow to marry and procreate. Only the bravest and best are brought together.

The children are raised by wet nurses in houses set apart for the purpose, and no mother is to know which child is theirs. The children that are born to inferior specimens, by accident, or the deformed are *"put away in some mysterious, unknown place."* Historically this means they are placed in houses with those who are already angry at being delineated to work in such a hated sphere, and the children have a very unenviable life. An unsanctioned child *"steals into life,"* and is included in those put away.

After they are past childbearing age (women at forty, men at fifty-five) the members of the State are allowed to "range" at will, just so long as they don't come together with close relations (anyone born in the month which his/her child would likely be born).

Notes of Interest

The Republic is a discussion of what an ideal city-state would look like; to be fair to Plato, he states it is not necessarily something one would see in the real world. It contains two of his more famous arguments, the Cave Analogy and a discussion of Plato's Forms.

The Kingdom of the Wise

Book Base

Philosophical Skepticism Distilled, by Jeremy Cotes, copywrite 3356 Simon and Schuster.

Government Structure

The book is a two-hundred page overview of philosophical skepticism in in all its humors and variations, from the Greeks through the early 3000s, before the collapse of civilizations. It includes as its final chapter, "What Skepticism Means for Us," and that is where most of the quotes in this section originate.

In a nutshell, philosophical skepticism is the idea that a person cannot know anything for certain. Everything we see around us could be a dream, or created only for our senses by a malevolent demon, or even fed to us as sensory signals by a mad scientist while we exist as a brain in a vat. At first glance it seems ridiculous. At second glance it can still seem ridiculous, but the difficulty is (philosophically speaking) it is almost impossible to disprove. If we were just a brain in a vat, or in a series of dreams, we would have no way of knowing that was our situation.

When a nation of people took this as their basis, it naturally caused difficulty in creating a cohesive governmental structure.

If no one can know anything for certain, and everything from the raindrops on your head to the stone under your feet is called into question, how does one conduct business rationally?

The first council could not come to an agreement. Every attendee had a different theory on life, and government; most with themselves as the leader. It ended with the council members traveling home and setting up their own ideas in their own households. The Kingdom of the Wise evolved into a system of city states. Each one holds the same book base, and each one found it necessary to rely on the others to beat back attacks from other kingdoms in order to survive. Those two factors are what draws them into a cohesive whole; but each sector has its own governing body, its own army, and its own mini-feuds with the other sectors.

To the rest of the world, the sectors of the Kingdom of the Wise seem very similar, almost identical. One traveler termed them, "Anarchies with their own personal, delusional despots." Each sector has what might be termed a ruling house; some one family richer and more power hungry than the others, who becomes the figurehead of that sector. But in a country where rain can be doubted to exist even as it falls from the sky, anyone claiming to rule can be "brushed off," as it were, by being philosophically explained away. The individuals within the sectors live however they want, while trying not to fall afoul of the mercenary army controlled by their sector's ruling house.

The government of the Kingdom of the Wise presents us with a changing landscape, with the sectors' borders growing, shrinking, and shifting constantly as the ruling houses try to usurp each other.

Incompletes and Chimeras

"It is necessary that the world be peopled. Whether or not our procreation is actually happening or if a mad scientist is pulling the strings, it is still necessary to keep up the front, as it were, and replenish humanity."

There is no official statement on GIs or chimeras. But the sec-

tors tend to take the same theory as other kingdoms around them, and discourage GIs on the grounds of possible pollution of their fine state blood.

They have no objection to chimeras owned by citizens, so long as the chimera is contained and well trained. Those chimeras within the Kingdom of the Wise live as little better than animals, most as menial workers, a few as mercenaries.

Art and Music

"The senses might be lying. But even if it is all a lie, it is still pleasant to hear a good strain of music, or hang a painting on the wall."

The original art works that originate within the Kingdom of the Wise tend to be according to the popular trend. They are created to sell, for material purposes, to help increase the artist's comfort, not necessarily to make a particular statement. The same applies to music.

Science and Advancements

Styles Griffan was an entrepreneur in the Kingdom of the Wise during the years 31-107 of the Book Base Age. Other words used to describe him were "unscrupulous gangster," "brilliant commercialist," "bloody gunrunner," "kingdom shaper," and "greedy blackguard." When he was twenty-two he began to import and market the newest weaponry available. He marketed them first to one sector, then to the opposing sector. It was a lucrative business, but it was also a dangerous one as he worked among feuding ruling houses who had no compunction about killing anyone who annoyed them. When he was twenty-nine, Griffan made a discovery that amended his business technique. Griffan discovered a network of underground cavities lying underneath his home sector. Tunnel systems created by the past civilizations for transport ran underneath a large portion of the kingdom, and it was perfect for Styles Griffan. Instead of taking his merchandise to the sectors (risking death to run the borderlines), he began to invite people to come to him. He carefully selected his clients, and took care to outfit his own mercenaries with better equipment than he sold. It became a very exclusive market, a hub of the newest technologies.

Soon the Underground Market underneath the Kingdom of the Wise became the best source of technology in the world. Griffan repaired, built, and dug, and created a whole kingdom running underneath the sectors of the Kingdom of the Wise. It is a private kingdom, rife with vice and violence, but it ensures the Kingdom of the Wise a place among the best equipped countries on the globe.

Army

"This world may be a playground for us, or it might only appear that way while we exist in hell. It is impossible to know. But what we see we can still enjoy."

The Kingdom of the Wise does not have a cohesive army because it does not have a cohesive government. But each sectors' despots have a burning desire to enjoy what they have, which means they are willing to work to keep from being overrun by opposing sectors. Most are also power hungry, and a little spiteful of what feuding sectors already have.

Mercenaries are well paid, well trained, and abundant within the Kingdom of the Wise. The Underground Market provides them with updated weaponry, and they are formidable foes. As mercenaries, the soldiers of the Kingdom of the Wise have no love for the land or peoples they fight for, and if not paid well and kept in line, they can cause more damage than those they are hired to fight against.

Social Structure

"We know there is nothing we can know. The rest of the world exists in the old fashioned misapprehensions that the planet is a knowable place. We must pity their delusion."

The citizens of the Kingdom of the Wise tend to be arrogant about their own views.

It is an anarchist kingdom, which bows only to the might of those with the greater force. There is no real distinction between the men or women; one's gender might be an illusion, after all. The whole person sitting across from you having a conversation might be an illusion. But it is still a pleasant sensation to have a

good conversation. The practical outcome of this, is each individual or family unit lives as they choose to.

Mostly because of the Underground Market, it is a fairly prosperous kingdom. Travelers from all over the world come to the Market, and need housing and food and other amenities provided by those not employed in the Market itself. One might say the tourist trade is the strongest thing within the Kingdom.

Recipe

Cheddmusham Soup
(With Potatoes)

2 medium russet potatoes
Half Stick Butter
8 oz sliced mushrooms
1 cup diced or bite-sized ham (a great way to use leftovers from hams)
1/8 cup flour
2 tsp pepper
3 tsp fresh parsley
2 ½ cup half 'n half
1 cup water (or chicken broth)
1 ½ cup cheddar cheese

Peel potatoes and chop into bite sized cubes. Place in a pot, cover with water, and boil till almost tender (not quite cooked). Set aside.

Melt butter in a large saucepan. Add in mushrooms, and cook. As they're cooking, add in ham and spices. When you start to see little bits of brown on the 'shrooms, add the flour. Mix enough to coat the 'shrooms and ham. Pour in the half 'n half and water, then use a whist to make smooth. Add in the potatoes and heat until bubbling. Remove from heat, add in the cheddar cheese and let melt. Enjoy hot, with more cheese sprinkled on top, or maybe a dollop of sour cream.

Sign Language Alphabet

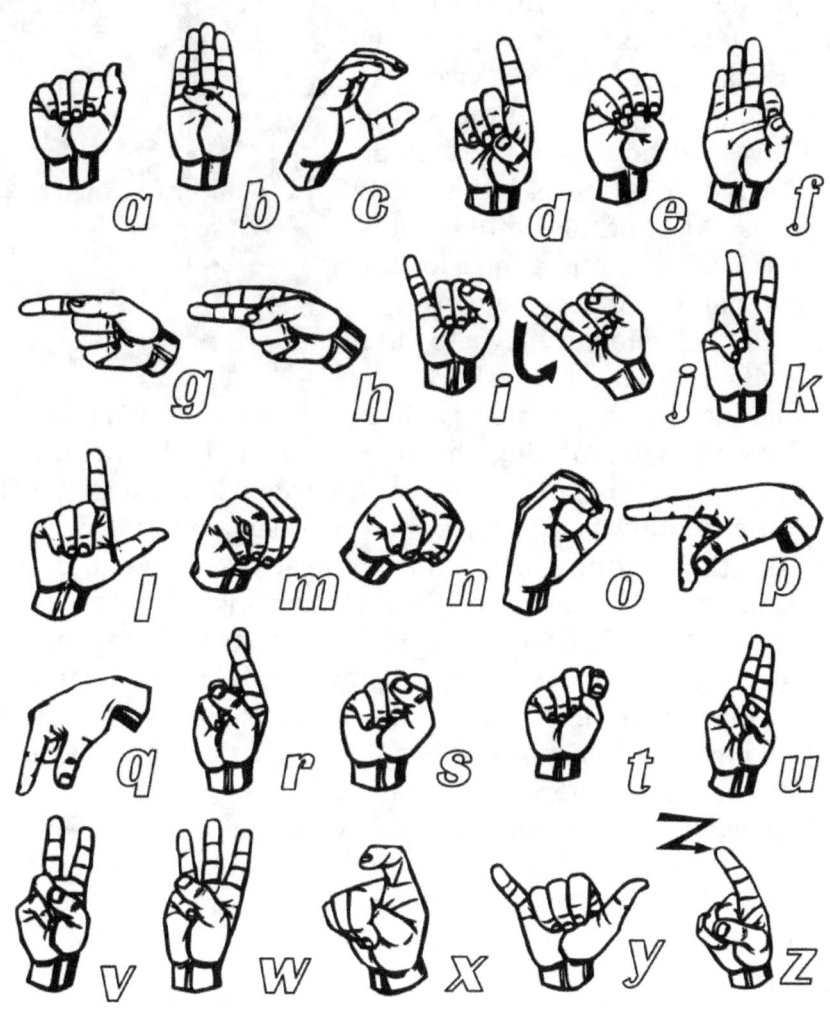

Author Bio

Catherine Gruben Smith lives in the middle of Texas, which she begrudgingly admits is probably better than a magical tower. She grew up mostly in a dusty town in the southern New Mexican desert and will always carry the quirks. (Yes, New Mexico is a part of the United States, and no, she was not a missionary, and yes, you can drink the water.) It is her delight and privilege to be a housewife, mother, and an Earl Gray  connoisseur. Another of her constant activities is trying to keep her dogs from terrorizing the house and neighborhood with their determination to be always underfoot and hungry. (The work of a dog lover is never done.) She has always been fascinated by the written word, philosophical reasoning, and good stories of bravery and honor. When not writing, reading, chasing children or dogs, Catherine can be found board-gaming, baking, hiking, or possibly broad sword fighting with her older brother. If you want a fuller explanation of Catherine, go and read Psalm 30. The heart and purpose of her life can be found there, especially in the last two verses.

Catherine prays reading her books will help her readers find the urge to get up off the couch and serve. The Lord of all life calls us to the battlefield, to mop up the enemy after He has won the war. Don't sit on the side-lines. We have the tools to fix this broken world.

Where to find more information, or contact Catherine:
catherinegrubensmith.com
catherinegrubensmith@gmail.com
postetenebrasluxbooks.com

Books by Catherine Gruben Smith

Parabaloni Series:
The Parabaloni
The Slingshot Effect
As the Eagle Flies
Solitaire
Adele Angst
Blind Leader

Dreaded King Saga:
A Son Rises
Reign Falls
Knight Duty
Heir Raising
Splitting Heirs

Faerytales of Deweot:
How to Unmake a Dragon
Faery Wings and Pirate Things

Sojourners:
Ravens Ruins
Ravens Rescue
Ravens Return
Ravens Refuge
Ravens Raid
Ravens Rebirth